# Backstage

The fourth novel in my *Tales from Great Yarmouth* series

– TONY GARETH SMITH –

Printed and bound in England by www.printondemand-worldwide.com

www.fast-print.net/store.php

BACKSTAGE
Copyright © Tony Gareth Smith 2017

A catalogue record for this book is available from the British Library

ISBN 978-178456-452-0

First published 2017 by
FASTPRINT PUBLISHING
Peterborough, England.

*This novel is dedicated to Shane*

# Chapter One:

*Ashes to Ashes*

*Thursday, 14 October 1971*

"Ashes to ashes, dust to dust..." The words did not register with Elsie Stevens; standing on either side of her were Jenny Benjamin and Rita Ricer. Brompton cemetery was crowded with faces and personalities from show business, many of whom over the years Don had represented. Several close friends of Don were also present, still reeling from the shock of his untimely and preventable death.

Don Stevens had been a small fish in the world of entertainment but he was well respected, to which wreaths from the Delfont and Grade families bore witness.

Elsie was led away to the waiting car by Rita and Jenny. A funeral tea had been laid on at the studios in Earls Court, where many of Don's shows were rehearsed before going on to the seaside resorts for the summer season. Elsie conducted herself well, shaking the hands of many whom she hadn't seen in years and some she had never met, but knew by name.

Rita, whose own husband, the comedian Ted Ricer, had died in the summer of 1970, felt the memories come flooding back; Jenny, who sensed that the funeral was a trying time for her friend, did her best to divert the attention of others away and engaged them in conversation. Mystic Brian was accompanied by his wife and children, Derinda Daniels with her husband Ricky Drew, Tommy Trent, Jonny Adams, dancers from the JB Dancing School, The Olanzos and even Dawn, Sue and Jill of The Dean Sisters were part of the entourage.

Back in Great Yarmouth the funerals of two more who died in the fire at The Golden Sands Theatre were taking place. Bob Scott, who had returned from his holiday early on hearing the news, had read the papers in disbelief. It was Matthew Taylor who had started the fire; Bob had engaged Matthew as the backstage manager of the Golden Sands, but he had come to Great Yarmouth with an ulterior motive: to seek revenge for the death of his sister Gwen, who had been the secretary and lover of Don Stevens. Gwen had been responsible for the attempted murder of at least two others, and met her own demise when she was rumbled by Veronica, the sister of June Ashby, whom Gwen was convinced she had murdered.

At least his assistant Beverley and Maud Bennett had managed to escape. At first, the galvanised bucket found by the fireman was thought to have been at the side of cleaner Mona Buckle, but Mona was found suffering from smoke inhalation at the rear of the auditorium and was still recuperating at home.

With Beverley, Barbara and Maud at his side, Bob attended both funerals in succession. One was for a young barman by the name of Pete, who had been on duty to help out while Don Stevens was interviewing acts in Ted's bar; the other was for "Grafter", as Andy was known to his friends, who worked backstage and was only at the theatre because Matthew had asked him to help out with some rigging. Both were young and the services were upsetting and moving.

As Bob took off his black coat and hung it up, he hoped it would be a long time before he had to attend another funeral. One was enough, but two on the same day seemed very wrong. Beverley, Maud and Barbara were visibly upset but, keeping a stiff upper lip, they shook the hands of the respective relatives following the services and attended the wakes afterwards. Maud and Beverley thought that it could so easily have been their own funerals.

It was a worrying time – the theatre was deemed unsafe and out of bounds. Bob waited, as did Beverley and other members of staff, for the decision from the owners on what was going to happen to the Golden Sands. Ted's Variety Bar had been totally destroyed by the fire and some of the backstage area and fly tower had been badly damaged. The safety curtain had prevented the fire spreading too far into the auditorium, but there was no doubt that a lot of work would need to be done if the theatre was going to open the following season.

The *Great Yarmouth Mercury* covered the story of the fire for a few weeks as further news of the Sands' future was released. Photographers had captured pictures of the blaze and the aftermath which for many readers was all too much. One photographer had taken aerial shots from a helicopter and it was clear to all that the rear of the theatre had been destroyed. The pier remained closed to the public, and locals who walked their dogs along the promenade stopped at the front of the pier and looked on in wonder, tutting as they did so that such a tragedy could have befallen the resort. Lucinda Haines read the news, keeping abreast of any titbits she heard, and began to put some details in place for the next meeting of GAGGA, when all of the landladies would no doubt be concerned how this would affect business for the 1972 season.

## Friday, 15 October 1971

In Brokencliff-on-Sea, Alfred Barton was taking steps to close down The Beach Croft Hotel for refurbishment, and also looking very carefully at the staffing situation. He had long known that some of the staff should have been given "their marching orders" – a phrase he had heard his wife repeat on many occasions before she had deserted him and gone to join family in Australia. Alfred had called upon the services of a personnel officer he knew to help him sift through the staff records. Maureen Roberts had studied and noted comments within the files. She made herself a short list and discussed her findings with Alfred.

"So, what you are saying is that I need to cut my losses and start all over again."

Maureen studied her friend's face. "Alfred, I have known you for many years and you have never struck me as managerial material. I would like to suggest that you need some training on that side of things. Unlike your late parents, your love is that theatre and not this hotel, but it is this hotel that brings in the revenue."

Alfred nodded in agreement; Jean had always been the hirer and firer. He readily admitted to himself he hadn't listened enough to her over the years and he should have listened to her when she had wanted to get shot of certain staff members.

"So, Alfred, my suggestion is this: I will sit in with you on all the sackings that have to take place. It will be a long and painful exercise. I know the staff have been told you are closing down until next year and I note that certain monetary plans are in place. You will need to give them severance pay. The hotel will reopen following its refurbishment and these staff will be able to reapply for jobs if they so wish to. However, in my experience they usually move on to other employment and are happy to remain where they are."

"What kind of money are we talking here?" asked Alfred, mentally trying to calculate what the exercise was going to cost him.

"Some staff are seasonal, there are a few employed all year round, but – as your bookings bear out – you are quieter during the months January through March. Full-time staff will be given a day's pay for every year they have worked, plus any outstanding holiday accrued, and I think as a parting gesture a further week's salary." Maureen noted the look of horror on Alfred's face. "Don't worry, Alfred, it is all accounted for – if anything, Jean ran a very tight ship where salaries were concerned. I assure you that you will still have the amount you need to do the changes here."

Alfred sighed.

"When the hotel is completed you can advertise for staff."

"Oh my goodness, there is so much to think about. I will be useless when it comes to advertising and interviewing for positions – Jean took care of all of that."

"It seems to me that Jean took care of a lot of things, Alfred. Well, Jean isn't here anymore, so it's down to you, matey."

Maureen gave Alfred time to drink in all that she had said to him. "Look, Alfred, if you need a hand I am willing to throw my hat into the ring. I do take on private work from time to time, but it will cost you, I don't come cheap."

Alfred ran a shaking hand over his head. "Give me a figure, Maureen, I will need help."

Maureen reached for her pen and wrote a figure on a piece of paper and slid it across the desk to Alfred.

"As much as that?"

"Yes, Alfred, as much as that, but that will include an assistant. I have someone in mind."

Alfred nodded. "Draw up the plans and I will sign them off."

"You will of course need a hand in rewriting some of your job descriptions. As a favour, I will take that on at no extra cost. This place needs to move slightly upmarket, you need good calibre staff here and not the likes of that madam on reception. Where on earth she came from I shudder to guess. I will have everything drawn up by the end of the week and have it delivered to you by hand."

"You are a lifesaver, Maureen," said Alfred, getting up to shake her hand. Maureen picked up her briefcase and walked towards the door. "Remember, Alfred, professionalism is the key here, this place could be good – very good – but you really need to be more hands on."

Alfred escorted Maureen to the steps of the main entrance and waved her goodbye, feeling some weight had been lifted off his shoulders.

\* \* \*

## Tuesday, 19 October 1971

Enid had just sat down when Maud drew her attention to the news report on the television. There were Pearl and Sidney Arbour on the steps of the court and behind them, coming down the steps, was Rita Ricer with her solicitor.

"A total miscarriage of justice," said Sidney to the television reporter.

"We were stitched up," said Pearl, dabbing her crocodile tears. "We are a professional couple, never have we been subject to such treatment. It has ruined our reputation in the business."

Sidney took Pearl's arm. "Don't take on so, my sweet. We will be back on the stage in next to no time, you'll see."

"Well," said Maud, turning to her sister. "I didn't think Rita would go through with taking them to court, but she has. Rita can be a tough cookie when it comes to business."

"I expect she has to be," said Enid, picking up her embroidery. "It's a man's world, despite what they keep saying in the papers. I know how hard it is to deal with reps and companies in my little shop. Some may snigger behind my back, but it is no picnic I can tell you."

Maud looked at her sister and smiled.

\* \* \*

Rita turned the television off. "Well, they have only themselves to blame, leaving us in the lurch like that."

"I bet they didn't think you meant it when you said you would sue them," said Elsie, pleased to take her mind off her own worries for a few minutes.

"Well, let that be a lesson to anyone who thinks they can mess with Rita Ricer. Now, Elsie love, can I get you anything? You have hardly eaten anything today."

Elsie shook her head. "I am not really hungry," she replied, but then catching the look on Rita's face, she relented. "I could manage some cheese on toast though."

\* \* \*

## *Wednesday, 20 October 1971*

"Firstly, I must say how very sorry I was to hear about the tragedy," said Malcolm Farrow, looking across the desk at Rita.

Rita shifted the papers on her desk to one side. "It is certainly a tragedy, Malcolm, and on behalf of Elsie Stevens thank you very much for the floral tribute you sent."

"It was the least I could do," said Malcolm. "Of course, I didn't have the pleasure to know Don Stevens personally, but I had heard so very much about him. I am pleased I did have the opportunity of seeing him that evening at the Beach Croft."

"Ah yes, the Beach Croft," said Rita, casting her mind back to that evening. "I expect you have come to see me about the conversation we had concerning the Sparrows Nest."

"It seems a little indelicate now," said Malcolm, "but I have to make plans for next season's show."

"Business goes on," replied Rita, "as life does, even at times of sadness. I have to say, Malcolm, I really haven't had much time to give the matter any thought. However, now you are here, one possibility did cross my mind – how about a professional pantomime at the Nest this Christmas?"

Malcolm looked bemused. "They usually entertain an amateur production and I believe we have the Lowestoft Players booked in for late January."

"So, a professional pantomime is out of the question, yes, I see that."

"Do you have something else in mind?"

"Well," said Rita, sitting back in her chair, "before I commit to looking at a summer season, I would like to see how things would work at the theatre as I'm not over familiar with the Nest. I could suggest a Christmas show to run for three weeks."

"Really, who had you in mind to top the bill?"

"Derinda Daniels. Derinda is at a bit of a crossroads at the moment, and she cannot make her mind up whether to settle in France, keep her home on in Norwich or do another tour with her husband, Ricky Drew. I am sure I could persuade her to do a Christmas show."

"Isn't it too late to start putting such a show together?"

Rita opened her drawer, took out a pad with some notes written on it and laid it on the desk.

"We are talking professionals here, not amateurs, who – forgive me for saying so – take at least three months to rehearse a production."

Malcolm picked up the pad and read what Rita had written. "I see you have sketched out a pantomime and a show."

"Malcolm, me old lover, you have to be prepared for all kinds of eventualities in this business. I remember when I was signed up to play Fairy Godmother in a production of *Goody Two Shoes* and there was a change of heart and I ended up learning the lines to play principal boy in *Jack and the Beanstalk*, and we were due to open the following week. All the posters and programmes had to be changed – it was a complete fiasco but I dealt with it. Some of the cast were in tears, the young girl playing Goody was beside herself and couldn't get her head around playing Jill to my Jack, but we got there in the end."

"So, three weeks you are thinking?"

"Certainly no more than four, it could open early December and close first week in January. It will give you something different, Malcolm, and may well put you on the map as the person who introduced a Christmas show to the Sparrows Nest."

"I am flattered," said Malcolm with a smile. "I think when I take this idea back to the team they will be surprised. Any ideas for the summer season?"

"I am really going to need more time to work that one out. But perhaps we can put a date in the diary when you and I can meet. We will include Jenny and possibly Elsie, if she is up to it, to discuss possibilities."

Malcolm smiled. "I had heard you were good, but not this good. I came here to discuss next season and you have sold me the idea of a Christmas show."

"One always has to keep one's options open. Speak to my receptionist, Julie, on the way out and she should be able to give you some dates. In the interim, I will have a chat with Derinda, get Jenny on board and come back to you by the end of this week with a plan for the show."

Malcolm stood up and fastened his briefcase. "You have been most helpful, Rita. I am really looking forward to working with you."

And as Rita shook Malcolm's hand, she smiled. "And I am looking forward to working with you, Malcolm. Goodbye for now."

## *Wednesday, 21 October*

Lucinda Haines had called a meeting of The Great Yarmouth and Gorleston Guesthouse Association, known as GAGGA. The venue was a meeting room inside the Two Bears Hotel, as nowhere else was available. With Muriel Evans (Treasurer) and Erica Warren (Secretary) either side of her on the raised platform, Lucinda addressed the members.

"You will all know about the dreadful fire at The Golden Sands Theatre which killed three innocent people."

Heads nodded around the room and Freda Boggis was heard to sniff loudly.

"Erica, our secretary, did arrange floral tributes to go to each of the funerals from us all here at GAGGA. My committee and I"—said Lucinda with a nod to Muriel on her left and Erica on her right—"have been discussing how the loss of this theatre could affect our business here in Great Yarmouth. Of course, we still have the other venues, like Wellington Pier and the ABC Regal, but the Golden Sands is very close to all our hearts."

Freda Boggis let out a big sob and blew her nose loudly.

"So many of the artistes that have appeared there have become friends to us, and it is only right to say that the Golden Sands is the only venue of its kind in the resort to have invited the likes of our association along to their opening and sometimes closing nights."

"And the parties," shouted out Gloria Winstanley, egged on by her friend Ethel Winters. "They've been like family to us. I remember that dear old Ted Ricer, what a lovely man he was."

Lucinda banged her gavel. "Thank you, Gloria, as you rightly said they have been like family to us."

"Some more than most," said Ethel in a whispered voice that carried across the room. "You know Lucinda nearly had that Ted in bed."

Gloria jabbed Ethel in the ribs. "Quiet, Ethel, I think she heard you."

Unperturbed, Lucinda carried on. "We have no idea when – or indeed if – the theatre will open again, so we must come up with our own plans to make sure that business doesn't suffer."

"If I may interrupt, Lady Chairman," said the voice of Fenella Wright, who was until a few months previously the secretary of GAGGA (and sitting beside her was Agnes Brown, one-time treasurer). "One need look no further than Brokencliff, they revived their theatre this last season to great acclaim – maybe we should approach the owner, Alfred Barton, and get him to extend his season."

"Thank you, Fenella dear," said Lucinda, "we were thinking along the same lines."

Nettie Windsor, never one to keep quiet, also added her thoughts aloud. "How will the theatre at Brokencliff help us in Great Yarmouth, surely it will benefit the landladies nearer to Gorleston?"

"My dear Mrs Windsor," said Lucinda in her most sickly condescending voice, "we are all one here at GAGGA, several among you have guest houses in Gorleston, we even have one or two from the Hopton area and that is on the other side of Brokencliff. I think what is needed here is a combined effort. As the head of GAGGA I will enter into talks with the respective proprietors and see if I can bring a plan of action to the table."

There were mutterings around the room and Lucinda banged her gavel again. "And now we come to our convention. I will hand you over to our secretary, Erica, who has news for us all."

Erica stood up. "Thank you, Lady Chairman. As you all know I am new to this role, as is my colleague, Muriel. We both looked over the venues that GAGGA have frequented in the past. Unfortunately, neither the Cliff Hotel nor the Star can accommodate us this year. Normally these events are held around October or November but, at the request of our new chairman, we have decided that a Christmas gathering would be most welcome. We are very fortunate to have secured the use of the ballroom at Owlerton Hall in Brokencliff, which is undergoing something of a refurbishment. Our chairman has been able to secure a deal with Sir Harold and Lady Samantha Hunter which is far less than we have paid in previous years."

"And how on earth are we all getting to Brokencliff?" called out Gloria. "That's what I would like to know."

Erica smiled. "Worry not, ladies, that has all been taken care of. With the money saved on the venue we will be able to provide coaches to ferry all of you to and from the venue."

"And how much is that going to cost us?" shouted out Ethel.

Erica turned to Muriel. "Perhaps our treasurer can give us a figure."

Muriel blushed and stood up. "I have calculated a cost of three pounds per head, which includes a buffet and two drinks at the bar. Oh yes, and we have a raffle in hand too."

Erica continued. "You will all be able to bring along a guest, and we have secured Maurice Beeney and his All Rounders to supply the dance music."

"I thought he was dead," said Gloria, looking at her neighbour.

"I think you will find he has retired from full-time work, but he kindly agreed to get his boys together for us."

"His boys," said Ethel, "now there's a laugh, the youngest must be eighty-two if he's a day. I expect you got them cheap. Why can't we have that nice Vic Allen or rock and roll group Rick O'Shea and the Ramblers?"

"All fully booked, I am sorry to say," said Erica, "so Maurice Beeney it will be."

"Are we going to have any kind of cabaret act?" asked Gloria, who enjoyed a bit of entertainment. "A good comedian or a nice singer would be good."

Lucinda stood up and looked at her watch. "Time is of the essence, ladies, I am sure Erica will be looking at the possibility of some entertainment in due course."

Erica sat down feeling less than pleased.

"Now, ladies, just a reminder that we have another visit from Crocket, Crocket and Crocket who are displaying their wares in the adjacent ante-room and offering a ten per cent discount on all purchases made today. Details of the forthcoming Christmas party will be sent out, but I strongly advise you all to keep Saturday, 11 December free."

As Muriel left the platform with Erica, she couldn't help but comment, "Lucinda is becoming very grand – in fact she is nearly on a par with Shirley Llewellyn, and that's saying something."

Erica patted Muriel's arm. "Don't worry, my dear, every dog has its day, you'll see."

Freda was waiting for her friend Muriel to gather her papers together and the two went for a coffee in Palmers.

"You did well there," said Freda, not usually one for paying compliments and insisting on paying for the drinks. "I should think it can be quite frightening sitting there in front of all of us."

Muriel nodded and stirred her coffee. "It's Lucinda that is frightening, I have had several meetings with her and she is becoming quite demanding."

"I heard one or two saying that she was getting more up herself, like Shirley before her."

Muriel nodded. "You can say that again. Mind you, I have to say she does have some good ideas and she will be introducing something new after Christmas. I mentioned to her, and was backed by Erica, that everyone was getting tired of the same old presentations from Crocket, Crocket and Crocket. Anyway – and you mustn't breathe a word of this to a living soul, Freda Boggis – Lucinda has been in talks with Murdell and Pocock, the big cash and carry wholesalers, and they are willing to allow GAGGA to become members and be able to buy things in bulk."

"Won't that put the likes of smaller shops out of business? I buy a lot of my groceries from Mrs Jary."

"And so do I," said Muriel, "and we can still buy some things from Mrs Jary, but get better deals at Murdell and Pocock."

Freda sat quietly for a moment. "But how would we get the things home? Not all of us drive."

Muriel looked at her friend. "Where there's a will there's a way."

"So, when will all of this kick off then?"

"Not yet awhile, but I believe at the January meeting of GAGGA Lucinda will announce some details."

"Do you think they sell perfume, this Peacock lot?"

"Oh, I do hope they don't for all our sakes, Freda Boggis," replied her friend, getting a whiff of Freda's latest purchase. "What is the stuff you are wearing today called?"

"Teardrops," said Freda, looking at a woman eating a cream puff and wishing she had purchased one.

"Well, it's certainly making my eyes water," said Muriel with feeling.

# Chapter Two     *If I Had a Hammer*

## Saturday, 30 October

S elwyn Woods had always been a misery, something that his long-suffering wife, Sally, knew all too well from the day she had married him. But, in his favour, Selwyn was a grafter; he worked hard, made sure there was money on the table and in his own little way enjoyed his life. Being miserable was part of his persona. He had followed his father into the building trade and ran his own little business, employing casual labour if he took on a big job, and spent most of his life wearing his brown overalls, boots and cap. Quite a catch in his day, he had retained a good complexion, a full head of hair and a way with words. The only time Sally could recall seeing her husband in a suit was on their wedding day and at the weddings of their two sons and daughter.

The Woods lived a reasonably comfortable life in Corton, and his builders' yard was next to the house they had mortgaged, with a deposit from his parents as their wedding gift. Sally's parents had provided bed linen and a set of cutlery that had been handed down over generations.

Now in his mid-sixties, Selwyn, or Chippy as he was known in the trade, was standing in the large banqueting room of Owlerton Hall as Lady Samantha and Sir Harold Hunter told him the work that they would require in order to have the room functioning by the end of November.

Looking down at his boots that were tied with odd pieces of string, he sucked on his pipe.

"So, Mr Woods, what do you think – is this something you can take on and complete on time?"

Selwyn sucked on his pipe again and then slowly removed it from his mouth using it as a pointer to the ceiling. "Those cornices will be a bit tricky to replace – that one there is badly cracked. You see, what we have here is a very large room," he said, walking about and stating what was quite obvious to his audience. "I would have to bring in some long ladders and a platform to get up there. These walls will need re-plastering in places and this floor could do with sanding down and being re-varnished. My boys should be able to sort out those alcoves, we did some a short time ago over at Somerleyton."

Selwyn, not one to be rushed, put his head from one side to the other and tutted to himself.

Lady Samantha, who was used to his ways, said nothing; her husband on the other hand had plenty to say.

"So, Mr Woods, are you going to take on the bloody job or not? Come on, man, make up your mind. I've some serious fishing to get in before lunchtime and I can't stand around here all day."

Lady Samantha glared at Sir Harold, but he was having none of it. He had got out of bed earlier than usual at his wife's request, taken breakfast at the ungodly hour of seven, all so that he could be standing in the large hall to meet Mr Woods who had arrived on the dot of eight forty-five. He frowned. Gawd damn it, his copy of *Tatler* remained untouched on his bedside cabinet and he had hoped to get a sly look at the racing form in the daily paper – there was a filly running in the two thirty he quite liked the look of.

"By the end of November, you say," said Mr Woods, as if he hadn't heard a single word uttered by Sir Harold.

"That is what we are aiming for, Mr Woods," said Lady Samantha, playing with her pearl necklace. "I would like to offer the room to the landladies' association for their Christmas social."

Taking a pencil from behind his ear and fumbling for a piece of paper in his overall pocket, Selwyn scribbled down some figures. He sucked on his pipe again, made a few guttural throat noises and then looked Lady Samantha in the eye.

"I could start in two days' time. I have a little job to finish over at Belton, but my boys could move in here and prepare the canvas, as we say in the trade."

Sir Harold raised his eyes to the ceiling and snorted.

"And can you give me a figure on the cost?" asked Lady Samantha, beaming one of her most radiant smiles at Selwyn.

Selwyn handed her ladyship a slip of paper with some figures scrawled on it. Lady Samantha looked at the figure, took a sharp intake of breath and smiled again. "Well, that seems to be in order, Mr Woods, and you can start in two days' time."

Selwyn knocked his pipe against a windowsill and a piece of the sill broke off. "That will need fixing," he said, totally unperturbed by the incident. "I shall order some materials when I get back to the yard and we will get cracking, as we say in the trade."

Lady Samantha looked mournfully at the broken sill and prayed it was only a turn of phrase Mr Woods was using because much more "cracking" she felt the room couldn't stand.

A few hours later Alfred was speaking to Philippa Tidy in the small shop that stood on the opposite corner to his hotel. The shop had once been owned by his late Aunt Dolly, but Philippa had managed to put her own stamp on the small provisions store and enjoyed serving the Brokencliff community.

"I saw Chippy's van earlier," said Alfred. "He must be doing some work around here."

"Oh yes, he's landed a job at Owlerton Hall doing the ballroom there," came the reply. "He was in here soon after. It appears her ladyship is planning the whole place to be redone over the next few months, but I understand she wants the ballroom or banqueting room done first so that she can allow the guest house landladies to hold their annual get together there. I heard on the grapevine that Lucinda Haines is quite well in with her ladyship."

Alfred laughed. "Well, that will be one in the eye for some around here. Interesting about the work on the ballroom though. I need work doing at the hotel, but I think the job would be too big to offer Chippy Woods."

Philippa began putting Alfred's provisions into a carrier bag. "Chippy does do some good work – he sorted out my kitchen for me. Mind you, it took him and his boys two weeks, but I have to say he did a good job. What you need is one of those professionals in – surely the Cliff or the Star could give you some leads. You might even find something in the local papers. If I spot anything I will let you know."

"I am tempted to go and have a word with Lady Samantha," said Alfred, handing over some money, "but perhaps I will leave it a couple of days – I don't want her to think I am being pushy."

"From what I have heard Lady Samantha would welcome suggestions and help from any quarter. They are not as short of money as they like to let people think – they have just been reluctant to spend any more on Owlerton Hall."

"And where did you hear that titbit?"

"You hear all kinds of things in a shop of this size. Let's just say that I heard it from a very reliable source."

Alfred picked up his groceries, smiled knowingly at Philippa and waved a goodbye.

\* \* \*

"I wonder if there is anything that can be offered to Mona for next season if the Sands isn't back up and running," said Rita, sifting through some papers.

"I do wish you would stop working," said Jenny. "We are supposed to be having a day off and really, Rita, Mona isn't your concern."

"But she does work for us."

"Yes, but we are nothing to do with the contract she had at the Sands. Besides, that was only seasonal work – it was the same for Lilly Brockett when she worked there, only she also had the General Hospital in the winter months, and I am sorry but I don't think patients and Mona would go together very well, even if they did have a job going."

"Perhaps I could have her do some housework here," said Rita, looking round.

"But you and Elsie hardly need a cleaner," said Jenny. "You would be throwing your money away. How do you think Maud Bennett survives in the winter months? She helps her sister out in her gift shop. Mona needs to find her own solution and, if my memory serves me right, she didn't work last winter. At least that's what I heard."

Rita put the papers back in their folder and laid them to one side. "Perhaps we can increase her hours at the office. She could come in every day instead of the three, it wouldn't cost us that much more and she does keep the place looking nice. I enjoy walking up the stairs to the smell of furniture polish."

"Well, that's up to you, but I would hold fire on it for the moment and see what happens; besides, Mona may like being idle in the winter, perhaps that bucket and her go into hibernation."

"Jenny Benjamin, go and wash your mouth out with soap, you are getting too sassy for your own good," Rita laughed. "Now, this day off then, where shall we go?"

"Why don't we take a trip over to Norwich, have a look round the shops and a spot of lunch at the Berni Inn?"

"I'll grab my bag – your car or mine?"

"Why don't we take the train? I'll order a taxi to take us to the station."

Rita nodded. "Good idea."

* * *

Maud looked round the gift shop. "You know what, sister dear, this place could do with a spot of paint and sprucing up. Those shelves have seen better days."

"Are you in one of your bored moods?" asked Enid, putting some invoices to one side. "You are always like this when you are bored. Who is going to do the paintwork in here, may I ask? If you think I am climbing ladders at my time of life, you can think again."

"We can get a man in to do it. Must be plenty of workmen round here that would be glad of the work."

"If you think I am letting some fly-by-night loose in my shop with a paintbrush, you are very much mistaken. If it needs doing, as you say it does, we will get someone in proper to do it and that, dear sister, is going to cost money."

"Now, if that nice Dave Grant and his oppo were here, he would do it for us."

"But he isn't. Now, make yourself useful and put these bags on display – thought they might go well at Christmas."

Maud picked up a couple of faux-leather bags. "Well, these are hardly the latest in fashion, Enid. How much are we charging for these?"

"The ticket is on the strap."

"Good Lord above, daylight robbery," said Maud with a heavy sigh.

"How else can we pay for a painter and decorator to come in? I have profit margins to think about, besides, this new money is a rip-off, as I have said before."

Maud cleared a space to display the bags. "Yes, so you have said many times, Enid."

The doorbell jangled and Muriel Evans came in smiling. "Morning ladies, quite a nice morning out there considering we are nearing Christmas. I say, those are rather nice."

Maud handed Muriel one of the bags. "Not a bad price either, I think I will get one for Freda for Christmas. This red one will do fine, it will be sort of Christmassy. Now, what I really wanted was some small items to put in stockings – my Barry likes a stocking."

"Shopping early then, Muriel?" said Enid, taking the bag from her and wrapping it in some tissue paper.

"Well, I thought I would make a start," said Muriel. "I was at a loose end, as my Barry is decorating one of the bedrooms at the moment and it is best I leave him to it."

Enid exchanged glances with Maud. "Where's your sidekick today?"

Muriel laughed. "Oh, you mean Freda. She is a bit under the weather – I think she has a bit of a cold. I said I would pick up a few groceries for her on the way back."

"Give her my best," said Enid. "Now, things for stockings you said, here let me show you."

Maud coughed. "Is your Barry good at decorating, Muriel?"

Muriel smiled at Maud. "Oh, he is a dab hand with a brush. Why?"

"Well, Enid and I were just saying, only this morning as a matter of fact, that the shop needed a fresh lick of paint and neither of us is really up to climbing ladders."

"I could have a word with him if you like – he might be able to help you out."

"We would pay him, of course, and buy the materials."

Muriel left the shop with her purchases, waving goodbye, and the door jangled shut.

"Well, you didn't hang about, did you?" said Enid. "You were in there like a ferret up a drainpipe."

"Enid, if there was one thing our mother taught us, if you don't ask, you don't get. I'll go and put the kettle on."

* * *

Over their lunch at the Berni Inn, Rita relaxed a little and kicked her shoes off under the table. "This was a good idea of yours, Jenny, thanks for suggesting it. I really needed a break."

"Well, you do work hard," said Jenny.

"Well, we all do," said Rita, toying with the idea of whether or not to have a sweet. "One thing about show business is that it never stops."

Jenny nodded. "I think I will just have coffee, I couldn't make room for a sweet."

"Then let's have a brandy with it," said Rita. "We're not driving – might as well enjoy ourselves."

"A coffee and a brandy apiece, please," said Jenny, as the waiter came to the table. "This is a hard life, on your feet all day serving customers. I wouldn't fancy it."

"No, you have to have some stamina to do waiting," Rita agreed. "Now, where shall we go this afternoon? I need to pick up some tights and I wouldn't mind popping into Bonds for a look round."

"Jarrolds for me – there's a book on dancing I'm after and I thought it would make a present for Jill and Doreen at Christmas."

"Don't mention Christmas," said Rita with a groan. "It only seems like yesterday when it was here."

Jenny laughed. "It will be panto time before you know it. I bet all the amateur clubs have been rehearsing since the beginning of the month."

"And the rest." Rita smiled. "And what annoys me is when I hear people saying they are just like professionals. No, love, they are not. Professionals have a two-week rehearsal period if they are lucky and then they are on with the show, eyes and teeth!"

"Calm down, Rita, we're talking work again. Here's the waiter, let's enjoy the moment while we can."

* * *

## Sunday, 31 October

Barry Evans opened the front door.

"Hello Barry, is Muriel ready for bingo?" asked Freda, stepping into the hallway.

"You'll find her in the kitchen. I thought you weren't feeling well," said Barry, closing the front door and returning to watch the match highlights on the television in the lounge.

"Just a touch of the shivers, nothing more – feel as right as ninepence now."

Muriel put the milk away in the fridge and turned to greet Freda. "I thought you weren't feeling well, you were at death's door when I called in yesterday. Freda love, what on earth have you done?"

Freda looked at her friend in surprise. "Me, I ain't done nothing, and anyone that tells you different is lying."

Muriel ushered her neighbour into the adjoining room. "I am talking about your appearance, Freda Boggis. What on earth has happened to your hair, and did you know that you had green circles around your eyes? I know it's Halloween but right now you look a dead ringer for Margaret Hamilton in *The Wizard of Oz*."

Freda caught a look of herself in the mirror. "Oh, I see what you mean," she said, sitting herself down. "Well, as you will remember, I had my hair permed at The House of Doris a couple of days ago."

Muriel nodded. "And it looked lovely – a bit tight on the curl, but it was nice."

"Well, Sadie Rowan called round earlier."

"Yes, I know Sadie, what did she want?"

"Well, just a chat really," said Freda. "She hasn't been the same since she lost her Douglas. As you know, Sadie used to do the make-up and hair for the local amateur dramatics."

"Yes, she did," said Muriel, "about twenty years ago, before she started losing her sight."

"Well, she looked at my hair through those bottle-thick glasses of hers and said she could loosen it up, and then she said I could do with a bit of make-up and produced some eyeshadow she had bought off the market and started having a go at my eyes."

"Freda Boggis," said Muriel, going to her bag in the hope she had a pot of cold cream handy. "Why did you let her? We can't have you going to the Palace looking like that, you'll frighten the passengers on the bus for one thing, and the staff at the Palace will think I've turned up with Charlie Cairoli."

"I felt sorry for her," said Freda. "I was going to ask her to come along to bingo, but she wouldn't be able to see the numbers."

Muriel smiled at Freda; sometimes she despaired at her friend, but there was also no denying that Freda's heart was in the right place.

* * *

It was a few days later when Lilly passed her driving test that she announced the wedding to William was off. What did she need a man for, she had asked, looking in the mirror; she was quite capable of changing a washer and mowing her own lawn. She did feel a bit mean – after all, it was William who had taught her to drive and taken her to her classes in Lowestoft, but now she could drive herself. He seemed to take it well but insisted that he carry on doing her garden as he found it relaxing.

There was a certain amount of sadness expressed when the news got around. Many who knew Lilly had wanted her to find happiness again, but had agreed that maybe she had found it when she was able to close the door on a home she owned to write the novels that were flying off bookshelves quicker than the staff could fill them.

It was Reverend George's daily, Martha Tidwell, who told him the news about Lilly.

"I am sure that Lilly has made the right decision for her," he said, as Martha dusted the ornaments on the shelf. "I wonder if I should go and visit her?"

Martha put her duster down. "It wouldn't do any harm, Reverend, and I am sure she would welcome the visit."

Reverend George laid down his pen and stood up. "There is no time like the present," he said and moved towards the door. "The Lord moves in mysterious ways."

Martha picked up her duster and set about her task. "He surely does," she called after him. "I won't bother with the coffee this morning – I expect Lilly will offer you something."

Lilly was busy at her desk when she heard the doorbell ring. She invited Reverend George into the lounge and sat down.

"I just wanted to make sure that you were okay, Lilly. I heard about the wedding being called off."

Lilly smiled. "Well, that is very kind of you, and I was coming along to see you, but I've been caught up with a pressing storyline."

"How did William take the news?"

"Very well," said Lilly. "I think we both realised that we had become close because of the driving lessons and his help in the garden. I never felt any love for William and I think he was looking for companionship. I know how much he misses his wife, but I know how much I enjoy my independence. When he asked me to give up Rose Cottage and go and live with him when we were married, it dawned on me that to marry him would not be the right thing to do. He seems happy to carry on doing my garden and now that I have passed my driving test he won't have to worry about taking me to and from my lessons in Lowestoft. He has kindly offered to help me choose a car that I can manage and I am sure we will continue to remain friends, and I think that is what matters."

"You seem to have thought of everything and I am so pleased that you will both be able to remain friends."

"I think," said Lilly, looking at Reverend George thoughtfully, "that maybe William would appreciate a visit from you. Men aren't as resilient as us women. He may open up to you more than he has to me."

Reverend George stood up. "William is coming along to the vicarage this afternoon, so I will have a chat with him then. And remember, Lilly, if you ever need anything my door is always open."

Lilly thanked him and showed him out.

Martha was just on her knees dusting the feet of the armchairs when Reverend George came back into his study. "Well, that didn't take long I must say," she said, putting the lid back on the tin of polish. "I suppose you'll want that coffee after all."

* * *

Maud Bennett looked at the boxes surrounding her sister, Enid. "I said I would give you a hand. What on earth have you ordered?"

"It's some Christmas stock," said Enid, smiling at her sister.

"Who did you order for, the whole of Norfolk?"

"There was an offer on, one of the reps showed me some discontinued stock at very good prices and I thought I could shift it and make a few pounds."

"There are enough boxes here to start a wall between the counter and the customers."

"Oh, I expect a lot of it is just packing," said Enid, taking a knife and attacking the packing tape of one of the larger boxes."

Maud took off her jacket. "We are having lunch out today, there is no way I am going home and doing a roast after helping you with this lot. We can go to the Star. I will phone Derek and reserve a table."

"A bit extravagant," said Enid, pulling out some of the brown paper packing.

Maud began dialling, "Well, if you make as much money as you think on this little lot, it will be but a mere dent in the profits."

Enid was unpacking ornaments depicting the stable of the nativity and placing them on the counter. Each one was a complete scene – the shepherds, the wise men and Gabriel the archangel standing on top. Maud picked up one of them. "These are quite big," she said, taking a closer look at the one she was holding. "These shepherds have wonky eyes. This one needs a white stick, never mind a crook."

As each of the cribs was unpacked another fault was found – some sheep had only three legs, one of the wise men's camels had an extra hump and a couple of the Marys looked as if they were hiding something under their headdresses.

Maud shook her head. "I have counted twenty-four of these monstrosities. Please tell me there are no more."

Enid looked at her packing note. "No, that's the lot of those."

"How much were you planning on selling these for?"

"I think they could sell at five pounds at least."

Maud laughed. "Well, I suggest you display them in a very dim part of the shop, sister dear, anyone mad enough to part with a fiver for this heap of rubbish needs their bumps feeling."

Enid huffed and began opening another box, this time revealing sets of coloured glass baubles which, on close examination, were all intact. There were Christmas fairies, napkin holders, candles and a few very strange-looking gnomes dressed in Christmas outfits holding what looked like a knife and fork in their chunky hands.

When Enid went to put the kettle on, Maud sneaked a look at the invoice. Admittedly, the total wasn't as much as she dreaded it would be, but how on earth any of this faulty stock would be sold was anyone's guess.

# Chapter Three     *Superior Interiors*

*Monday, 1 November*

L ooking through the adverts in the local paper, Alfred Barton's eyes hovered over one for "Superior Interiors – let us change your décor and do the work for you. Private Houses, Hotels and Theatres a speciality, please call or write for details."

Picking up the receiver, Alfred dialled the number and was astounded by how quickly the call was answered. A warm Brummie female voice said hurriedly, "Superior Interiors, how may I be of service to you this morning?"

Alfred explained his requirements and asked if it would be possible for a representative from Superior Interiors to visit the hotel.

"Just one moment, please, I'm just checking our diary for you. We are very busy at the moment with the Christmas season fast approaching."

"Really?" said Alfred. "I wouldn't have thought that many people would want the upheaval at this time of the year, which is why I thought I would chance a call to your good selves."

Looking at the blank diary pages lying on the desk in front of her, she continued, "Oh, you would be surprised, Mr Barton, we get a lot of enquiries at this time of the year. I am just looking through the diary now and I am finding it difficult to find a rep that might be free to visit."

Looking at the open pages of the *Eastern Daily Press*, Alfred glanced at an adjacent advertisement. "Thank you for your time, I do have a couple of other companies to try, so maybe I will call you back if I don't get anywhere."

"Wait!" screamed the voice down the phone at him. "I think I have found someone, how would tomorrow afternoon suit?"

"As soon as that," said Alfred, "I thought you said you were busy."

"This is a cancellation that came in and I hadn't spotted it. The lady in question passed away and her daughter phoned to cancel."

Alfred's finger was poised over "Randolph Carlton's Hotel Refurbishments". "Maybe I will just call a couple of other places."

"We give a twenty per cent discount if more than six rooms are refurbished," came the gushing tones of the woman at the end of the telephone, "and we can also offer a wonderful selection of furniture direct from the suppliers at rates you wouldn't find anywhere else."

"Perhaps you could send me a brochure and I will think about it. I am not planning on opening the hotel again until April next year, so I have plenty of time."

"We are awaiting delivery of some new brochures from our printers. If you would like our representative to visit tomorrow afternoon we can waive the consultancy fee, how does that sound?"

Alfred paused to think.

"Are you still there, Mr Barton?"

"Yes, I am still here," said Alfred. "Okay, if your rep can be here at two o'clock tomorrow afternoon, I will see him."

"Let me see, it won't be David Drummond, he is frightfully busy on a project in Huddersfield, but we can send over our queen of Superior Interiors, Sandie Cross."

"Would you like the exact location of the hotel?"

"That won't be necessary. We pride ourselves on being fully au fait with all areas in the country. Sandie Cross will be with you at two on the dot."

At two on the dot, Alfred greeted Sandie Cross in the hotel reception; she was swathed in a purple cloak and was wearing stilettos, a turban and large dark glasses. She held out a gloved hand which Alfred shook politely.

"So, this is the Beach Croft," she said in a strange accent which Alfred couldn't quite place – it had the sound of Bristol about it, but he wasn't sure. "One has heard of it, of course, but never actually seen it." She moved from the reception area and headed straight into the lounge. "Oh my goodness, I see the problem here, my dear. Those curtains and this carpet – they are not at one with each other. The furniture is very dated, too dark for a room of this size and you have such heavenly windows looking out onto that wonderful vista."

Alfred went to say something but was swept aside by Sandie who walked back into reception and over to the dining room. "You see, too much, too much, too much!" she exclaimed, examining the tablecloths and the stand that held the cutlery. "No, I can see the problem here – it needs updating. These tablecloths are so fifties – no, I am wrong, forties – they remind me of an old ladies' teashop. This cutlery is very of its day, but I am surprised someone hasn't broken their wrist trying to lift the damn things. Are those really the kind of glasses you serve drinks in? No, Mr Barton, this simply will not do, my dear man."

Marching by a bewildered Alfred, she headed for the staircase. "This could look so lovely, but the pattern on these stair treads would give you nightmares." She began her ascent to the first floor. "Oh, these walls are dreadful and where on earth did you get these paintings from? They are hideous. Was there a closing-down sale at Miss Havisham's?"

Alfred wanted to tell her they were his late grandfather's, but Sandie had flung open a bedroom door. "Just look at this décor and those spreads – one doesn't have tassels anymore – it really is very dated indeed. Where on earth did that mirror come from, and is that really a stuffed ferret on that shelf above the picture rail?"

She moved to the bay window overlooking the front of the hotel and onto the cliff beyond, and muttered and tutted under her breath as she did so. "These nets will have to go, Alfred. When were they last laundered? They smell of stale cigarette smoke."

In spite of her high heels, she strode across the room with her cloak billowing out behind her and flung open the oak wardrobe. "My goodness, one would expect Edmund and co to emerge from here – I can see what C.S. Lewis was getting at when he wrote those Narnia stories. Never mind Narnia, you could lose the whole of Asia in there."

She went out of the bedroom and walked along to inspect one of the bathrooms. "Lord preserve us, I haven't seen tiles like this since I was last taken short in Calcutta. I didn't even know they still produced things like this. Are those the original taps? My goodness, how on earth are you supposed to turn the handle – you supply a pair of pliers I suppose?" She tutted loudly and shook her head.

Alfred struggled to actually say anything as Sandie Cross went from room to room and floor to floor, tutting, making withering remarks and dismissing anything that might have been of value in its day.

She found herself in Alfred's private apartment at the top of the hotel and sighed. "Well, at last," she remarked, looking around her. "I can see someone has given some thought to this area, unlike the hotel that time forgot. Your wife's touches I presume?"

Alfred nodded.

Sandie flung herself down on the sofa and looked up at Alfred. "Why on earth didn't you allow your wife to have some say in the furnishings? Look around you and then compare them to what I have just seen."

Alfred sat down in the armchair opposite.

"Well, Mr Barton, we have a lot of work to do here. I can see warmer colours, lighter furniture, new beds and mattresses – in fact, practically everything needs to be replaced. Now, if you will get me a coffee I will write some ideas down and somewhere in my car I have some sample fabrics. We can go and look at carpets together, but I suggest that the reception area is tiled at the edges with a centre walkway to the reception desk. The lounge will need gutting and that bar area must be replaced. The dining room needs a lot of attention, and when I have had my coffee I would like to see the kitchens and storage area – I expect they could also do with the Superior Interior touch."

Alfred sat stunned and didn't know what to say.

"Jump to it, man, coffee please, quick sticks – time is of the essence here."

Once they had their drinks, Alfred stirred his own cup of coffee as Sandie continued, "I took a look at the cellar area while you were otherwise engaged. That's a big space down there and, with the basement windows giving some light, I think you should seriously consider making it into a club of some sort. The guests would be able to enjoy a night or two and when opened up to the public you could see yourself well and truly on the map for entertainment."

"I'd never thought about it," said Alfred. "We've used the area mainly to store furniture and crockery."

"It is a space that needs investment," said Sandie. "It could open up a whole new world of possibilities. You could have a pianist and hold dances and cabaret nights – the possibilities are endless."

"I will give the matter some thought," said Alfred, his mind ticking over the idea. "But for the time being, the hotel is probably more in need."

Sandie nodded in agreement, but she could tell that the seed had been sown and Alfred would be on side within a month or two.

When Sandie Cross left some two hours later, Alfred was unsure whether or not he had agreed for Superior Interiors to carry out the work. He hadn't actually signed anything but had been totally swept away by Sandie who seemed to be making a lot of decisions. He wished now that Jean was here to deal with Miss Cross – she would have spoken up. He poured himself a large scotch and went over the ideas in his head one more time. Perhaps he really should go and have a word with Chippy Woods after all.

\* \* \*

## Friday, 5 November

Bob Scott tore open the envelope and read the letter from Goldberg Holdings who owned The Golden Sands Theatre and pier. A cheque was enclosed which would cover the next few weeks of his employment. Goldberg Holdings had now assessed the damage at the theatre and had decided to sell the pier and theatre as seen.

"I don't understand why they didn't send someone to speak to us personally," said Beverley, who had met Bob in Matthes coffee bar. "It's so callous to just write a letter and enclose a cheque. Now I am without a job – something that at this time of the year I don't relish. Sorry to put this on you Bob, you are in the same boat."

"Maud won't be too happy," said Bob, "or any of the backstage crew. All you can say in their favour is that they are seasonal staff. Me and you are permanent."

"I wonder who will buy it?" said Beverley, playing with the sugar shaker on the table. "I like working at the Sands, I don't really fancy taking on a Christmas job somewhere, but I am going to have to."

"Hello you two, and what brings you into Matthes?"

They looked up and the smiling face of Rita beamed down at them. Ordering some tea, she sat down beside them and heard their tale of woe.

"Look, it isn't much," said Rita, looking at the pair, "but I have just taken on some extra work for the Sparrows Nest, not only that, but I am going to help Alfred Barton sort out the theatre at Brokencliff and an extra pair of hands wouldn't go amiss."

Beverley looked at Rita and knew she wasn't telling the whole truth. "Rita, that is really kind of you, but I know you have enough staff to help you with that sort of thing, there wouldn't be enough to keep me and Bob busy."

Rita smiled and touched Beverley's arm. "Look, I admit there may not be enough for two, but seriously, Julie my receptionist could do with a hand. She does all the paperwork and looks after my diary, and that of the JB Dancing School, so you wouldn't be idle."

"Take it," said Bob, looking at Beverley. "It will tide you over for a few weeks."

"It wouldn't be long term," said Rita, "but if it helps you out."

Just then the voice of Malcolm Farrow interrupted them. "Rita, there you are, I thought you meant us to meet upstairs in the restaurant."

Rita introduced Beverley and Bob.

Malcolm sat down and motioned for the waitress to bring a pot of tea and some sandwiches and fancies. "I am sorry to hear about the Sands," he said, hearing the news first hand. "It is a lovely venue. I wish I could offer you something at the Nest, but I am only just in there myself."

Bob nodded his thanks. "I will find something eventually. Look, I have to be going."

"But I've just ordered some tea and cakes," said Malcolm, "please don't leave on my account."

"I ought to be off too," said Beverley, getting to her feet. "I have to go and get Ian something for his tea. I think I will get some steak, he won't be too happy when he hears my news. Rita, thanks for your offer, can I let you know in a couple of days' time, please? I am still trying to get my head around this letter."

Malcolm stood up and shook hands with them both and then as they watched the pair head out towards the front of the bakery he said, "I wish I could offer them something at the Nest."

"Something will turn up for them, me old lover," Rita replied, watching the pair head out towards the front of the bakery. "Bob won't stick around waiting for a buyer for the pier if what I have heard is anything to go by. He will be off to London or another seaside resort. He has years of managerial experience behind him. Beverley will sort herself out, strong sensible head she has."

"So, Rita, now that you have tried to sort out their problems, have you given mine any more thought?"

"As a matter of fact I have," said Rita, taking a notepad from her bag. "Jenny and I thought a variety show, something along the lines of the one we presented at the Sands this year. I think I can get the heartthrob all the ladies are talking about – Christian Lapelle. His appearance on *Opportunity Knocks* has made him a household name. He has no agent to speak of and I have managed to get him on to my books. Prior to his recent television fame, he mainly worked the nightclub circuit, but found it punishing. You know what these places are like – two shows, in a smoky atmosphere and you don't get home until all hours of the night."

"Wow, Christian Lapelle," said Malcolm. "I am impressed."

"It would have to be once nightly I think and, if my observations of him are right, he may only wish to appear at the end of the show and not enter into all the other stuff we expect variety artists to do."

"So, there are no sketches or speciality numbers."

"I may be able to get him to agree to an opening number with the dancers, but I would be pushing my luck with anything else."

"It sounds okay to me," said Malcolm.

"I'm meeting with him this week – he's at The Talk of Norwich nightclub and I will report back with all the news."

The waitress arrived with the order and laid out a selection of pastries and cakes and a pot of tea enough for six people.

"I hope you're thirsty," said Malcolm with a laugh. "We may be here some time."

As Beverley went about her shopping she began to think over what Rita had suggested to her. She put the two steaks in her bag and thanked the butcher and made her way down the road. At least it would tide her over for a bit and something was bound to turn up.

As she opened her front door the telephone was ringing. It was Bob Scott.

"I have made a decision," said Bob, sounding quite excited. "I am going to rent the house out and travel the world for a bit. I have often wanted to visit places like Australia and America and this may be my only chance."

Beverley was very surprised; she had never heard Bob mention wanting to travel before. "If you are sure that is what you want to do, Bob. Well, let's face it, you have nothing to lose."

"I've been thinking too," said Beverley. "I am going to take Rita up on that offer and wait and see what else comes along."

"Good for you," said Bob. "Look, before I head off I would like to take you and Ian out for a farewell meal. I will invite Maud and co, of course, and I will get back to you with a date."

Beverley replaced the receiver and went to the kitchen. Life certainly was full of surprises.

\* \* \*

## Wednesday, 10 November

"So, Alfred, my suggestion is this," said Rita, looking across her desk at him. "We bring back plays to the Little Playhouse."

Alfred looked surprised. "But we weren't doing good business towards the end, that's why we pulled them."

"Ah, but what audiences were you aiming them at?" Rita said with a knowing smile. "I asked Jenny and Elsie to do some research on my behalf. With the Golden Sands out of action we can turn the attention to Brokencliff. We already know that big plans at Owlerton Hall are underway – Lady Samantha is keen to attract large coach parties and 'we' can get in on the action."

There was a pause before Rita continued. "It has long been the opinion of many that closing the Little Theatre in Great Yarmouth was a mistake. Visitors like to have a choice of things to go to, especially the older people. They don't always want to go and watch a variety show and hear loud music. So, the idea is that we stage two plays, alternating them daily Monday to Saturday, but matinee performances only, at two o'clock. One should be a thriller and the other a comedy or a farce. The plays must be no more than two hours including a fifteen-minute interval. Each play should have one set – this will cut down on unnecessary scene shifting. With the plays finished by four o'clock, we could arrange with Owlerton Hall to lay on afternoon tea for those who wanted it. Thinking along those lines, Lady Samantha may be agreeable to a tour of the Hall followed by the play, or vice versa."

"I think I am following you," said Alfred, who was now fully engaged with Rita's suggestions and sitting bolt upright in his chair. "So, in the evenings we could show a film – or bingo that everyone keeps going on about."

Rita laughed. "My dear Alfred, I know how much you hate the thought of running bingo sessions, though of course you could consider it. I have another solution. We stage a simplified variety show in the evening at eight o'clock."

Alfred looked at Rita in astonishment. "But how would that work? You would need extra sets and there will be the play sets to change."

"All furniture from the sets would be removed at four. By using flats from the fly tower and many different curtain formations you will not be relying on big staircases and the like. I said simplified."

A silence fell and the only noise came from the clock ticking on the wall. Rita sat back in her chair and waited; she watched Alfred carefully and could almost see his mind throwing around the idea.

"I would need to source some plays," said Alfred, finally.

"If you take care of that side of things I will get my team working on the bill for the show. I don't know much about theatre proper so I will have to rely on your judgement to ensure that the actors and actresses that you employ are of the right calibre. You must know of some you can call upon – after all, they were part and parcel of your world before."

Alfred nodded. "Yes, I think I know who I can approach. Who were you thinking of for the variety show, out of interest?"

"I think I can get Lauren Du Barrie back, Jill and Doreen will supply dancers and I will sound out Jonny Adams. I have one or two other ideas but I will need to check them out before I commit."

"This really is very good of you, Rita," said Alfred. "I thought you would be concentrating your time on the Sparrows Nest."

"That is in hand," said Rita. "Besides, I have Jenny and of course Elsie working alongside me. Elsie is losing herself in the job, as I did when I lost Ted. I know how much she misses Don. His empire was larger and wider spread than many people realised. Elsie will eventually fold the agency in London, but there are a lot of contracts to be honoured, so it's all hands on deck at the moment."

Julie Porter popped her head round the office door. "Sorry to interrupt you both, but Jenny has just been on the phone to remind you of your meeting with Christian Lapelle."

"Thanks, Julie," said Rita, "call her back and tell her I am on my way."

"Wasn't Christian Lapelle on *Opportunity Knocks* a few weeks ago?" asked Alfred, getting up to leave.

"Yes, me old lover, he was," said Rita, grabbing her car keys from her drawer and picking up her handbag, "and if I am lucky I may be able to bag him for the season at the Nest before the big time comes calling."

"French, isn't he?" said Alfred, holding open the door for Rita.

"As French as a beret and a string of onions," said Rita. "I am hoping that the old Ricer magic will pay off."

And as Alfred followed Rita down the stairs to the main door, he knew that it would – Rita Ricer made things happen.

On his way back to the hotel, Alfred called in at Owlerton Hall at the request of Lady Samantha who had telephoned him earlier.

"You see what a great job Selwyn Woods has made of the ballroom, as I like to call it. I also got him to fix up a few other things while he was here. He may be a grumpy so-and-so but he does deliver."

Alfred nodded. "I wonder if he might be able to do something with the theatre entrance. The box office is really too small and I would like to see it made bigger, but keep it central. There is also a bit of work that needs doing on the dressing rooms."

Lady Samantha motioned for Alfred to follow her through to her private lounge. "There is no harm in approaching him," she replied. "He will probably huff and puff a bit but once he goes through his funny little ways I expect you will find him willing. Now, allow me to offer you some tea, cook has been busy and made a wonderful Victoria sponge with fresh cream."

Alfred sat down.

"You mentioned on the telephone that you were meeting with Rita Ricer – pray tell, how did that go?"

"Well," began Alfred, "she has suggested a number of things and I think you and I will be able to do some business together."

There was no time like the present, so on his return to the Beach Croft he dialled Selwyn's number and was surprised when it was answered by Chippy himself.

An hour later, Alfred was standing in the foyer of the Little Playhouse as Chippy measured up. He tapped his pipe on the wall and relit his pungent tobacco.

"I think I will be able to extend it by two foot width-wise and bring it forward by another two foot without people standing outside the front door, so to speak. You better show me what you will be wanting in those dressing rooms of yours, might as well get it all on paper whilst I am here."

Alfred showed Chippy the dressing rooms and pointed out where he thought changes could be made to make them more comfortable and to provide better wardrobe facilities.

"You see, what I would be inclined to suggest, Alfred, is this," said Chippy, taking a long puff on his pipe. "When you have these actor people of yours, you could have dividers to separate the areas and make them a bit more private. Fold-back doors would do it – either way, you could use them or not, depending."

"I hadn't thought of that," said Alfred.

"And if you take my advice, for what it's worth," Chippy continued, "you would consider having a proper area out front for a small band. You need only lose the first row and it would mean not having them cluttering up the stage when you have those dancers on. I came to see your show with the missus and was mightily impressed with those variety girls. Old Jenny Benjamin used to be behind those dancers, you know. My wife knows old Jenny from when she was a Bluebell girl. Some say Jenny lost the plot a few years ago, but I am of the opinion – and you don't have to take my word on this – that old Jenny still has a lot to offer the world of entertainment. Good old gal that she is."

This was quite a speech for Selwyn, and Alfred was amazed by the passion in his voice and wondered if in days gone by Chippy hadn't been a bit sweet on Jenny.

"I like your ideas," said Alfred, getting the subject back on track. "Perhaps you can do some figures and send them on to me."

Selwyn gave a huff. "I can do better than that," he said, taking a pencil from behind his ear and producing a piece of paper from his overall pocket. Licking the tip of the pencil, he jotted down some figures and handed the paper to Alfred.

"This looks very reasonable."

"It does include materials, but I think I can have this all in hand within the next couple of weeks if it suits?"

"As soon as that?" said Alfred. "Then the answer is yes."

Chippy put his pencil back behind his ear and shook Alfred's hand. "I understand you have employed the services of another company to do over your hotel. I hope they are keeping to their schedule, I hear you want to be open again in time for Whitsun."

Alfred blushed. "I was going to approach you, Selwyn, but I thought the job might be too big and I know how busy you are. Lady Samantha was delighted with what you did with the ballroom."

"Ah yes, well, Lady Samantha knows craftsmanship when she sees it. I'll be off now then, Alfred. I should be able to start on Wednesday. I will give you a call. Remember, if it all goes wrong with them people you've got in to do the hotel, give me a call. I am sure I will be able to sort you out."

And with that parting gesture, Selwyn "Chippy" Woods took his leave as Alfred's face resembled the look of a rabbit startled in car headlights.

## *Thursday, 11 November*

"Was that Rene Sparrow I just saw coming out of the shop?" asked Maud as she entered carrying a box of fancies from Matthes to cheer Enid up, who hadn't been feeling too good.

Enid looked up from the counter. "Yes it was, she has been chatting away for the last half hour. You know they took her mother to Spain?"

"Really, at her age? To my knowledge she has never been further than Lowestoft."

Enid put down her pen. "Well, they thought it would do her good, a change of air, but of course she falls asleep at the drop of a hat."

"Well, on a flight that can be a godsend, especially as she has problems with her dentures. The last I heard was they were chafing something chronic."

"Well, apparently," said Enid, wanting to tell her news, "and I am not one for gossip as you know, but when they arrived back in London, she fell asleep near the baggage-claim carousel. Of course, Sid and Rene hadn't spotted it at all – you know what Rene is like when she travels, very nervous."

"Oh yes, that time on the train when she pulled the communication cord thinking it was to open the windows."

"Well, her poor mother fell onto the carousel and went round three times before Rene or Sid even noticed."

"Did she hurt herself?" asked Maud, laying down the Matthes bag on the counter.

"A bruise on her left leg and she came off the carousel clutching a straw donkey."

"Oh! Nasty."

"Yes, I can't say I'd be too pleased taking one of those blessed things home," Enid replied with feeling. "Do you remember her mother used to do a turn down at the Dying Swan, she did have quite a good voice?"

"That's right," said Maud, "she did impersonations. Ethel Merman was one, I remember, though the night I saw her she sounded more like Bernard Bresslaw."

"Well, sister dear, I hope you are going to make a pot of tea," said Enid, peering into the bag. "Oh good, you got a couple of vanilla slices and a couple of iced buns."

"I was going to get fresh cream," said Maud, heading out to the back of the shop to put the kettle on, "but they were having problems with the cream machine."

"No matter, these will go down a treat," said Enid, licking her lips; she really fancied a cake, good old Maud.

*Tony Gareth Smith*

# Chapter Four        *Seasonal Felicitations*

*December 1971*

Posters for the Christmas show starring Derinda Daniels at the Sparrows Nest Theatre had caused quite a stir since they had been pasted up three weeks before. Advertisements in the *Eastern Daily Press*, *Great Yarmouth Mercury* and *Lowestoft Journal* had become a talking point. No one had ever staged a Christmas show before and some of the locals were quite excited about not having to rely on the usual pantomime offerings.

Derinda had agreed to do a three-week season and would appear with the largest ensemble to be seen in the area. There were to be twelve female and six male dancers. Ricky Drew was also to be on the bill along with an act that had been seen in the pre-season at the Golden Sands in 1969, The Dean Sisters, who did a rollerball act – rolling on large glitter balls up a three-tiered ramp while juggling. They would normally have been busy with a Christmas circus abroad but happened to be free for the three weeks of the show. Rita was delighted that she had been able to entice them back. Tommy Trent would be providing the laughs. There were a couple of new acts – The Long Islanders (a male folk group) and Lucy Locket and her ventriloquist doll, Dainty Daisy.

Beverley had taken up her position at Rita's Angels and her thoughts of not having enough to do were unrealised – on some days she didn't know whether she was coming or going.

Bob Scott had left for Australia and his house had been let to a couple he knew, so he went away with a clear head.

The market place was once again decorated with a beautiful Christmas tree and carols from The Salvation Army could be heard on Wednesday and Saturday market days. Palmers and Arnolds once again had their own Father Christmas grottos, with Palmers winning hands down with their Winter Wonderland Walk to Father Christmas's workshop. Arnolds had gone with the less exciting option of a small hut where children queued eagerly to meet Father Christmas and receive a gift. Shoppers wrapped in their winter best went in and out of shop doorways with worried and stressed faces as they checked off their Christmas lists.

The Golden Sands pier stood ghostly and unloved against the seascape beyond. Barriers, where once the entrance to the pier had been, were put in place to prevent anyone going onto the pier to view the charred remains of the theatre. With its future uncertain, many thought that the Golden Sands would never be the same again. As Rita walked along the seafront she stopped and looked at the barriers and thought of the lovely bar that had been created in her husband's name which was no more.

Many a local spoke their thoughts over the dinner table, "They will probably pull the whole thing down." – "Who in their right mind is going to take that lot on?" – "You never know, a company may just snap it up." to the "Well, I never went there anyway so it don't matter much to me."

The Beach Croft Hotel in Brokencliff had been taken over by an army of builders and electricians under the supervision of Sandie Cross, who turned up every morning at the hotel dressed in a totally inappropriate colourful outfit. Alfred did his best not to interfere but he watched furniture being loaded on to trucks, walls being knocked through and floors ripped up. He began to think that he would never see the hotel occupied by guests again and retreated to the haven of his rooms at the top which he had forbidden Sandie to enter.

Despite the Christmas stock being not one hundred per cent, all of Enid's bargain buys were flying off the shelves, much to Maud's amazement. When Maud was helping her sister in the shop, she couldn't help but point out one or two flaws for fear of customers returning the item after Christmas. Most customers accepted that the goods were seconds and for the few who didn't, they purchased something of a better quality so, all in all, Enid was having a bumper season.

The landladies enjoyed a wonderful Christmas gathering at Owlerton Hall and Lucinda worked the ballroom with aplomb, managing to speak to every landlady present. Maurice Beeney and his boys supplied the dance music and Freda, who was worse for wear in the drink department, treated everyone to her own version of the Rumba! Several men were seen heading to the facilities, as the sight of Freda's latest creation rising and falling as she kicked her legs in the air was more than they could stand. Lady Samantha agreed to make an appearance and hand out the raffle prizes, wearing a gown she had had made for the occasion and a tiara that caused quite a sensation. Talk turned to Shirley Llewellyn who hadn't been seen for weeks. Her guest house was on the market – it was clear she had left the area for good. Lucinda smiled to herself and looked at everyone enjoying the party and was pleased that at last she was able to do things her way without all the flash that Shirley had been so keen on. Ruby Hamilton had reluctantly attended and even she admitted to Petunia Danger that the organisation of the event had been second to none.

Something that Lucinda would dine out on for many a night to come.

The Christmas offering at the Sparrows Nest opened to rave reviews and Derinda Daniels had another hit on her hands. The Dean Sisters had changed their act from when they had appeared at the Golden Sands during the pre-season summer show with the addition of balancing on each other's heads. The audience was in awe. The Long Islanders proved a hit with their folk tunes and ended the act with a couple of Christmas favourites set to alternative folk music. Tommy Trent delivered laughs aplenty and Lucy Locket and her doll Dainty Daisy were both funny and a delight. The dancers were a sensation, never had such a large troupe of dancers been seen at a theatre venue on the Suffolk coast. The dancers provided glamour and glitz along with Christmas magic at its best. The costumes of feathers, spangles, top hats and tails were worthy of a show on their own. Ricky Drew provided a Christmas singalong and everyone agreed that a Christmas show should be on offer every year.

Rita Ricer stood at the back of the auditorium every night with Malcolm Farrow and watched to see that the show kept its pace.

"There is no doubt about it, Rita." said Malcolm, handing Rita a gin and tonic. "You have produced a wonderful show and I cannot wait to see what you come up with for the summer season."

Rita smiled. "Thank you, Malcolm. I will drink to that."

And as the two clinked glasses, there was the hint of a spark between them that they both felt.

## *Early January 1972*

Elsie Stevens was finding it hard to get over the loss of her husband. Everywhere she looked she was reminded of Don – at the offices in London, at their home and even at the offices of Rita's Angels. There was no getting away from the fact that her husband had played a large part in the world of variety. At the office in Regent Street, Elsie went through the folders for venues where Don was due to present summer shows. As was Don's way, some acts had been contacted, others had been auditioned and deals had been struck with the seaside theatres up and down the country. These would all need honouring, but Elsie knew that she couldn't do it alone. For the time being she would retain the young man that Don had engaged to run the office, but with Elsie feeling the need to sell up and move down to the East Coast, that arrangement would be short-lived and she didn't like the idea of not giving the young man enough notice to find another job. Norman Howard was hard-working; he had replaced a previous employee who on paper had looked fine, but in practice hadn't a clue. Obviously, Norman had become aware of the situation since Don's death, but he had carried on regardless, not wanting to let Elsie down, and besides, he loved his work and in the short time he had been working for Don Stevens had learned a lot about the world of variety. The office walls were covered with posters advertising the many shows that Elsie and Don had been behind. Norman had given the matter serious thought and had decided that he would like to stay in the business if at all possible and he wanted to broach the subject with Elsie, but the time never seemed to be right.

Taking the bull by the horns, he decided to call Rita Ricer and ask her advice. Rita listened carefully to what he had to say.

"Well, me old lover, I cannot speak on behalf of Mrs Stevens, but if you are really as serious as you say you are then I may be able to help you. There is no denying that there is a lot to sort out for the summer season and I know Mr Stevens would want to honour those bookings. I will speak with Mrs Stevens and make a few suggestions to her. I will also come up to London and meet you and we will see if something can be worked out. In the interim, please can you send me your CV so that I can look over your previous experience? I know you mentioned working for Rank for a short time. Oh, and before I go, Norman, if we did manage to keep things going, would you be willing to relocate?"

Norman replaced the receiver and began putting his CV together – he intended to strike while the iron was hot.

When she had come off the telephone, Rita ran the idea by Jenny.

"Do you think we could keep things running?" Jenny asked. "We have quite a lot on ourselves."

"We need to convince Elsie not to give up the agency – it would be too sad if the name of Don Stevens died with him. He was well respected in the business."

Jenny looked pensive. "I am not sure that Elsie could cope with things, everything is pretty raw at the moment."

"Look, if we can move this Norman Howard down here, we could run things side by side. We have Beverley on board now and she could act as his secretary."

"Exactly where are you thinking of putting this other office?" asked Jenny, looking around her.

"We can use the attic above that we currently use for storage. It's big enough and it does have windows."

"It would need some work done on it and that back staircase would need replacing. It would also need cleaning. I wouldn't want to be the one to approach Mona Buckle with the idea of cleaning another floor."

"She would be glad of the work," said Rita. "We can't be sure that the Sands will be back in operation, and besides, we could offer her more hours. It isn't as if she would have to clean all the offices every day."

Jenny sighed. "Well, first you had best get Elsie on side and then go and see this Norman. From what Elsie has said about him he sounds okay. I hope you know what you are doing, Rita."

Rita smiled at her friend. "You know, me old lover, I don't think I do, but let's face it, what have we to lose?"

It was some days later when Elsie had returned from London that Rita broached the subject of what to do with the agency. Elsie listened and shook her head.

"I don't think I could do it," said Elsie. "I wouldn't want the responsibility of running the agency without Don. Norman has kept things ticking over 'tis true, but maybe I should just give it all up. I have already put the house on the market. I am going to look for a bungalow down here."

"Steady on, me old lover," said Rita, taking Elsie's hand. "If you want to, you can move into my house – there is plenty of room and we wouldn't get under each other's feet. It's been working well the last few months."

"You are very kind, Rita, but I cannot encroach on your hospitality any longer."

"Stop your nonsense, of course you can. Look, Jenny and I can sort out the business side of the agency and if Norman is all he is cracked up to be then we shouldn't have too many problems. I am sure you would like to see the Stevens name kept alive."

"No, I am sorry, Rita. I want to close the agency. When Don died, the agency died too. I have no problem with you taking on some of the other acts or even striking a new deal with the venues Don had lined up for the season. I just couldn't bear to see Don's name on posters, it would break my heart."

This gave Rita some food for thought. She sat down at her desk and began to scribble down some ideas. After a couple of hours, she went and found Jenny who was with Jill and Doreen discussing some routines.

Jenny followed Rita into her office and sat down. "What's to do Rita?" she asked, looking at her friend's face, sensing some excitement there.

"Elsie is adamant that she wants nothing more to do with Don's agency, she wants it to close and for us to take his artists on to our books. I've thought of an idea."

Jenny laughed. "I guessed as much."

"Why don't we take on the offices in Regent Street ourselves? Buy the lease and have Rita's Angels in the West End as well as here. If Norman is as good as he says he is, we could leave him in charge for the time being and find another suitable person to join him."

Rita looked at the expression on Jenny's face. "Don't worry about the money, me old lover, I have a nice little nest egg stashed away. Besides, I could move my offices up to the attic here and we could let this office out. There is always someone wanting office space."

"Well, you can count me in," said Jenny. "I've got some capital I can use, and besides, it would be great if we were based centrally. We're a bit cut off down here when you think about it."

"I wonder if Bob Scott would be interested in becoming an agent based in London. He seems to have the wanderlust."

Jenny thought for a moment. "He might be open to the idea, but we mustn't forget his strengths lie in their management."

"So we get the boy Norman to do the leg work. He sounded as if he would be keen. Bob could keep things running in Regent Street. We can soon find him a secretary. Norman could gain experience by going around the country with me or you and then let him loose. Now, I wonder where I can find Bob, I hope he hasn't taken off again on his adventures, I need him here."

"Steady on, Rita, we're jumping the gun a bit. What if Elsie doesn't like the idea, or Bob says no, or Norman runs away screaming?"

Rita stood up and walked around the front of her desk. "Jenny me old lover, you see problems, I see solutions. Let's strike while the iron is hot. I will talk with Elsie, you find Bob."

Elsie listened to what Rita had to say and nodded. "If you think you are able to make a go of the offices in Regent Street then you have my blessing. You won't need to worry about buying out the lease; it has another twenty-five years to run. Changing the agency's name shouldn't be a problem and I am sure you will find the acts on the books willing to be represented by Rita's Angels. You have become something of a name in the business since you started taking things on."

"Are you sure you will be comfortable with it, Elsie?" said Rita, who knew how difficult it must be for her. "I don't want you to feel you are being railroaded into a decision that you are not happy with."

Elsie smiled. "I feel nothing of the sort I can assure you. If anything, you have taken a great weight off my mind."

\* \* \*

It didn't take Jenny too long to track down Bob Scott. He listened to the ideas that Rita was proposing, and said he would give it some thought and get back with his decision in a couple of days.

Rita and Jenny took the train to London and went to meet with Norman. It was also an opportunity for them to see the offices again. Norman was a very pleasant young man and Rita knew that she liked him from the off. Jenny could see that the offices had potential to include part of the dancing agency, but kept the thought to herself for the time being. While they were in town, the two took the opportunity to stay over a couple of nights at the Kensington Gardens Hotel, do some shopping and get better acquainted with Norman.

They arrived back in Great Yarmouth to a "yes" from Bob Scott, who was returning from his trip down under. He was going to stay with a friend in West London until he found himself a flat to rent.

All in all, it was going to be all change in the world of variety – Rita would now be competing with the big boys, and with the combining of two agencies she would certainly have the ammunition she needed to succeed.

## Mid-January 1972

It wasn't often that Lilly had time to read a novel. However a book by Dorothy L Sayers had had her spellbound since Christmas Day. Lilly had been thinking about a new twist to one of the stories she was working on and this story had given her an idea. Lilly had never written about a character being murdered; she had written about death in all shapes and forms, but never murder. How did you go about using poison to murder someone and what were the consequences? She went to her bookshelf and took down a small book about mushrooms, toadstools and other fungi. Dorothy L Sayers had killed off a character using fungi in a food dish. Lilly sat down to see what she could learn and how she might weave a similar idea into her plot. She began to make some notes in her exercise book and then sketched out some possible scenarios but none seemed right when she looked at them on the page. She closed the book and walked to the window. The wintry sunshine was lighting up the bare flower beds. Pulling on her winter coat, Lilly locked the front door and decided that a walk along the top of the cliffs would clear her head. She would walk over to Hopton and have a coffee in the café there. The sea air would get her writing flow working again, and it usually did the trick.

\* \* \*

"So, Alfred, how is the hotel coming along?" asked Rita as she looked at him from across the desk. "I have to say I was much impressed when I saw what you had done to the foyer at the Little Playhouse when I popped in to see how the local panto was faring."

"Oh, Superior Interiors didn't have anything to do with the foyer, no, that was Chippy – Selwyn Woods – he did some work at Owlerton Hall. Looking at the mess I see every day I can't help wondering if I shouldn't have offered the work to Chippy. Sandie Cross arrives on site every morning in the most ridiculous outfits and uses a megaphone to shout out her orders to the workmen who, I have to say, do get on with things."

"I have never heard of Superior Interiors," said Rita, putting the top back on the biro. "But then I have never had to call upon such services."

"They are relatively new," said Alfred, coughing and trying to hide how embarrassed he was feeling. "Based in Norwich. I have to say, whenever I phone them I usually get one or other of the staff there – one with a strong Scottish accent, the other is from Birmingham I think."

"So, Alfred, any more thoughts on how you intend to get plays back into the Little Playhouse?"

Alfred took some papers from his briefcase. "As a matter of fact, Rita, I have. I got on the blower to my old pal Ray Darnell who used to present the Clifftop Players. He was thrilled to hear from me and thinks he can put a company together for the season. He liked your idea of matinees and said he had often thought about that when things were not going too well. He will call me in a day or two so I should have more news then. He does know some good people and he will also look up a couple of plays with the same number in the cast – a thriller and a farce, as you suggested to me."

"That is good news, Alfred," said Rita, smiling. "I admit I did wonder whether we had left things too late. I've been working on a line-up for the variety show but I will tell you about that another time. I have another appointment in fifteen minutes with our accountant and I mustn't be late."

Beverley knocked and walked into the office. "Sorry to interrupt, I have those figures you need."

"Thanks Bev," said Rita, as Beverley left the office. "What a treasure she is. I am hoping I may be able to keep her on if the work is here. Sorry day when she lost her job at the Sands."

Alfred stood up. "Well, I shall be in the market for some staff myself when the hotel is finished. I really need a manager and an assistant, and then I can concentrate on the theatre."

"Well," said Rita, picking up the papers and her handbag. "Why don't you ask Beverley if she would be interested? She's a grafter and knows what she is doing. Bob Scott often said that everyone should have a Beverley – maybe you need one too!"

* * *

The call from Ray Darnell was positive. "You see, dear boy, I have managed to track down a few old stalwarts and I am delighted to say that I have Constance Anderson and her husband William Forbes on board. Neither has appeared at Brokencliff before but are seasoned professionals. You will remember Julia Burton, Fred Hughes, Patrick Prowse, Edmund Green, Edith Harris and Sue Wilson. They were all delighted to hear that you were putting plays back in the theatre."

Alfred beamed. "That really is wonderful news, Ray. Can I ask if you have come up with any ideas about the productions?"

"My dear boy, it is all in hand. You mentioned a thriller, and I have come up with *Death Nap* by Mildred Miles. It's quite gripping and I am sure the audience will lap it up. I have also sourced a farce, *Wardrobe Doors* by P.J. Proctor. It's along the lines of a Brian Rix and very funny."

"Will you be directing the plays?"

"Dear boy, of course. We will rehearse in a studio here in London and then spend a week at the theatre. I will post on the details of the sets. All in hand, dear boy, so they will be delivered to the theatre a week before the technical rehearsals."

"I cannot tell you how relieved I am," said Alfred, shouting above the banging of a workman who was on the floor below.

"Sounds like you are having something done there, old boy," said Ray.

"Having the whole place refitted," said Alfred. "Thought it was time I spent some money on the hotel."

"Wise man," said Ray. "Sorry to hear about Jean, nice filly as I recall. I am pleased I managed to steer clear of marriage lines. I don't think my lifestyle and a wife would go together. As a matter of interest, what company did you get in to do the hotel for you?"

"Superior Interiors," Alfred replied. "And the woman who manages the business is something else."

"A woman?" said Ray in a surprised tone. "That's unusual, but then I suppose the world is changing. Before you know it we will have a woman in 10 Downing Street."

Alfred laughed. "I think that's stretching things a bit."

"Anyway, old boy, must dash – have visits to make, people to see – toodle-pip for now."

"Toodle-pip," said Alfred, replacing the receiver with a smile. The thought of Ray Darnell with a wife amused him; the man was as camp as Christmas!

The loud banging of Sandie's army of workers was beginning to get on Alfred's nerves. It seemed that every morning twenty men would turn up, who spoke little English, to be told by Sandie the tasks for that day. Her commanding boom could be heard bouncing off the walls of an empty room she was currently giving her attention to.

Whenever Alfred asked Sandie how things were going, she held up her hand and came back with her standard reply. "My dear Mr Barton, when you see the finished product you will be stunned by the magic we are weaving here."

Something that Alfred was secretly dreading. As another piece of discarded furniture flew down to the car park below, Alfred, who had been watching from the window of his turreted living room, winced. "There goes Dad's desk."

Materials for the jobs in hand arrived daily, but all were covered in wrappings or dust sheets as if they were items being smuggled in. Alfred was beginning to feel quite alarmed. As he headed down the back stairs and out of the back door of the kitchen area, a curtain rail just missed him as it hit the tarmac. At the far end of the car park a medium-sized truck was parked, bearing the name Superior Interiors, and a tarpaulin covered whatever was hidden on the open back. Feeling like a schoolboy on a mystery adventure in an Enid Blyton story, Alfred looked around him and then up at the windows to ensure that no one was watching. He ran gingerly across the car park and crouched down at the side of the truck. Sneaking round the far side, where he thought he would have cover, he pulled back the tarpaulin to see what treasures lay beneath. He found large pots of paint bearing names he had never heard of. On closer inspection, the writing on the tins was in a language he didn't understand. The only thing he could fathom was the colours that the tins contained, marked by a square of colour on the lids – vibrant reds, yellows and greens; he held his breath in panic. In his mind he had visions of his hotel resembling the running order of a tube of Rowntree's Fruit Pastilles. As he looked closer he spotted rolls of wallpaper, again bearing no English wording. Through their plastic covering he could just make out some garish patterns of a dubious nature – one appeared to have half-naked men on. He quickly replaced the tarpaulin and crouched at the side of the truck putting his head in his hands. His beloved family hotel was to become a house of ill repute and, as another piece of furniture was hurled out of a window, he wondered how on earth he was going to take control of the situation. Sandie Cross was quite a scary lady.

*Tony Gareth Smith*

# Chapter Five

*All of a GAGGA*

## Wednesday, 26 January 1972

Once again the venue for the meeting was the Two Bears and several landladies had arrived early in order to bag the front seats. The Christmas evening at Owlerton Hall was thought by many to have been a great success. Lucinda had done away with the Landlady of the Year award, much to the relief of some but to the disappointment of others. There had been a raffle with twelve prizes and the top prize was a twenty-five pound gift token from Palmers, the second prize was lunch for two from Matthes and the third was a pass for two at the Regent cinema.

Maurice Beeney and his boys had provided a good selection of dance music and there had been a cabaret offering from Jonny Adams who did table magic with decks of cards. He managed to produce a rabbit from Muriel's bag, much to the surprise of all present. As promised, coaches had been laid on to ferry everyone to their homes and a good time was had by all.

Lucinda rapped her gavel, bringing the meeting to order, and asked Muriel to give a breakdown of how the Christmas evening had worked out. Lucinda thanked Erica who had secured all the prizes for the raffle and a round of applause rang out around the room as many nodded their approval.

Then Lucinda announced that all landladies should sign up to the cash and carry giant, Murdell and Pocock. She then called on Muriel to explain the pluses of joining the scheme.

Fenella turned to Agnes. "Have you noticed how Lucinda delegates these proceedings? If Shirley had still been at the helm, she would have been delivering this news, and she wouldn't have asked one of us to do it."

Agnes smiled. "Well, I will say this in her favour, it's a step in the right direction – she is letting people have their say and despite the mutterings of her being grander than her predecessor I would say that she has thought that one out and decided to change things. She didn't swank it too much at Owlerton Hall – we didn't all have to line up to shake her hand, and she was in with the rest of the crowd."

"I don't think Ruby Hamilton was too impressed though. She was heard to say she thought it had been well organised," replied Fenella.

"She didn't get her own way when she tried to insist that the Landlady of the Year award remained. As I seem to recall, didn't she leave early when the raffle was announced?" said Agnes.

"I think you are right, she didn't even buy a ticket."

Several of the ladies put their hands up to ask questions about how using a wholesaler would affect local business and Lucinda was happy to address this issue head-on.

"I am a great supporter of local business as Mrs Jary will tell you. I have been a customer there for years and that will not change," said Lucinda, smiling. "Murdell and Pocock will help you cut down some of your overheads, especially when it comes to buying in tea, for example. There are other benefits of using frozen produce – being able to buy in pies, fruit and vegetables. I have recently invested in a small chest freezer that will enable me to stock up on essentials to offer evening meals at a lower cost than I am able to at present. Instant mash potato is a great boon to the catering trade and being able to make Angel Delight or Instant Whip with water rather than milk will be a great saving."

"I don't like the sound of that," Nettie Windsor called out, feeling that she had kept quiet for long enough. "People will be able to tell the difference – that instant mash has a funny twang, and how can something normally made with milk taste the same if it's made with water?"

Lucinda smiled and turned to Erica. "Erica, over to you I think."

Erica stood up. "Well, ladies, this has certainly got us all talking and even I was sceptical at first, but you have to try these things first and I am delighted – or should I say 'Angel Delighted' – to have with us representatives from Murdell and Pocock who have prepared some of their frozen produce and their catering packs of custards for you all to try. So, if you would all like to make your way to the adjacent meeting room you will find this morning's coffee break totally supplied by the cash and carry chain. Feel free to sample anything you choose and don't be afraid to ask questions. I think you are all in for a pleasant surprise."

As everyone made their way out of the room, Lucinda took Erica by the arm. "You delivered that very well, thank you very much and, Muriel, the figures you produced are spot on. Now, let's join the others. The proof of the pudding, as they say, is in the eating."

\* \* \*

## *Thursday, 27 January*

"Beverley, thanks for these," said Rita, looking at the letters she needed to sign. "I wonder, when you get a minute can you see what you can find out about Superior Interiors? Alfred Barton mentioned them to me and I was thinking that maybe we should go ahead with the conversion of the attic upstairs here. It would give us some extra office space."

"Wouldn't you be best to ask Selwyn Woods?" said Beverley, taking the accounts book from the tray. "He is very good and locals swear by him."

"Yes, you are probably right. Tell you what, see if you can get a quote from both of them. I believe Sandie Cross is the designer at the superior lot, though according to Alfred she can be difficult to get hold of."

"I'll speak to Selwyn first," said Beverley. "He can probably pop over within the next couple of days with him being local."

"I will leave it with you," said Rita with a smile. "Oh, and on the subject of Alfred Barton, he may have a job offer for you."

"He has already approached me, but to be honest, Rita, I would sooner not get involved in the hotel business. It would mean being on call all the time and travelling over to Brokencliff every day. I have friends who work at the Star and it really is all hands on deck. Alfred really needs someone with a hotel background and one who doesn't mind putting in the long hours."

"You are right, of course. Well, if all goes well you may find yourself with a permanent position here. Now that Bob has agreed to take on the London office and Norman is staying on, the workload here will only increase. I have seen the way you work and Julie is really pleased to have you working beside her."

"Thanks, Rita. Staying here would be ideal."

"As soon as I have had time to sit down with Jenny and Elsie I will give you a definite answer."

\* \* \*

## *Wednesday, 9 February*

With their membership cards in place, Freda and Muriel decided to take a trip to see what Murdell and Pocock had to offer. Apart from the samples they had tasted at the last meeting, they were keen to see how much money they might save.

Muriel, armed with a pad and pen, took notes as they walked around the large aircraft hangar of a place.

Wall-to-wall shelving housed branded and less well-known grocery items. Chest freezer cabinets housed every kind of frozen food. Freda looked carefully at ready-made dinners and decided to buy two beef and Yorkshire pudding ones to try out.

"It says here it's from their 'could have tasted worse' range," said Freda.

"Who makes them? Not Birds Eye," said Muriel, looking at some packs of beef burgers.

"No, they're made by a company called 'Lings Luscious' — they do all sorts of things."

"Never heard of them," said Muriel, deciding on some burgers and fish fingers. She looked carefully at the packet of fish fingers. "Oh, these are made by them as well, also from their 'could have tasted worse' range. Well, I'll give them a go. My Barry likes a fish finger."

With other purchases of instant whip made with water, frozen vegetables and instant coffee, also from the new range by Lings Luscious, they were both pleasantly surprised at what they were charged. As neither of them drove a car, the fare for a taxi home saw the savings on their shopping dwindle.

Muriel telephoned Lucinda and told her about their experience.

"Well, it will be worth giving these things a try," said Lucinda. "You know as well as I do, the cost of things keeps going up. I will certainly be using their instant desserts and frozen meats. I have tried their own-brand teabags; they are quite good and will do for my guests. I prefer loose tea myself, but the thought of not having pots of loose leaves to deal with when I have a full house does take the edge off things a bit."

Dick looked at the meal set before him, to which Freda had added vegetables. "We don't normally have a roast dinner mid-week," he said, licking his lips.

Freda smiled to herself and sat down, watching as Dick took his first mouthful of sliced beef and Yorkshire.

"This gravy is very tasty. Aren't you using Bisto anymore?"

"Trying out some different brands," said Freda, tasting a roast potato, which in fairness was nothing like her own, but was okay. Dick seemed to enjoy his meal and the only problem was he wanted more.

"Sorry, love, it was only a small piece of meat," said Freda. "I have made a pudding."

Dick seemed satisfied with the explanation and Freda cleared away the plates and returned with tinned peaches and instant whip made with water.

Dick ate it, said nothing, and Freda heaved a sigh of relief.

On the other side of the wall, Barry was trying the fish fingers with frozen vegetables and some tinned potatoes.

"We usually have chips," he said. "Are these them tinned potatoes? They're too perfectly shaped to be anything else."

Muriel nodded. "Yes, I did them for quickness, been shopping this morning and I have committee work I need to catch up on. How are you finding the fish fingers?"

"These aren't the ones I've brought home from the factory," said Barry. "But they could have been worse. Did you get these from Mrs Jary?"

"No," said Muriel, "she doesn't stock them. They're from that cash and carry place I mentioned to you."

"Oh right," said Barry. "Well, they are some unknown fish I expect, no doubt they didn't cost as much, but they will do me."

Muriel raised her eyes to the ceiling and whispered under her breath, "Thank you, God."

It wasn't long before Mrs Jary got wind of her customers turning to the likes of the large cash and carry emporium. However, she remained silent on the subject and was pleased that, even though her regulars didn't buy all of their groceries, they still shopped with her. Looking around her, Mrs Jary knew that times were changing and the smaller shops were being overtaken by supermarkets with their cheaper goods. In a couple of years' time, she decided, it would be time for her to move. Standing behind a counter day in and day out, she felt she was reaching an age when she deserved to take things a little slower.

Doris – who owned her hair salon, The House of Doris, on Lowestoft Road – was also considering what she should do in the future. She still had her own flurry of regulars, but as they got older and died, her bookings were not as healthy as they had once been. Several hair salons with modern interiors and equipment had opened in Gorleston High Street and more and more were opening in Great Yarmouth. Doris had to admit to herself that the service she offered was probably being seen as old-fashioned. With so many modern products flooding the once-barren market, the days of perms and a wash and set were numbered. She either had to move with the times or get out, and it was the latter that was setting alarm bells ringing in her head. She was getting too long in the tooth to change her ways. A couple more years and then maybe it would be time to call it a day. Retiring to a small home in Corton might just be the ticket.

Doris looked at the clock and went to rinse off Mrs Cornell's perm solution. It wouldn't do to leave it a minute longer than usual, otherwise her customer would resemble a dark-haired version of Shirley Temple. Not a good look at seventy-five.

She gently combed out the damp hair and began putting rollers in. "Are you going anywhere special later?"

Mrs Cornell coughed. "Just to the Palace Bingo with Vera and a few chums. It does me good to get out of the house once in a while in the evening. I won't know which way to turn when our Steven gets married next month. He is of a mind to move in with us, but Stan's not having any of it and told him he and his bride-to-be will have to find rented accommodation until they can get their own place."

Doris nodded. She heard so many tales like this during the course of a day. She never commented, allowing her clients to get things off their chest. Many a time Doris had wanted to say something, but years of practice had enabled her to keep her thoughts to herself. As she placed the hairnet over the curlers and moved the large-domed hairdryer in place, she reflected that all through her life she had never had anyone she could turn to, unless she counted the time when she had called the Samaritans when she'd had that funny turn. She set the dryer on medium, handed Mrs Cornell a copy of the latest *Woman's Realm* and moved to the next cubicle where Sarah Hines was waiting for a wash and set.

\* \* \*

Philippa Tidy – or Phil, as she liked to be known – was running through a quick stock check in her small provisions store, "Tidy Stores". She did quite a good business with the locals in Brokencliff, but was aware that many went to the larger supermarkets to do their shopping. However, that wasn't true of Joe Dean who had a regular order with Phil for his weekly groceries. Phil and Joe had become firm friends and often passed the time of day together when business was quiet.

The Reverend George was another regular customer; he was a great believer in supporting local business and, although his housekeeper Martha Tidwell complained to him that he could buy the goods cheaper elsewhere, he was happy to continue shopping with Phil.

Another regular was Alfred Barton, a hangover from when his Aunt Dolly ran the shop. He always purchased bread, milk, cheese and biscuits, never once considering that his own hotel kitchen could supply him with whatever he needed.

During the summer months, the members of the company that played the theatre were always popping in and out for a packet of biscuits, cigarettes, matches and all manner of other things. Judging by the amount of sweets and chocolate they purchased between them, Phil wondered how they ever managed to fit into their costumes.

She was just coming down the stepladder as the shop door jangled open; it was Joe Dean.

"Morning, Phil, how is my favourite girl today?"

"For someone who shows no sign of an Irish accent, you are full of the blarney, so you are," said Phil with a laugh.

Joe acknowledged the sentiment. "Funny that, it's only when I go back to the Emerald Isle that I slip back to the accent, you are not the first to comment on it. My mate Reverend George says it often."

Phil smiled at Joe. "You two are such great friends. It is nice to see how well you two get on. I am sure he must have somewhat of a lonely life in that draughty old vicarage."

"The Reverend, lonely?" said Joe. "Not a bit of it, his door is always open to his flock. And the women of Brokencliff are always dropping off food parcels."

"I think some of them carry a torch for him," said Phil. "He is a very handsome man."

"Now, enough of your match-making, bejesus, I've forgotten what I came in here for."

Phil put a small box on the counter. "I think this is what you came for – you put a note through my door last night."

"So I did, what an eejit. How much do I owe you?"

"You can settle up at the end of the week, Joe, there's no rush."

Joe put his hand in his pockets and laid a ten-pound note on the counter. "Best take it now, while I've got it. I need to go to the bank later."

Phil rang up the amount on the till and handed Joe some change.

The door jangled open again and in came Reverend George. "Morning, Phil. Hello there, Joe, getting some shopping in I see."

Joe smiled. "Yes, I need to get this back to the park. If you fancy, pop in on your way back and I will make some coffee."

"I would love to, Joe, but I've some parish calls to make, another time perhaps."

Joe nodded, said goodbye and left the shop.

"He is a nice fella," said Phil.

"One of the best," replied the Reverend. "A quarter of tea and a couple of slices of ham, please. I am planning on making myself some egg and chips, but I mustn't let that get out – the ladies in Brokencliff would think I was letting myself go."

Phil laughed. "They do seem to take good care of you."

"Sometimes too much. Thanks, Phil, you have a good day now."

Phil watched him leave the shop and not for the first time had she realised there was a spark between the Reverend and Joe. She was about to go back up the stepladder when Alfred came in.

"My goodness, it's like Piccadilly Circus in here this morning."

"Hello, Phil, having a busy morning? Just thought I'd pop over and get a packet of custard creams and if you have any ginger cake, I'll take that as well."

"Having a party?"

"Not really, just fancied something for my afternoon tea."

"I am closing up at four today, so if you fancy having a bit of tea with me back at the cottage, you'd be most welcome."

"That sounds champion," said Alfred. "Thanks, Phil. I will still take the cake and biscuits though, always good for a standby."


Later that afternoon, Phil listened to Alfred as he told her his story. "My advice to you, Alfred, is to call a meeting with Sandie Cross, but perhaps before you do that, you should gain entry to the rooms – after all, it is your hotel."

"I keep telling myself that. The problem is the labourers don't appear to speak a word of English, there are barriers everywhere and Sandie Cross is in the hotel for fleeting moments giving out her orders and then she disappears."

"Have you tried calling her office?"

Alfred nodded. "Oh, nearly every day, but I always get the brush-off from one of her office staff. Miss Cross is at another site; Miss Cross is in a business meeting."

Philippa sighed. "Yes, I see your problem. Perhaps you should lay a trap for her. Leave her a note saying there is no more money and you are not sure how you will be able to pay her for the completion of the job."

"Yes, that might do it," said Alfred, feeling slightly better; it was always good to hear someone else's take on things and again his thoughts went back to his wife, Jean, who would have had this neatly sewn up in next to no time.

That evening, when all the workers had gone, Alfred answered the door to Selwyn Woods.

Selwyn tapped his pipe on the wall and snorted. "I just had a look at some of the materials stored out back, Alfred, and if you want my honest opinion they are knock-off."

Alfred looked horrified. "When you say knock-off, you mean..."

"Stolen," said Selwyn, taking a deep breath. "That stuff is off the foreign boats in Yarmouth and beyond. I was offered some by a couple of the blokes who work on the docks there at knock-down prices. I wouldn't touch them with a barge pole. I'm not saying that the quality isn't good – some of that wallpaper would sell for a fortune in a hardware shop – but it ain't right. Someone is making a profit on the backs of others and I don't hold with things like that. Besides, if I was to get caught handling these goods I would be out of business and I don't think the missus would be any too pleased about that."

Alfred listened in silence, quite stunned by all that Selwyn was telling him.

"I know people may think that I charge a lot for my labour, but I am a small business, Alfred. My workers are skilled and they need paying. You won't find foreign names on the materials I use. I get mine from a wholesaler – Dulux and Crown are names to be trusted and I stand by that. I bet this Sandie Cross lady is charging you a fortune for this work. Now, let's have a look at one of the bedrooms, shall we."

"They're all locked and Sandie Cross has all the keys," Alfred replied sheepishly.

Selwyn sucked his teeth and looked Alfred in the eye. "If your missus was still here you wouldn't find yourself in this mess. I wouldn't say she was the easiest lady to deal with, not many women in business are, but she knew proper when she saw it. Now, I will just get my crowbar from the van, I'll have these doors open in a jiffy and then we can see what's what."

*Tony Gareth Smith*

# Chapter Six     <u>*Relatively Speaking*</u>

### *Thursday, 10 February*

**B**ob Scott looked at his new surroundings and was pleasantly surprised. His friends had found him a flat to rent in West Kensington, just off the North End Road, and he felt he could make it a good base. He was close to local transport and wouldn't need his car to travel to the West End every day. A stone's throw from West Kensington tube station and a short walk from Earls Court and bus routes, he had several options to hand. His meeting with Norman had proven fruitful and with Rita's guidance he was happy that they would develop a good working relationship.

Bob was hesitant at first about taking on this new position; he had never been an agent before and the concept was unknown to him. Over the years of working at the Sands, he had watched and listened as acts were booked for the venue and had heard from the late Don Stevens the many tales he had to tell concerning contracts. However, he felt that there was all to play for and, with the help of Norman and some guidance from Rita, he was more than willing to give it his best.

### *Friday, 3 March*

Lady Samantha was reading the *Great Yarmouth Mercury*. "I see they have announced the company for the Playhouse."

Sir Harold, who was studying the *Racing Post*, looked up. "What's that, Sammie old thing?"

"I said, Harold dear, they have announced the cast for the theatre and guess who they have in the line-up?"

"Thora Hird," said Sir Harold. "She would pull them in no problem, loved her in *Meet the Wife*."

"Well, I am sorry to disappoint you, it isn't Thora Hird. But it is someone you know, dear."

Sir Harold looked puzzled and laid down his paper. "I don't know anyone in the theatre, do I?"

Lady Samantha smiled and leant across the table and took her husband's hand. "Harold darling, I am sure Constance would be most upset to hear you say that."

Sir Harold shook his head and coughed nervously. "Constance – you don't mean Connie Anderson?"

"The very same, Harold, perhaps we should invite her and that husband of hers to stay here for the season."

Sir Harold pulled his hand away from his wife's grasp. "I say, old thing, there's no need for that, besides, it was a total misunderstanding; Connie and I were never...well, Gawd damn it. A man is entitled to look at another woman without there being any hanky-panky."

Lady Samantha smiled to herself at her husband's discomfort. "Well, perhaps Constance can enlighten me when I invite her for tea one afternoon. I am sure she would like to see the Hall again."

Sir Harold stood up and banged his newspaper on the table. "I say, old thing, that's a bit below the belt. You wouldn't invite them here, would you?"

Before she could answer, a cough was heard from the open doorway. "My lady, there is a lady wishing to speak to you in the hallway."

Lady Samantha rose from her chair. "Thank you, Penge, that will be Mrs Dawson about volunteer recruitment. Harold dear, close your mouth, you might catch a goldfish."

And as her ladyship left the room, Sir Harold was sure he saw a knowing smile on Penge's lips.

* * *

Rita looked over the paperwork again and then she addressed Jenny and Elsie. "So, ladies, we are in agreement that we can offer Beverley a full-time position here."

Elsie nodded. "It's not for me to say, but Beverley is such a joy to have around. Don was always singing her praises."

Jenny smiled. "She has fitted in so well here and with Bob now ensconced in London we can begin to build the empire."

Rita laughed. "You've been watching too many old films, Jenny. I've had a quote in from Selwyn Woods concerning the attic and his figures are well within our budget." She handed the quote to Elsie.

"Weren't you going to get a quote from the company that Alfred is using?" Jenny asked.

"Beverley couldn't get anyone at their offices to agree a date when to call round. She explained what we wanted to do, but, according to the secretary who answered, Miss Cross was booked until next Christmas."

"But surely they could have sent someone else."

"My sentiments precisely," said Rita, adjusting the bow on her blouse which had tangled with the gold pendant she had been given as a Christmas present. "These companies do make me smile; they advertise their wares and then don't employ the manpower to carry it out."

"Where are they based?" asked Elsie, handing Jenny the quote.

"Norwich, I believe. Beverley has all the details."

"I am thinking of taking a trip to Norwich," said Elsie. "I thought I would treat myself to a spring outfit. I could pop in there if you like."

"This quote is very reasonable," said Jenny, "for old Chippy."

"Well, let's go with it," said Rita. "Keep it local. I've been meaning to go and have another chat with Alfred and to see how the hotel is coming along, but we have been so busy."

"Look, maybe I could go over and visit the hotel this afternoon," said Elsie, "and report back. In the meantime, hadn't someone better let Beverley know our decision?"

"Of course, of course, let's get Beverley to come in and join us. No time like the present, and I think I have a bottle of sherry in the cabinet – we can have a little toast with that."

\* \* \*

Elsie parked her car and went up the pathway to The Beach Croft Hotel; she walked through the main entrance into the reception area, which she thought was decorated to a very high standard, a stunning black and white design with a centred red carpet strip that led to the reception desk and went off like the yellow brick road to the adjoining bar and dining area either side.

Elsie spotted Alfred who was just coming out of one of the lifts. "Hello, Alfred, I hope you don't mind me calling unannounced."

"Hello, Elsie – it is okay to call you Elsie?" Elsie nodded.

"I wanted to see how things were taking shape here. Rita wanted to come and see you but she is very busy at the moment and I am at something of a loose end not quite knowing what to do with myself, if I am honest."

Alfred nodded; he knew what it was like to lose someone close, even if in his case they hadn't died.

"I have to say this reception area looks most impressive," said Elsie, admiring the décor. "Superior Interiors have done you proud."

Alfred shook his head. "Yes, it is most impressive but it isn't the downstairs that's the problem." He showed Elsie the bar area which was carpeted in a beautiful peacock-blue carpet; heavy velvet drapes hung at the windows, held back by matching tassels. The bar area had mirrors at the back, making the area look more spacious. Mirrors etched with the Beach Croft emblem hung on the walls and in the corner that Rita had spoken of with Jenny stood a grand piano adjacent to a small stage. The leather and wooden seating combined with the etched-glass coffee tables made the room look inviting and special.

The dining area had been transformed with a black and white tiled floor, the tables were covered with white table linen and the heavily padded dining chairs looked comfortable. The rear of the room leading to the kitchen serving area now housed a proper waiter station, and the single door to the serving area was now double – one in and one out.

At the windows hung lighter drapes than those in the bar area, with white blinds that could be adjusted accordingly.

"It's beautiful," said Elsie, remembering how things looked before.

"As I said, it isn't down here that is the concern. Allow me to show you one or two of the bedrooms."

Elsie followed Alfred to the lift and they got out on the third floor. The hallway leading to the bedrooms looked fine. Neatly papered in a beige design, wall lights and one or two tasteful seascapes adorned the walls. Alfred used his master key and opened one of the bedroom doors.

"Oh, my word," said Elsie, looking around her. "Please tell me that they are not all like this!"

"Oh no, Elsie, they are not – some of them are worse."

Elsie held her hands to her eyes as she tried to take in the fluorescent-green painted walls; the pattern on the green carpet screamed at her; the curtains were another shade of green and the green-painted wooden furniture almost blended into the walls; lime-green lamps stood on green bedside tables. The only variation in colour was the white linen bedspread and pillow shams on the twin beds.

"They all look like this?"

Alfred nodded his head slowly. "We have a blue room, a lemon room, an orange room; in fact, it would be safe to say that if anyone did want to go over the rainbow, they only need book in here. We even have a black room."

Elsie walked into the adjacent bathroom. "Well, at least this is white."

"Yes, all the bathrooms have been done in white," said Alfred, signing relief.

Following Alfred, Elsie viewed three more bedrooms, each more bizarre than the last.

"What are you going to do?" asked Elsie. "Surely you won't be able to let the rooms as they are now. Your guests would be having nightmares. I take it that Sandie Cross is going to redo this work?"

"Sandie Cross thinks they are a work of art," said Alfred, "and she is most offended that I should want her to change her colour scheme."

"Have you paid her in full?"

"Not quite," said Alfred, "and I won't settle the account until she has made the necessary changes."

"So, has she agreed to meet you halfway?"

"Well, after much persuasion and a couple of drinks, she has agreed to redo ten of the bedrooms. But of course that is going to take weeks and I was hoping to have reopened by now. Apparently, she has let half her workforce go and the others have moved on to another job."

"What on earth are you going to do?"

Alfred closed the bedroom door and they made their way towards the lift. "I will have to roll up my sleeves and paint some of the walls and, bless him, Selwyn Woods has agreed to have some men come in and help out – at a cost, of course."

"So, you are going to be out of pocket," said Elsie, pressing the button for the ground floor.

"Looks like it."

"I have an idea," said Elsie. "Perhaps we could round up some of the boys that used to work at the Sands and, if you are of a mind, Rita can help you sue this Sandie Cross for what she has left you with."

"To be honest I would sooner not have her or her men back in the hotel."

"Then don't," said Elsie. "Let's give Beverley a call and see if she can contact some of the backstage boys – you know they are all a dab hand at carpentry and paintwork."

"Elsie, you really are a lifesaver – let me make you a drink. You can use the phone in my office, which thankfully hasn't had the touch of Superior Interiors."

* * *

Beverley made a few phone calls, an agreed rate was set and Alfred was informed that a group of seven would be reporting for duty the following day. Alfred called in some favours with a friend he had in the carpet trade and they came to an arrangement to re-carpet all the bedrooms in a standard pattern.

Rita came out of her office just as Beverley finished her last call.

"Who was that?"

Beverley explained to Rita what Elsie had asked her to do and Rita smiled to herself; if Elsie was getting involved in business it meant she was feeling better than she had been, which was only a good thing.

Leaving Alfred much happier than when she had arrived, Elsie drove to Lowestoft and found an outfit in Tuttles that she liked; Norwich would have to wait for another day. As she drove back towards Great Yarmouth, she felt that the heaviness she had been carrying was lifting. Don would always be in her heart and her thoughts but, as she had often said to others, life had to go on.

The following morning Selwyn Woods arrived and was pleasantly surprised to see he was going to be helped by seven others plus his own workers.

"Well, Mr Barton," said Chippy, sucking on his pipe, "someone has certainly been busy since our conversation."

"I wonder, Selwyn, if you could take charge of the extra men and then you will be able to supervise them to your high standard."

Chippy's chest swelled. "I can soon get this sorted, don't you worry about that. I will assemble the men in the backroom, if that is okay, and we can look at the rooms one by one. You mentioned that you were going to have some carpets re-laid, I will arrange it so as we finish the decorating the carpet fitters move in. To my mind that would seem to be the best solution."

Alfred handed Selwyn a business card. "This is who will be doing the carpets and they can start in three days' time."

Selwyn looked at the card and sucked on his pipe. "Ernie Stokes, yes, I know old Ernie from way back." Selwyn tapped his pipe on the wall and looked up. "I remember old Ernie when we played footy together as young lads. Funny he moved into carpets, his old dad always thought he would try and become a professional footballer, sad it weren't to be. Ernie worked for Platterns in the Row for many years and then set up on his own. Good worker, old Ernie, knows his onions."

Alfred, aware of the time, interrupted. "That's good to know. So, if I can leave everything in your hands, I have some other business that needs my attention. I am interviewing staff today over in Great Yarmouth at the Two Bears."

Selwyn, who was obviously in reminiscent mode, ignored Alfred and continued. "Ah, now you see, I know for a fact that Ernie did some of the rooms at the Two Bears. It's had a bit of a mixed reputation over the years, but I did some jobs there and I always found the management well organised and friendly. They always stood me a pint at the end of the day and my boys appreciated that."

"I've left some bottled beers in the kitchen fridge for you all," said Alfred, remembering he had heard about the little extras Chippy enjoyed, "and a friend of mine is coming in to provide you all with a hot lunch."

Selwyn smiled. "That's mighty decent of you, Mr Barton. Now you mustn't keep me talking, I have some men to sort out." And with that, Selwyn Woods left the office.

\* \* \*

Later that day, with the men working under his instruction, Selwyn called in to Rita's Angels.

"Thank you for coming in so promptly," said Rita, shaking his hand. "I think Beverley has mentioned to you what we would like to do with the attic area. There is no rush; I understand how busy you are."

Selwyn removed his cap and put it in his overall pocket. "I will take a look at what needs doing; your secretary explained that the attic here does have windows, so that won't be too much rebuilding, although a proper staircase will need to be put in. I can't promise when I can do the job, but let's say it will be within the next three months."

Rita nodded. "I will leave it with you, Mr Woods. You can send a quote to Beverley and we can take it from there."

"Right you are, missus," said Selwyn, "you leave it to me."

# Chapter Seven    *A Change of Personnel*

## *Wednesday, 8 March*

With Maureen Roberts at his side, Alfred Barton prepared to interview staff for the hotel. The interviews would take place over three days, as there were a lot of vacancies to fill. Maureen had noted that Alfred had tried to run the hotel on a shoestring, and that it had ended up with Alfred and his estranged wife doing most of the work. Maureen had prepared plans that would allow Alfred to step back. First impressions were important and reception staff had to be of the calibre of the larger hotels in the area. Rooms should be managed by a housekeeper with responsibilities for managing the maids, cleaners and front-of-house staff.

A chef would need at least three commis chefs and a kitchen porter on hand. The dining room would require experienced waiting staff and the bar area would need at least three staff in order to cover the various shifts that would be in place.

Maureen had also looked at the hotel tariff and had suggested a slight rise in the room rates with parking charged as an extra. A deal had been struck with Owlerton Hall to take any overspill that the hotel car park could not accommodate.

Alfred had been reading through the various CVs and had drawn up his own shortlist of possible candidates and, in tandem with Maureen's own findings, letters to attend interviews at the Two Bears had been sent out. It was going to be a long three days, but, as Maureen had assured Alfred, a rewarding three days; she intended to make sure that Alfred had the right personnel in place to make the Beach Croft a hotel to be proud of.

Janine sat in front of Alfred and Maureen, dressed in a very smart black two-piece, white blouse, black stockings and kitten-heel shoes. Her hair had been cut shorter and was coloured a shade more in keeping with her natural colour, which was not blonde, and her make-up was toned down considerably. The only thing remaining of the old Janine was the thick false eyelashes which she was still struggling with. When Janine's application had been received, Alfred felt obliged to interview her, but with Maureen at his side, Janine would have to impress greatly if she was to succeed. Maureen had rewritten job descriptions and changed the titles accordingly, so Janine was applying for one of four Guest Coordinators, which basically meant she would be working at reception, answering the telephone, but with some added duties that changed her previous receptionist role considerably. The Guest Coordinator would report directly to the General Hotel Manager or his/her assistant, who was yet to be appointed.

Janine had obviously taken on board previous comments about her behaviour. Since being made redundant by the Beach Croft, she had found a temporary position with a bigger concern in Great Yarmouth who had obviously put Janine through a vigorous training programme with a view to making the position permanent if Janine delivered. When asked why she didn't want to stay with her current employer, Janine had answered that she felt happier working for a smaller family concern and saw the Beach Croft as part of her family.

Only three other previous employees of the hotel had submitted an application and all three were to be offered a position – two cleaners and one barman whom Alfred knew he could rely on.

After the three days, there were three piles: "employ", "interview again" and "no". Janine was between the "interview again" and the "no" pile.

The position of Executive Housekeeper was offered to Minnie Cooper, whom Maureen had approached a few weeks before. Minnie had worked in many of the top London hotels and had a proven track record. She had decided to return to her Norfolk roots when she felt she needed a quieter life away from the ever-changing London hotel scene. In her mid-fifties, she had planned on finding herself a part-time job in Great Yarmouth, until Maureen had tracked her down. Once Minnie knew she had a challenge on her hands, she was ready to roll up her sleeves. She had a bungalow in Crab Lane, Gorleston, so was not so far away from Brokencliff.

The appointment of General Manager went to a single man in his forties, Stephen Price, who had worked in the catering industry all his life. The Assistant Manager's post was offered to Caroline Hutton who had worked as front-of-house manager for many of the Trusthouse Forte hotels around the country and was looking for something nearer to her ageing parents in Winterton.

Over their lunch, on the third and final day of interviews, Maureen said, "Janine is a no, Alfred; if you allow her back into the business your reputation will plummet. I know the Janines of this world."

Alfred nodded. "Yes, I understand what you are saying; Jean wanted shot of her a long time ago. I just feel sorry for her."

"Sentiment and business do not go hand in hand."

"I was thinking of offering her something at the theatre, but Maud and Barbara have agreed to run the box office between them and I have my old standbys for usherettes."

Maureen smiled. "Look, Alfred, this is a new beginning for you and the hotel. Once you have everything in place you will see the plans we have made bear fruit."

"I do hope so," said Alfred.

* * *

## Monday, 13 March

Due to his heavy workload, Selwyn had taken on more labour to oversee the changes that Lady Samantha was making to Owlerton Hall. Despite her husband's protests, Lady Samantha had sat down with Selwyn and gone over her ideas. Several of the rooms needed paint work; others needed more attention, replacing floorboards and fittings. She had also employed the services of a professional gardener based in Ormesby who, with his work force, was bringing the gardens back to their former glory.

"And another thing," said Lady Samantha, looking over her glasses at her husband as he ate his breakfast, "we are going to start employing staff again. We have been very fortunate to have the volunteers, but we must get things back on a more professional level when it comes to business."

Swallowing a mouthful of toast, Sir Harold groaned. "This is going to cost a pretty penny, Sammie old thing."

"I have gone into the finances with a fine toothcomb. I had my accountant look things over."

"Since when have you had an accountant?"

"Since the day I married you, Harold. You have never been good with money. You think that you can keep taking from the pot, but if we are not careful, the pot will be empty. Owlerton Hall can once again be somewhere people want to visit, and with the theatre and the Beach Croft being revamped I thought it was high time we got on board. Look at the money we made letting out the car park, that can only be improved upon, but in order to get it done properly we need a few staff."

"How many had you in mind?"

"Well, we will keep the volunteers on, of course, but we need a couple of cleaners, a kitchen help for Mrs Yates and I am sure Penge could do with an extra pair of hands about the place."

Penge coughed as he came into the room. "Begging your pardon, your ladyship, I couldn't help overhearing your conversation about taking on staff."

Lady Samantha removed her spectacles and laid them on the table. "My dear Penge, I will discuss all of this with you before I make any further decision and of course I would want you present at the interviews, you have been with us for a long time now."

Penge duly nodded. "Thank you, your ladyship. Did you or Sir Harold require anything further from the kitchen? Only it's Mrs Yates's pantry day."

"No thank you, Penge, I think we are quite suited," replied Lady Samantha. She smiled warmly and added, "Perhaps you and I can have a little tête-à-tête this afternoon?"

Penge bowed. "As you wish, your ladyship."

"Damned good man that, what?" said Sir Harold as Penge left the room. "Wouldn't want to lose him."

"And we won't, Harold dear, but we must make some kind of provision for him. Mrs Yates has her own home and family in Gorleston, Penge has no one. He lives in those two rooms at the top of the house – it can't be much fun."

"What are you suggesting, Sammie old thing?"

"I thought we might give Penge the run of the cottage, give him some independence away from the house."

Sir Harold nodded. "I say, old gal, that mightn't be a bad idea. It would need some attention. I can't remember the last time I went in there. Used to play there as a child when the old gardener and his wife lived there – old Mangle – he was a nice old gentleman, and his wife made the most delicious shortbread, used to sneak down there sometimes when mater and pater weren't watching."

"Harold dear, you haven't changed very much over the years – I know you sneak down to the kitchen and help yourself to Mrs Yates's homemade biscuits from time to time."

"I say, steady on old gal, a man has to have some pleasures in life."

Lady Samantha laughed. "Which is why you married me, Harold dear. Now, finish your breakfast and I will take you through some of my ideas."

Sir Harold sighed. "Could have gone a tad more toast."

"You heard what Penge said, it's Mrs Yates's pantry day."

"Whatever that means," thought Sir Harold, and drank the last of his tea.

\* \* \*

"A quarter of tea and a jar of Nescafé," said Lucinda to Mrs Jary, "and if you have some fancies I will take six of those, I have a couple of the committee coming over this afternoon."

Mrs Jary nodded as the door jangled and in came Muriel followed by Freda who was sneezing.

"You sound as if you have a bit of a cold there, Freda," said Muriel with a smile.

"My chest is something awful," said Freda, acknowledging Lucinda. "My Dick has been full of it and now he has passed it on to me. That man will be the death of me."

"And of everyone else," said Muriel with feeling. "Barry has been sniffling since yesterday. I hope I don't get it, I can't be doing with colds. Of course, it would happen when I was planning to redecorate the lounge. Barry has got the week off."

"First I've heard about you decorating," said Freda, blowing her nose. "You've not long done some."

"Well," said Muriel, "my three-piece suite has seen better days and I thought it was time for a change, so I thought, well, if I was going to do one thing I might as well do another."

"Fancy," replied Freda, picking up a packet of biscuits and then deciding to get a cake instead. "It was a shame about Lilly calling off her wedding."

"That was weeks ago," Lucinda said, handing Mrs Jary a five pound note.

"I know. I was just saying, that was all."

"Freda had planned a new outfit for it," said Muriel to Lucinda with a smile. "Freda does like a new creation every so often."

Freda beamed with pride. "My Dick says I am a clothes horse when it comes to fashion."

"Not how I would have put it," said Muriel quietly.

"What was that?" asked Freda, raising her voice slightly. "Only this cold is blocking my ears something chronic. I had to turn up the telly last night, right in the middle of *Coronation Street*."

"You need to get a packet of Tunes," said Muriel. "Mrs Jary keeps them over there near the sweets."

Lucinda, who had heard enough for one day, picked up her purchases and headed for the door. "Don't forget, Muriel, this afternoon three thirty, committee meeting, see you then."

"Her and her committee meetings," said Freda. "I don't know what you lot find to talk about."

"That's for me to know," said Muriel, handing Mrs Jary a list.

"Fancy," said Freda and blew her nose louder than before.

* * *

"But, Mr Barton, my men will need paying," said Sandie Cross, shouting down the telephone. "You cannot just stop payment, I have done a lot of work on your hotel and I am proud of the results, you should be too."

Alfred remained calm. "As I have told you, Miss Cross, the work you have done on my hotel is dreadful. I do agree that you have done a wonderful job on the downstairs areas but any guests booking into one of the bedrooms would be having nightmares. What on earth possessed you to think that bedrooms would look good in such garish colours? I have tried on numerous occasions to speak to you and to no avail. Only now in the light of a letter from my solicitor have you telephoned me."

Sandie, who was feeling slightly the worse for wear following an all-night party, tried to keep her thoughts together. "But, Mr Barton, I am a creative spirit, my work is my life. I have letters here on file that congratulate me on my work. I wanted to give you something that no other hotel had to offer its guests."

"What was that, Miss Cross – migraines?"

"Mr Barton, I ask you, I plead with you to reconsider – I can make some changes if that is what you require."

"Too late, I have another company doing that right now. I have wasted a great deal of money on your foolhardy colour scheme and I intend to claw back as much as I possibly can."

"But you will put me out of business," cried Sandie, beginning to feel most unwell at the end of the telephone.

"If it prevents you from putting other good, honest, hard-working people like me out of business then so be it," said Alfred, beginning to feel he had at last taken responsibility for his livelihood. "Good day to you, Miss Cross, you will find your tools and other items belonging to you in the hotel car park which I would like collected by the end of the week. I would advise you very strongly not even to try to enter my premises again."

As the phone went dead, Sandie Cross screamed out, "Margaret, coffee now, with brandy!"

\* \* \*

## *Wednesday, 15 March*

With the hotel now beginning to take shape, Rita decided to pay Alfred a visit to discuss further plans concerning the theatre.

"Elsie said that the reception areas looked lovely. Seeing them for myself, I have to concur. Alfred, it looks splendid."

Alfred smiled. "She told you about the bedrooms, of course." He handed Rita a couple of photographs. "I took these before Chippy and his men got to work."

"My goodness," said Rita. "These are horrendous. Have you seen anything of this Cross woman since?"

Alfred explained what had happened and Rita nodded with a smile. "At last, Alfred, you have seen the error of your ways – your wife would be proud of you."

"It's a shame she won't ever see it."

"So, there are no thoughts of a reconciliation then, Alfred?"

"Jean is happier where she is," said Alfred. "I've accepted that. We have filed for divorce – it seems the best solution for us both, then we can both move on."

"Will that mean you selling this place?"

"No, I don't think so," said Alfred. "Jean has said she wants nothing from me, but I can't accept that. When everything is done and dusted here I will sort something out. She put a lot of hard work in here and it shouldn't go unrewarded."

There was a pause before Rita continued. "Well, let's get down to business, shall we?"

Alfred led Rita through to the office.

"Everything seems to be coming together. We have a company for the theatre and I have got Lauren Du Barrie on board. She will fare better here with a smaller audience, I feel. I shall be steering her towards some good old-fashioned tunes that your audiences will enjoy."

"I have got Maud and Barbara on board for the box office," said Alfred, "and Chippy has done some sterling work on the foyer and backstage area. Old Jack from the Sands has agreed to come and be stage doorkeeper, not something we have had at the Playhouse before, but I thought it would be a nice gesture to help him out as there won't be much in the way of work for him. I have also offered him a couple of shifts as a night porter here at the hotel."

"That really is most kind of you," said Rita. "I am sure that Jack appreciates that."

They talked about the programme, ticket prices and the advertising, both ticking off things on their respective lists as they did so.

"I thought we might go up to Owlerton Hall and see Lady Samantha," said Alfred. "She has agreed to the use of her car park and seems to want to help out generally speaking. She is making arrangements to take on some more with her to open up the Hall once some more work has been carried out."

"But not by Inferior Interiors," said Rita with a laugh.

Alfred joined in the joke. "Your Ted could have made a proper joke about that."

Rita acknowledged the sentiment.

Alfred picked up the telephone and called Lady Samantha. "That would be great, your ladyship, you can expect us in half an hour."

"Lady Samantha is offering us smoked salmon and cucumber sandwiches followed by her cook's cherry cake."

"That sounds lovely. She really does seem very down to earth," Rita replied. "Do you want to take my car?"

"Why don't we walk there?" said Alfred. "We can go out of the back of the hotel through the car park and walk up the hill; it seems quite pleasant out there today."

"What a good idea, I don't walk as much as I should do."

As Alfred closed the back door, Rita drew his attention to someone in the car park. "Who is that over there? She seems to be loading material into that van?"

"That will be the infamous Sandie Cross," said Alfred. "I gave her instructions to remove her stuff by the end of the week."

"I've a good mind to go and introduce myself; I'd like to see exactly what this Sandie person looks like."

Alfred followed Rita across the car park. Sandie Cross was dressed in her usual strange attire, sporting a flowing top, thigh-high boots and her hair covered by a large floppy hat with her eyes shielded by sunglasses; she turned as the pair approached.

Sandie took in a sharp gasp of surprise. "Mr Barton."

Rita eyed Sandie Cross and remained silent.

"I am doing as you asked me."

"So I see," said Alfred.

A smile played on Rita's lips as she observed Sandie more closely.

"I think one more trip will do it," said Sandie, turning back to her duties.

"I believe we have met before," said Rita, finding her voice.

Sandie's back remained turned. "I don't think so."

"Sorry, I should have introduced you. Miss Cross, this is Rita Ricer, a friend of mine."

"Oh, we don't need any introductions," said Rita with a mischievous laugh. "Audrey Audley and I go way back."

\* \* \*

# Chapter Eight

## Cocktails for Two

*Friday, 14 April*

Minnie Cooper called the staff together in the bar lounge where she stood on the small stage and gave them their instructions for the day.

"Now remember, ladies and gentleman, Mr Barton has spent a lot of money to bring the Beach Croft to this high standard and it is our duty to ensure that we are seen and not heard. By that I mean that as we clean, change bed linen, we move like ghostly spectres, do our work and move out. Guests should feel that they are seeing everything for the first time, whether that is a napkin on their side plate or a glass from the bar. Everything must look new. The reception area should be a haven of social interaction with each guest. Nothing is too much trouble, the guest is always right. The bar area is a retreat for those who may be on a business trip wishing to escape the toils of a long day. The service must be friendly, unobtrusive and above all swift and sure. Waitresses and waiters must serve the meals with precision, as each plate is cleared the next will appear after a short interval. Drinks served at tables must arrive on silver trays. The kitchen must be ready to take orders and keep things flowing without any hitches. We have spent several days training together and you have each been given a staff handbook. Your uniforms must be changed regularly and can be laundered by the hotel. Ensure that your appearance is immaculate, hair neatly tied back, caps positioned thus. Pockets should not be bulging with wallets or personal items; these are to be locked in your allocated lockers at the beginning of your shifts. Tonight, Ladies and Gentlemen, we will open the doors of the Beach Croft to invited guests and we will wine and dine them. They will be given carte blanche to view any of the bedrooms. Following their meal, they will enjoy our bar lounge where Mr Barton will address his guests to be followed by a cabaret."

Minnie Cooper, who had looked at every member of the assembled staff, paused for a moment. The room remained silent, no one spoke, no one moved.

In a booming voice, Minnie continued. "Tonight, ladies and gentlemen, will herald a new beginning for The Beach Croft Hotel. Wear your name badges with pride and remember our Beach Croft motto, 'Today, Tomorrow and Beyond, We Will Serve You, Our Guests, with Excellence.'"

Alfred Barton and Maureen Roberts had been watching from a distance.

"My goodness, I haven't heard a speech like that since I heard them play a recording of Churchill."

"I told you she was good," said Maureen. "You see how she has them all lined up. Look at their shoes – they are polished glass, even the maids. I bet if you measured the exact spot of everyone's name badge they would all be in the same place, regardless of how tall or short a person is."

"I have to say, I've been impressed how she has brought everyone together, and all done without any intervention by me."

"That's the key here," said Maureen. "If Minnie keeps the ship sailing, the need to involve the general manager will be lessened. Too many times I have heard of staff running to a general manager when really they should have spoken to someone like Minnie."

"It was a good idea of yours to have the kitchen and catering staff reporting to their own supervisors who, in turn, report to her. It leaves the manager the room to do what he or she should be doing."

"Let's go up to my apartment and have a little snifter and relax," said Alfred, "it will be a long evening."

"Lead the way, Alfred," said Maureen. "I could just go a nice gin and tonic."

"Harold dear, do try and sort out your clothes. Penge has put out a white shirt and your shoes have been polished. But please make up your mind whether you are going to wear a dinner suit or lounge attire. Remember, we are guests of Alfred Barton and we have a certain standard to maintain."

"All this nonsense about this new décor at the hotel, I have no idea why we should have to attend."

"Because, Harold, we are seen as VIPs in the community," said Lady Samantha, deciding on a pearl or diamond necklace with matching earrings. "I think we should stand shoulder to shoulder with Alfred Barton. He needs our support and we need his if we are to make this place pay again. He is a very nice man once you get to know him, and get to know him you will."

Sir Harold sniffed. "I bet he doesn't go shooting, not one of the old school I'll be bound."

"And how often do you actually go shooting, my dear? You and your friends can't seem to manage getting past a public house without popping in for a quick one, as you term it."

"It's all gossip, all gossip, and the locals like nothing more than to gossip about things they know nothing about."

Lady Samantha smiled to herself. "Penge will be here in a moment so I will leave you to it. Perhaps he can help you decide what to wear and, Harold dear, I don't want you having a drink before we arrive at the hotel. I have instructed Penge to lock the cabinet."

"Typical!" he exclaimed. "A man is not the king of his own castle anymore."

Lady Samantha closed the door behind her and, smiling to herself, went along to her private dressing room.

As the guests began to arrive, locals who were out walking their dogs or just taking an evening stroll were intrigued by the arrivals at The Beach Croft Hotel. Of course, several faces were familiar, but some not so familiar. It was sure to be the talk in the Fisherman's that evening and in Tidy Stores the following day.

Deanne Williams at the Fisherman's was not impressed that she had not received an invitation. Tom, her husband, was less bothered.

"Probably an oversight, Deanne, I wouldn't worry about it."

"But we are publicans and known to Alfred and that wife of his, Jean," she said indignantly as she pulled a pint for one of their regulars. "You want nuts with this, Doug?"

Doug waved and nodded, engrossed in his *Sporting Life*.

As she handed Doug his change, Reverend George and Joe Dean walked in, both dressed in what Deanne termed "their Sunday Best".

"And where are you boys off to, then?" she asked, smiling at Joe and giving only a passing nod to Reverend George.

"We've been invited to attend the Beach Croft's opening, thought we would have a swift half before we went over there."

Deanne was not impressed. "It seems everyone has been invited except the Williamses at the Fisherman's. Tom, serve these two gentlemen, please – I have one of my heads coming on."

Tom came to the rescue and smiled sheepishly. "So sorry about that, gents, only Deanne is a bit put out not receiving an invite." He pulled two halves of Infinity and put them on the bar. "Have these on me, please."

"It must have been an oversight," said Reverend George, thanking Tom and turning to Joe. "I am sure Alfred Barton wouldn't have left Tom and Deanne off his guest list."

"I was surprised to be invited to be honest," said Joe, taking a sup of his beer.

"Well, you were very friendly with Alfred's Aunt Dolly."

Joe nodded, "I guess so, but I really don't have much to do with Alfred Barton."

"Well, maybe that will change after this evening. I know Alfred is keen to see Brokencliff get back on the holidaymakers' trail, even Lady Samantha is on board and some money has been spent on the theatre too. And Joe, I don't think you have ever called me by my Christian name. I am only Reverend George when I am on duty."

Joe laughed. "But I always think of you as Reverend George, the thought of calling you Charles never crossed my mind."

Reverend George smiled. "Whatever you feel more comfortable with, Joe, but when we are out socially, Charles is fine."

They finished their drinks and walked along to the hotel.

Greeted by staff, each guest was offered a sherry and shown into the dining room. There were gasps as each guest drank in the new décor for the first time – it was making the impression that Alfred had hoped for.

Half an hour later, the guests were served with a three-course meal and the finest wines that Alfred's cellar could offer.

Rita was looking radiant in a beautiful red gown and was sitting beside a rather dapper-looking Malcolm Farrow. Jenny and Elsie were at another table with Maud and her sister, Enid, who had been coaxed out of the house amidst protest that she didn't enjoy social gatherings. But in true Enid style, she soon drank two glasses of wine and was looking merrier than she had done on arrival.

Lady Samantha and Sir Harold were at the top table with Alfred Barton and Maureen Roberts, along with some local dignitaries from Great Yarmouth and Lowestoft. There were several other well-known faces, including Lucinda Haines with Muriel Evans and Erica Warren representing GAGGA. Beverley was also present with her husband, Ian, who had hated the idea of being "togged up", as he termed it, but he was happy enough to escort his wife, knowing that her job was important to her and to the contribution to their household.

Bob Scott and Norman Howard had been invited from the London offices of Rita's Angels and were staying in the hotel overnight. Jill Sanderson and Doreen Turner were also present and even Selwyn Woods who, with his wife Sally, had made a concerted effort to look smart.

In the bar lounge, Alfred mingled with his guests and he made a short speech thanking everyone for coming. He said he hoped that with all the works that had been going on in Brokencliff it would bring in more revenue and help boost its future.

Lady Samantha had been most impressed with the hotel, the food and the excellent service, and in conversation with Maureen Roberts asked if she might be able to find her suitable staff for Owlerton Hall.

"I am pleased you could come along, Joe," said Alfred as he worked the room. "I must come over and visit the caravan park one day soon."

"You would be very welcome," said Joe. "Can I just tell you that I was in the Fisherman's earlier and Deanne Williams was a little upset that she hadn't received an invitation."

Alfred looked alarmed. "Oh dear, I did wonder why we had two spaces empty at one of the tables. They were sent an invitation, I can assure you. Oh, I feel bad about this. I think I had better get over there now, thank you for telling me."

Excusing himself, and leaving Maureen to deal with the guests, Alfred walked swiftly along the parade and into the Fisherman's.

Tom looked up. "Mr Barton, what brings you here, I thought you had a do on at the hotel tonight?"

"And that's the very reason I am here. I understand you didn't receive my invitation. I wondered why you and your lady wife weren't with us. My head waiter alerted me to the fact that there were two empty spaces at one of the tables. I really cannot understand how this happened."

"Don't worry about it, and thank you for coming over to explain. Deanne was a bit perturbed earlier when Joe and the Reverend popped in on their way to you."

"Look, if there is some way I can make it up to you both – perhaps you would both like to dine one evening in the restaurant, if it's cover you need for the bar I am sure we can help out there."

"That's jolly decent of you. I will let the wife know, she is upstairs at the moment with a headache."

Alfred said his farewells and returned to the Beach Croft.

"Was that Alfred Barton's voice I heard?" asked Deanne as she appeared behind her husband.

"It was. Something of a mix-up, he is sure they sent an invite – there were two places set at table for us."

Deanne didn't seem impressed. "Well, he would say that wouldn't he."

The cabaret for the evening was a husband-and-wife duo known locally. Peter and Joy Partridge were based in Lowestoft and were often booked for birthdays and special occasions. Long-retired from the business, they were still on top of their game and enjoyed the occasional booking. Peter played the piano and Joy sang well-known songs; sometimes she was joined by Peter in a duet they both particularly liked. The guests at the Beach Croft enjoyed them immensely, but their cries for more fell on deaf ears; it was a thirty-minute set and Peter and Joy never entertained encores.

"You see, Alfred, that is something you could have more of in here, the odd evening's entertainment – a piano player or, as we've just seen, a duo. There are plenty of good acts out there. I could see who I could get for you."

Alfred smiled warmly at Rita. "I will keep it in mind and let you know."

Malcolm returned to Rita's side with a tray of replenished glasses. He handed Alfred his.

"I have to say, Alfred, I am very much impressed with the hotel, and it looks positively stunning."

"Thank you," said Alfred. "It has turned out alright after all."

"I am now about to have some work done on my house in Oulton Broad. It was in need of redecoration when I moved in and I have only just got round to doing something about it."

"Are you doing it yourself, then?" Alfred asked.

"Dear Lord, no," said Malcolm, handing Rita her drink and passing the empty tray to a waiter. "No, I have called in a specialist. Have you heard of Superior Interiors?"

Alfred nearly choked on his beer and Rita gasped. "No, Malcolm, please tell me you have got the name wrong."

Malcolm looked puzzled. "No, I am sure it was Superior Interiors. They are sending a woman round on Monday – Sandie Cross I think her name was. Why, do you know something I don't?"

"How long have you got?" said Alfred and Rita burst out laughing.

"Well, it's nice to see those two enjoying each other's company," said Elsie to Jenny. "They do make a nice couple, I must say."

"I agree, but we will just have to wait and see on that score. Rita isn't one to rush things; besides, she may not be as interested as he obviously is."

"I wouldn't say that," Elsie replied. "Did you see him give her that rose at dinner? She's wearing it on her dress lapel. Romance isn't dead, it is alive and well."

Lucinda was enjoying the function and was pleased when Lady Samantha came over and interrupted her conversation with Muriel and Erica.

"Lucinda dear, you are looking marvellous – I love that outfit. Palmers, Windsmoor, I bet?"

Lucinda smiled at Lady Samantha. "Yes, it is. I decided to treat myself. Allow me to introduce the secretary and treasurer of GAGGA, Erica Warren and Muriel Evans; this is Lady Samantha of Owlerton Hall."

Pleasantries were exchanged and Lady Samantha excused herself to have a quick chat with Alfred.

"She is a charming lady," said Lucinda, "and so down to earth."

Erica smiled and Muriel looked on.

"Allow me to get you ladies another drink," said Lucinda, tapping a waiter on the shoulder. "Two gin and tonics, please, and a sweet sherry – thank you, my good man."

"It was a lovely meal," said Reverend George, "and a very pleasant evening."

"It was indeed," said Joe.

"I think I ought to be making a move, but do stay and enjoy the rest of the evening, Joe."

Joe finished his drink. "No, I am ready for the off too, I have work tomorrow; sadly, that park does not run itself."

The two said their goodbyes and expressed thanks to Alfred and headed out of the hotel.

"It's a fine evening, Charles, to be sure," said Joe as the two walked along the parade while the sounds of the waves rang gently in their ears.

"Would you like to come in for a nightcap?" asked Joe as they reached the caravan park.

"I had better not, Joe. I have parish business tomorrow and I must be up quite early." He tapped Joe on the arm. "But we will sort out some theatre dates. If you are of a mind, drop by one morning and have coffee, I can check my diary."

Joe smiled warmly. "I will. Goodnight, Charles."

"Goodnight, Joe."

Joe went into the park and unlocked his front door. He poured himself a small whisky, sat down in his favourite armchair and had a long think.

Later, when Tom was clearing the bar, he looked down the side of the till for some cash bags and discovered some unopened mail. Among it was a gilt-edged envelope bearing the logo of The Beach Croft Hotel. Then it dawned on him. A couple of weeks previously, when he had been dealing with the draymen, the postman had called and he had put the mail down the side of the till meaning to deal with it later. He now faced the task of telling Deanne the news. Taking a large measure of scotch, he went upstairs to their living quarters with some trepidation.

## *Thursday, 20 April*

"I see the fair is setting up on the market place," said Elsie, coming into the office with a Palmers bag swinging from her arm.

Rita looked up from her desk. "Let's hope the weather holds out, nothing can put a dampener on a fair like bad weather."

"Perhaps we girls should all go over there tomorrow when it opens and try our luck on a coconut shy. I bet Jenny will be game."

"I worry about you sometimes," said Rita with a giggle. "We could give it a whirl I suppose. If they have a helter-skelter then I say we all climb those stairs and whizz down on a mat."

"It just gets better." Elsie put her bag down. "I had a quick tidy round this morning before I came in."

"Well, I don't know what for, that's what we employ Mona for."

"I just like to leave things nice."

"Elsie dear, Mona Buckle has cleaned a lot worse places than our lounge and kitchen."

Elsie settled down at her own desk and began to look through her post. There were still a lot of things to sort regarding Don's artists and she'd had her mail redirected to the office. She opened the envelopes and then sorted things into two piles. She took a deep breath and began to tackle the first.

In the adjacent office, Doreen and Jill were having a disagreement about a routine they were intending to use in a show in Clacton.

"It's no good you changing your mind every five minutes," said Doreen firmly. "We have six dancers and don't have the capacity to manage what you have suggested. The girls would not be able to change quick enough. The idea of a *Follies* routine is a lovely one, but it is hardly going to work on that stage. We need to stick to the tried and tested."

"So, in other words, we knock out the same old thing," said Jill. "Six lavish costumes is all I am suggesting, and each dancer will come down the staircase separately. Not so much a routine as a montage. I swear, if I have to use another one of those sailor or soldier routines I will explode."

Jenny came into the office, having just been to see her solicitor about some pressing business regarding leases. "I heard raised voices, is everything okay here?"

"It would be if madam here would see reason," said Jill. "We are supposed to be reinventing the dancers, not staying in the nineteen-fifties."

Jenny smiled to herself. "Tell me what it is you are suggesting, Jill, and then Doreen can voice her opinion. I will see if I can offer you some advice; the decision will be yours alone – I really don't want to get too involved."

Jenny listened to Jill's proposal and then to what Doreen had to say. "I like the *Follies* idea, I have to say." Doreen shook her head. "Hear me out, we do have a surplus of costumes and with a few added feathers and sequins Jill's idea could work, even on that small stage. It would make a change to open the show with something a bit different. I am thinking along the lines of 'A Pretty Girl is Like a Melody', something like that."

"My thoughts exactly," said Jill.

"But we don't have the room backstage for big costumes at Clacton," said Doreen. "Getting the six girls into that dressing room is bad enough, but just imagine having six overly large costumes in there as well, not to mention all the other costumes and wigs."

"So, you're not opposed to the idea, just the costumes?"

"Well, when you put it like that, yes."

"Okay," said Jenny, "here is my suggestion – the costumes open the show, once the routine is done, they are then wheeled away on a rail and stored in the back area with other props."

"But won't that cause a hazard for artistes to cross behind the backdrop to get to the other side of the stage for their entrances?"

"Hardly," said Jenny. "Think about it, at the end of each act a front cloth or tab descends, anyone not on the right side for their entrance need only go across the stage."

"That makes sense," said Doreen.

"Another suggestion, get on to Mr Massey at the Shrublands Youth and Adult Centre and ask him if you can borrow the stage there for a dress. It's the same size as Clacton and has the same problem, no dressing rooms on one side of the stage. Find some costumes and take the girls through a suitable routine. If you need music you can borrow my cassette player, which I treated myself to at Christmas; you can even record some music on a blank tape from my stereo, so you won't need the band."

Doreen looked at Jill and they both looked at Jenny; common sense prevailed once again.

*Tony Gareth Smith*

*Chapter Nine*    <u>A Bird in the Hand is</u>
<u>Worth Two in the Nest</u>

The Sparrows Nest Theatre – Lowestoft
Opening Thursday, 8 June at 8.00pm
For the summer season – nightly Mon–Sat at 7.45
Rita Ricer proudly presents

# CHRISTIAN LAPELLE

*"Dreamboat French Tenor direct from Opportunity Knocks"*

| *Puppet Sensation*<br>**"The Black Theatre of Milan"** | *The Comedian's Favourite*<br>**Tommy Trent** |
|---|---|
| The JB Showtime Dancers<br>Featuring *Dean, Morris, Glen and Sean* | **The HIT SHAKERS**<br>Girl and Boy band with Popular Hits from the sixties |

| And Special Guest Stars<br>Direct from their World Circus Tour<br>**Miss Pauline**<br>*Fire Eating, Knife-Throwing and Juggling*<br>*while swinging by her hair*<br>**assisted by Simon** |
|---|
| Produced by Sparrows Nest Co. and Directed by Rita Ricer<br>Choreography – Jill Sanderson and Doreen Turner |
| The Showtime Orchestra under the direction of VIC ALLEN |
| **Bookable in Advance** – 75p, 55p and 45p<br>**OAPs** – 50p all performances except Sat evening |

When Christian Lapelle had left his parents' home in Paris to come to England to enter the television contest *Opportunity Knocks*, he had done so believing that he would return home after having the exposure he craved on a television network. The British audience had raved about his singing voice and he had quickly picked up cabaret dates. Rita Ricer had stepped in just at the right moment and offered him her representation so that he could expand his bookings. Had the Golden Sands been on offer, she knew she would have liked him to have appeared there first, with plans to send him off to Blackpool for the lights season and then on to the London stage. She had approached Christian during his week in Norwich and a deal had been struck. Offering him the Sparrows Nest was poles apart from the London venues he really wanted to play, but she persuaded him to take baby steps first and she would ensure that he gained the experience to go further.

Christian was tall, dark and handsome, with chiselled features. His long, manicured fingers were often spoken of during interviews. He dressed in designer Italian suits and leather shoes that shone when a spotlight caught them. He dismissed the talk of his good looks and was only interested in his singing voice.

His parents had paid for him to have singing lessons from a very early age and encouraged him to enter the entertainment world. Before his car accident, his father had been a classical pianist; now confined to a wheelchair and with only one hand, he hoped his son would achieve the dizzy heights of fame that now eluded him. His mother had given up her career as a dancer to have a family, so it was fair to say that show business ran in the family.

However, unbeknown to his adoring public, Christian had a girlfriend, Fleur, who had been his childhood sweetheart and whom he adored. Christian's parents had not encouraged the romance for fear of it interfering with their son's ambition.

Fleur had remained in France and tried her best to keep a low profile. Her own parents wished for her to find a normal young man with whom she could spend her life. But, undeterred, Fleur continued to carry a torch for Christian and went to work every day at a local restaurant owned and run by her Uncle. With Christian now in England, all she could hope for was regular letters and the odd telephone call. She intended to save up her tips in the hope that she would be able to go across the Channel to see him.

Christian had met with something of a culture shock; everything was very different from what he had been used to in France, and although his appearances on *Opportunity Knocks* had meant that doors were opened for him, he hadn't reckoned with some of the places he would be appearing in or the accommodation he would be expected to stay in.

While appearing in Norwich, he had been staying with a theatrical family who allowed him the freedom to come and go as he pleased. His room was pleasant and overlooked a well-kept garden. His hosts were actors and actresses alike and he saw little of any of them as they busied themselves going to auditions.

The summer season in Lowestoft meant he had to take up residence in a boarding house in the area. Christian hadn't passed his driving test and was therefore reliant on public transport or the favours of others.

Rita had been more than happy to move him from Norwich to his new digs in Lowestoft, which even she considered "grim", but it was all the boy could afford and she wasn't open to mollycoddling her artists.

The digs in question were a modest terraced house just off the main Esplanade and had been suggested by Jack, the doorman, who said that he knew many theatricals who stayed there and had been quite happy. But as Rita pondered, Jack was harking back to the days before most houses had inside facilities.

The landlady was a Miss Gaunt; she was tall and slim, with sharp features, her nose supporting black-rimmed glasses which hid her beady eyes in their sunken sockets. Her dark hair was tied back in a bun and her thin lips sported a mere touch of red lipstick. Her feet were clad in heavy black support shoes and her legs lagged in thick black stockings. She wore a wrap-over pinafore with just a glimpse of a starched white blouse showing at the top that had a red enamelled brooch fastened at the neck.

She opened the front door and eyed Christian and Rita up and down as if scrutinising their very being.

Rita smiled and introduced Christian.

Miss Gaunt stood to one side "I was expecting you" she said motioning with her hand for them to step into the hallway. "I thought you were due to arrive earlier I don't hold with people being late."

"The traffic from Norwich was quite heavy" said Rita by way of an explanation.

"I don't hold with traffic" said Miss Gaunt closing the front door and turning to face her guests. "You don't have a car Mr Lapelle?"

Christian shook his head.

"I don't have parking" said Miss Gaunt "I tell all my guests that. I like to scrub my step of a morning; the last thing I want is a car blocking the pavement out front."

Miss Gaunt opened a door to her left. "This is the dining room, breakfast is at seven thirty sharp and I don't do fancy food. I don't hold with fancy food, if guests want fancy food they need to book in at The Claremont or The Thistle."

"I believe Christian will be eating out in the evening" said Rita looking around the dining room. There were seven tables, all with a white linen tablecloth, the carpet was a swirl of colour and the walls were papered in what once was a claret pattern. The woodwork was brown and the bay window housed a small radiogram with a doily on top, on which stood a vase of artificial flowers.

"What a lovely radiogram," said Rita, trying to make conversation, "my late husband had one like it, and he loved to listen to the World Service when he wasn't on the road."

"I have the Light Programme on in the mornings for the guests," replied Miss Gaunt, moving forward to straighten the curtains that hung at the window. "My guests seem to enjoy that."

"Is there a television lounge?" asked Rita.

"I don't hold with televisions," said Miss Gaunt, "and every room here has a comfortable armchair should someone wish to relax. I was under the impression that Mr Lapelle would be out most evenings at the theatre. Most of my guests are out in the evenings."

Miss Gaunt motioned for the two to follow her up the stairs. "I have given Mr Lapelle the front bedroom on the second floor as it has a nice view from there. Some of my guests don't care too much for views."

Rita followed a hesitant Christian up the stairs whose knuckles had turned white from gripping his suitcase so tightly.

The room was clean, but a smell of mothballs hung in the air – the candlewick bedspread had seen better days. There was a dark-oak wardrobe and matching chest of drawers, on which stood a wash basin and jug. As Miss Gaunt had mentioned, there was a leather armchair near a disused fireplace, which now housed a one-bar electric fire. The walls were papered in a design of forget-me-nots and pink roses; the carpet was showing signs of wear but was clean.

"There is a lavatory at the far end of the landing, you will find a bathroom on the first floor, but please be sure to let me know when you plan to take a bath as I will have to turn on the immersion heater. Baths are extra and I don't provide towels."

Christian put down his suitcase on the bed; Miss Gaunt grimaced. "I don't hold with suitcases on my beds – that was made up fresh this morning, the sheets were laundered at the local laundry."

Christian quickly moved the suitcase to the floor.

"As I told Mr Jack, payment is a week in advance. I will give you a front-door key and I ask all my guests to be quiet as they leave and enter the house. I don't hold with noise after nine in the evening. I will let you settle in and, as you have a friend with you, I shall provide a tray of tea and biscuits in the breakfast room in fifteen minutes – there will be no charge." Miss Gaunt attempted a smile and left the room, closing the door behind her.

Rita put her arm round Christian. "It won't be so bad when you get settled in and you'll be able to enjoy the sea air during the day and the café at the Nest does some good lunches. Besides, once you get to know the rest of the crew you'll be out and about and you can always come over to Great Yarmouth for the day, there is plenty to do there."

Christian managed a wintry smile and opened his suitcase. It was going to be a long summer season.

Rita had been fortunate, through her many contacts, to secure some acts that had not been seen in the area before. The Hit Shakers, who were a young quartet of two boys and two girls, had been formed a couple of years before for the sole purpose of appearing on the summer show circuit. They had clocked up successful seasons in Bournemouth, Clacton and Paignton and Rita was pleased to have them on the bill; The Black Theatre of Milan had toured Europe and this would be their first UK appearance and Rita thought they would be a great bonus to the show.

Her biggest success, however, was securing Miss Pauline and Simon. Miss Pauline, of Russian origin (aka Svetlana Smirnov), and her cousin Simon (Spartak Volkov) had been born into a circus family. Miss Pauline had followed in her grandmother's footsteps, the art of swinging by her waist-length hair while juggling with fire, soaring high above the audience and spinning.

She had recently introduced knife-throwing. Simon, who both managed and appeared in the ring with her, was responsible for ensuring that Miss Pauline's waist-length hair was combed and twisted correctly and then threaded through a ringed leather strap attached to the flying equipment that would secure her as he managed her air manoeuvres from below. Rita had to ensure that the Sparrows Nest would not be fire-damaged when Miss Pauline swung across the stage. A special fireproof canopy above the area where she would fly would be in place to ensure safety regulations were followed.

Because of the nature of the act, it was decided that they would open the second half, giving stage hands the necessary time to see that everything was in place. Miss Pauline was happy to adjust her act accordingly and would appear in a top hat and tailed trouser suit and dance across the stage. Then, handing the top hat to Simon, would have her hair clipped to the flying ring and begin by being taken slowly upward as she stripped from her attire to reveal a spangled leotard that would catch the spotlights and dazzle the audience. Being lowered back down onto the stage at regular intervals, Simon would hand Miss Pauline the various skittles she juggled with and the act would end with her juggling fire sticks while swinging above.

The knife-throwing was done in the middle of the act, when Miss Pauline threw knives as Simon was rotated on a spinning board. She had tried to perfect knife-throwing while swinging by her hair but during initial rehearsals, when there had been several near misses, it was thought that it was safer to do it the traditional way. It had often been reported that this kind of act could only be performed for six months of the year. The artiste could lose at least six waist-length hairs per day and suffer from terrible headaches, wearing dark glasses during sunny weather to help counteract the condition.

## *Friday, 19 May*

Rita and Jenny walked down the aisle of the Sparrows Nest Theatre just as Miss Pauline walked on to the stage. She smiled at Rita and came down the side steps.

"Hello, Miss Rita," she said in a strong Russian accent. "We have been checking the rig for my act. Simon, he knows people at the circus in the other town and they come to advise us – this is our first time performing in a theatre."

Rita shook Miss Pauline's hand. "This is Jenny Benjamin who works with me."

Miss Pauline tapped Jenny on the shoulder. "I heard of you. You were a bluebird girl, yes?"

Jenny smiled. "Bluebell girl – yes I was, many years ago."

"Is Simon your brother?" asked Rita. "There does seem to be a resemblance."

"He is my – how you say – cousin. Spartak and I work together many years. He was once a high-flier."

"In business?" queried Jenny, missing the point completely.

"I think Miss Pauline means he did a trapeze act," said Rita with a smile and motioning for them both to sit down. Jenny blushed.

"And your name isn't Pauline, it's Svetlana, is that correct?"

Miss Pauline nodded. "You say that well. We have to use names people understand. Spartak doesn't speak good English, but he is very good at French."

"We have a French singer topping the bill," said Jenny, "so that will be nice.

"They meet," said Miss Pauline. "I think Christian miss his girl. Spartak too, she back in Russia."

Spartak called from the stage as he walked on. "Good, good, all good."

Miss Pauline waved. "I think I need to rehearse now, you stay and watch."

"Indeed, we shall."

Without the aid of music, Simon operated the rigging from the wings as Miss Pauline, now hooked by a ring through her hair, was gently taken upward.

"That must hurt," said Jenny, "but she makes it look so graceful."

Pauline shouted some instructions to Simon in Russian and she came back down onto the stage. They exchanged more words and then up she went again, this time juggling with clubs. A wire had been fixed from the centre of the stage to just above the first few rows of the auditorium and Miss Pauline swung out above Jenny and Rita. Then, swinging across from side to side, she continued to juggle.

When she came back down again, Miss Pauline secured Simon to a rotating circular board and, as he spun, she threw knives at him, making an outline of his body.

"Are we insured for accidents?" said Jenny, alarmed.

"Maybe I will have to ask her not to juggle above the audience, but you can see how special this act is."

"In more ways than one," said Jenny, averting her eyes.

They both walked back up the aisle, leaving Miss Pauline and Simon to continue rehearsing.

"Tell me again why we booked a circus act into a stage show?"

"Well," said Rita, "I thought we needed something a bit different with this being our first full-season outing here and it was through The Dean Sisters that I got wind of these two. I had a word with my contacts at the Hippodrome and they said they were keen to book them at some time. They come from a family background of circus. Miss Pauline's grandmother swung by her hair and her mother was a high wire walker, and also worked with elephants. I believe that on Simon's side of the family they were jugglers, trapeze artistes and clowns too, I was told."

"I have to say, she is quite heavy round the hips," said Jenny.

"Most circus performers are muscly; you must remember that The Dean Sisters had strong thighs – all that rolling around on balls takes stamina."

Jenny held the door open. "Yes, they were now you come to mention it."

They walked out of the theatre and through the garden area. "If I'm not mistaken, that's Christian sitting on that bench over there."

"Want to go and say hello?"

"Let's leave it today, Jenny, there will be plenty of time to chat when we get into rehearsals proper. Now, we had better get back to the office – I have one or two calls I need to make and, if my memory serves me, you were meeting with Jill and Doreen to discuss the dancers' contracts for the season."

"Gosh, yes, I had forgotten about that. Can we stop off on the way and pick up a few pastries? I have a feeling that the meeting may go on a bit. The boys are trying to up their wages above the girls and I am not going to allow it. The show can go on with or without them; they knew the wage when we agreed the contracts, and they get a digs allowance."

Rita got into the car and smiled to herself. Jenny really was firing on all cylinders today and she hoped Doreen and Jill were ready to face battle. She started the engine and they set off back to Great Yarmouth.

* * *

"Some of these boys can earn more in variety shows in London," said Doreen, trying to put their point of view across.

"Then why have they chosen to work in a summer show in Lowestoft?" said Jenny, tapping her pen with impatience. "I will tell you – because they couldn't secure the work. The package we offer is far better than many others around the country. I've done my homework."

"But couldn't we see our way to paying a little bit more?" asked Jill, siding with Doreen.

"We have a strict budget to adhere to, as you are both well aware," replied Jenny, trying to control her frustration. "We could advertise for these dancers again and we would have a queue round the block. You go back to the boys and tell them if they don't like what is on offer then they are under no obligation to stay."

"But they've signed contracts," said Doreen, feeling somewhat alarmed by Jenny's forthright manner.

"We can overlook that and release them," said Jenny, steadily confident in what she was saying. "I don't want dancers in any show connected with our name being unhappy. As I have said, we can advertise again – we have a couple of weeks until we open, so finding replacements will not be a problem. An advert in the *EDP* should suffice. There is enough local talent without the need to advertise in *The Stage*. Beverley or Julie can sort out the arrangements for you and I will be on hand should you need any further advice."

Jill and Doreen exchanged looks and knew when they were beaten.

Jenny stood up. "Now, if you will excuse me, ladies, I have some other business to attend to. I will support you in whatever you decide is best."

"Well, that was a turn up for the books," said Doreen. "I thought Jenny might consider what they were asking."

"She did put over some valid points earlier on," said Jill. "We do offer them an allowance for their digs and not many seaside resorts do that. We both know she is right really, and there are plenty of other people out there."

"All of this started when we decided to take on the male dancers," said Doreen. "We should have stuck with the girls."

"That wouldn't have been progress, though, would it?" Jill stated. "Look how we had to coax Jenny initially – she was never in favour of male dancers, but now she has taken it on board."

"We will call a meeting this afternoon and see how they take it. Be a shame to lose any of them, but best we all know where we stand."

And Jill nodded in agreement.

\* \* \*

## Thursday, 8 June

The theatre was a hub of activity; last-minute lighting checks were taking place and the orchestra was running through some of the music as the backstage boys adjusted sets and ensured that microphones were working.

Malcolm Farrow, Rita and Jenny sat themselves down, centre stalls, and prepared to watch the final dress rehearsal.

"I understand there was a problem with some of the male dancers," said Malcolm, who was sitting between the two ladies.

"All sorted now," said Jenny. "They wanted to be paid more than the girls, but I soon put them right. At least Doreen and Jill did. I threatened to take away their contracts and recruit other dancers."

"Surely that was risky," Malcolm replied. "What if they had all walked out? It must have been a bit of a gamble."

Rita interrupted. "When you've been in the business as long as I have, me old lover, and indeed Jenny, this whole thing is a gamble."

"I agree. You sometimes put the wrong acts in that don't work with the rest of the company – I saw it happen many times. It can ruin the whole feel of a show," said Jenny.

"I am grateful that I have you two running things," said Malcolm. "I can sit back and watch it all unfold."

"That's what you think, me old lover," said Rita, offering some mints. "I shall expect you on parade at the opening-night party and making all the right noises."

A gentle squeeze of her hand assured Rita that Malcolm would do as she wished.

Vic Allen called out from the orchestra pit. "Okay, I think we are ready to roll. Can you bring the curtain down, please?"

The auditorium lights dimmed and the orchestra struck up an overture made up from some of the songs in the show.

The rehearsal reached its conclusion and Rita, armed with notes, went onto the stage to deliver her verdict.

"Right, everyone, listen up please. I will deal with the dancers first – you are all slightly off-centre during the opening and the second number needs tightening up before this evening." She looked out into the auditorium. "Jill, Doreen, I would be grateful if you would take the dancers through their paces again; for a final rehearsal this really isn't quite up to scratch."

"Is she always like this?" whispered Malcolm to Jenny.

"Oh, she can be much worse once she gets started." Jenny felt Malcolm twitch and she smiled.

Turning her attention to the Hit Shakers, Rita continued. "Sorry, me old lovers, but you were off-key in the second number, and in the fourth I could hardly hear you boys at all. Vic, sweetheart, maybe you need to tone down the brass. Tommy, keep up the pace, quick snappy and don't slow down when you reach the final joke, you need to keep the audience engaged, don't lose them. I've left you a couple of joke sheets in your dressing room; use them if you need to."

"She really is a terror," whispered Malcolm, and Jenny laughed. He didn't know the half of it.

"The lights are not coming down quick enough for the Black Theatre and it will spoil the opening of their set. Richard, me old lover, have a word, please."

A cry of "Yes, Rita" was heard from the wings.

Turning her attention to Miss Pauline and Simon, Rita smiled warmly. "You two are going to knock them dead, spot on, breath-taking, I cannot find the words."

Svetlana and Spartak both smiled and nodded.

"Christian, my flower, you got a bit lost in your Edith Piaf, perhaps Vic and the boys can run you through it one more time." She patted him on the shoulder and gave him a reassuring hand on his cheek.

"Right, everyone, that's all. We have a full house tonight and the great and the good will be in attendance; all are potential critics, word of mouth in this business is crucial. If they don't like you, audiences will stay away in droves. This is your chance to shine, oh, and I have it on good authority that Hughie Green is in tonight."

Christian blushed and smiled. "So, you see, you have everything to play for – be lucky, me old lovers, and don't let me down."

Rita strutted off the stage and down the side steps and back to Malcolm and Jenny.

"My goodness, it was like seeing the commander of a ship." Malcolm laughed, standing to attention. "You had them eating out of your hands."

Rita laughed. "And to recall an old joke of Ted's – well, it saves washing up."

"Come on, you two, a cup of tea and then off home to change, I think," said Jenny.

*Tony Gareth Smith*

# *Chapter Ten*    *It's SHOWTIME*

"Showtime at the Nest" – the programme

"Showtime Overture"
Vic Allen and the Showtime Orchestra

**The Show's the Thing**
The JB Showtime Dancers introduce
"Under the Bridges of Paris"
**CHRISTIAN LAPELLE**

**I Was Just Passing By**
**Tommy Trent**

**Chirpy Chirpy Cheep Cheep**
**The JB Showtime Dancers**

Tommy Trent

Juke Box Jury
**The JB Showtime Dancers Introduce**
**THE HIT SHAKERS**

Interval

The Girl with the Sun in Her Hair
The JB Showtime Dancers introduce
The Hair Raising
Miss Pauline and Simon

Tommy Trent

The JB Showtime Dancers introduce
The Star of the Show
The French Sensation
**CHRISTIAN LAPELLE**

The Company say "Goodnight"

In the theatre bar, Malcolm Farrow was shaking hands with the Mayor and local dignitaries, who were all congratulating him on a wonderful show.

"It is this lady I have to thank," said Malcolm, turning to look at Rita. "She is the brains behind this whole thing and along with her trusted team she has put a show together I am very proud of. But then, after her Christmas show here, I knew I couldn't have expected anything less."

Pleasantries were exchanged and Rita moved around the room closely followed by Malcolm.

"He really is smitten," said Elsie to Jenny as they enjoyed a drink.

"And I think it's reciprocated," replied Jenny. "You have got to admit, he's a bit of a catch and it would be nice to see Rita in a cosy relationship."

"Softly, softly, catchee monkey," said Elsie. "I think he is doing all the right things, he courts her, and that is something you don't hear of much these days. Have you ever wanted to marry, Jenny?"

"I had my moments, but let's just say it wasn't to be. I am quite happy as I am. Would you ever get involved again, Elsie? Sorry, that was crass, too early to be thinking of such things."

Elsie patted Jenny's arm. "Don't worry about it. Don and I were very happy together and of course I do miss the old beggar. I don't know that I would ever look at a man in the same way again. But who knows."

"And what are you two chatting about?" said Rita, interrupting.

"Life in general," said Elsie, taking the lead. "Great show, by the way – that Christian Lapelle knows how to woo an audience."

"Can I get you ladies a drink?" asked Malcolm, moving alongside Rita. "I am just about to get a round in for the backstage crew."

"I will have another Dubonnet," said Jenny, "and I am sure Elsie could manage another gin."

"Rita, would you like another?"

"I am okay for the minute, me old lover, thank you."

"Malcolm is a nice man," said Elsie. "I think he will do well here at the Nest."

Rita smiled. "Yes, he seems to be the business, he is very professional. Stands no nonsense and gets on with the job in hand."

"Handsome-looking brute too," said Jenny, and then stopped herself from going further.

"Yes, he wasn't at the back of the queue when they handed out the looks, that's for sure," said Rita. "I'll go and have a word with Christian. He is looking rather isolated over in that corner."

Elsie surveyed the room. "It seems strange not to see all the landladies here from Great Yarmouth, somehow."

"Oh, I expect there are local landladies here," said Jenny, "but of course we wouldn't know who they were, though by looking at some of the faces I could hazard a guess. They have a look about them, don't they, landladies? Like vultures awaiting the kill."

"Jenny Benjamin, how many of those have you had? It's not like you to be so outspoken."

"I'm making up for all those years when I was but a blushing wallflower, kept a civil tongue in my head and lost myself in my work."

Elsie laughed. "If anyone could hear this conversation they would think we were a right couple of gossips."

Photographers were taking snaps of some of the groups and two local reporters were seen interviewing a couple of the stars of the show, with Miss Pauline and Simon attracting a lot of attention and Miss Pauline doing the talking for both of them.

"A wonderful show, Mrs Ricer has done it again," said Lady Samantha, who for once was accompanied by her husband who was making free with the drinks on offer.

"I couldn't agree more," said Alfred, accepting another glass from Sir Harold. "Rita does have a Midas touch about her. She is able to change a negative to a positive. I wish I had her sorting out the hotel."

"I could do with someone like her at the Hall, Harold is quite useless."

Alfred laughed. "I think we could all do with a Rita."

"And a Beverley, if all I hear about her is true. That's her over there talking to Jenny, isn't it?"

"That's her alright," said Alfred. "I offered her a job at the hotel, but she prefers to remain nearer to home; besides, the unsocial hours of a hotel wouldn't suit her."

"I could do with someone to take on some of the administrative work," said Lady Samantha. "It wouldn't be a full-time position. If you hear of anyone, Alfred, please let me know."

After chatting with Christian, Rita moved her attention to Tommy Trent, congratulating him on his act. He had taken Rita's comments on board and was delivering the jokes in a quick-fire way that had the audience roaring with laughter. Rita spoke in turn with every one of the artists on the bill, including every member of the dancers and the orchestra, as Malcolm watched her, admiring her ability to make conversation.

"She doesn't miss anyone, does she?" he stated to Jenny as she walked by him on her way to the ladies.

"No, she doesn't. Rita has a way with her that many could learn from in this business."

"I am taking notes," said Malcolm, smiling as Jenny touched his arm and continued on her way.

* * *

## Monday, 12 June

The company of the Clifftop Players assembled at rehearsal rooms in Earls Court. Last to arrive were Constance Anderson and her husband, William Forbes.

Ray Darnell leapt from his seat to greet the couple.

In his usual fashion he stood on one leg, slightly leaning to the right, with a large open grin on his face. "Connie my darling, and William old boy, what a lovely surprise."

"Hardly a surprise," said Constance, removing her beige suede gloves and holding out her hand to shake Ray's. "You did book us after all, Ray dear, so a surprise it isn't."

Ray grabbed Connie's hand and then embraced her. "You are looking ravishing."

"You wouldn't have said that if you had seen me first thing this morning," said Constance, "without the make-up."

"That's what I love about you, Connie, you are so openly honest."

Constance smiled. "My dear, I make no bones about it, I am the wrong end of sixty and I see no reason to pretend otherwise. William, on the other hand, still believes himself to be in his forties."

William hugged his wife. "You exaggerate, my love, I confess to being fifty now."

"You're seventy-two, you old rogue, but you scrub up well and keep yourself fit."

Constance removed her coat and surveyed the faces of the others. "It is so lovely to see so many familiar faces. Edith, how the devil are you? I hope the problem with your knee has cleared up since we last saw each other."

Edith Harris beamed a smile at Constance and nodded.

Ray knew one thing that was certain – Constance and William would both be word-perfect from the off. Constance had never once gone into a production without knowing her lines; all she and William would require was some stage direction.

Constance and William worked the room, reacquainting themselves with Fred Hughes, an older character actor they had worked with a few times, and Edmund Green and Sue Wilson, both in their mid-forties, who had been on tour with Constance and William several times. The two youngest members of the cast were Julia Burton and Patrick Prowse who were new to the company, but had both appeared in a couple of Shakespearian plays where Ray had spotted their talent.

Bringing the company to order, Ray went briefly over the two scripts they would be working with, *Wardrobe Doors*, a farce and *Death Nap*, a comedy thriller.

"Sorry to interrupt at this juncture," said Constance, removing her reading glasses. "But when I read through *Wardrobe Doors* I did find it a bit weak. Of course, the part of Marcia Duke is right up my street but the whole thing lacks something."

Some of the company nodded in agreement.

Ray placed his pencil in his top pocket and looked up from his clipboard. "I had intended us to be performing *Wanted, One Body* by the wonderful Raymond Dyer, but it was performed in Great Yarmouth in sixty-nine and I thought it was too soon for it to make a reappearance."

"If I might say so," said Edith, looking up from her script, "*Wanted, One Body* is a wonderful play, I saw Brian Rix in it."

Ray sighed. "Sadly, we don't have *Wanted, One Body*; we have *Wardrobe Doors*, which I think, as we get into our stride, we can make something of."

William Forbes gave one of his snorts, for which he was renowned. "I think we have to give it a bash, old things, sometimes what doesn't look good on paper turns out to be quite different in performance."

Sue Wilson fidgeted in her seat; she wasn't one to speak up often, but felt the need to do so on this occasion. "I am with Ray on this; it might be the funniest thing since *Tom and Jerry*."

"I am quite looking forward to *Death Nap*," said Patrick. "I've never appeared in a thriller before."

"And reading the script as I have," said Constance, "you are not likely to. Such is the world of theatrical drama; we can't have the cream every time."

Ray looked crestfallen. "Not *Death Nap* as well, Connie darling, when I was casting it I could see you as Gloria Jarvis from the start."

"Well, if it makes you feel better, Ray, *Death Nap* is better than Wardrobe Knobs or whatever it is called."

Ray looked at his watch. "I think we should all take a little break here and get back together in, let's say, sixty minutes – call it an hour."

"But it is an hour, you silly old fart," said William with a laugh. "Come on, I spotted a nice little boozer across the road, let's all go and have a couple of bevvies."

Ray held his hand to his forehead; it was going to be a trying rehearsal.

# THE LITTLE PLAYHOUSE –
# Brokencliff-on Sea

Rita Ricer in association with Ray Darnell and
Alfred Barton
presents

For the Summer Season from
Monday 3 July until Saturday 2 September 1972

## Afternoons at 2pm (except Sun) –

## Wardrobe Doors – a farce in 3 acts
## by P.J. Proctor
## Death Nap – a thriller in 3 acts by
## Mildred Miles

featuring the Clifftop Players under the direction
of Ray Darnell

**Week 1** – **Mon** – **Wed** "Wardrobe Doors" / **Thurs
– Sat** "Death Nap"
**Week 2** – **Mon** – **Wed** "Death Nap" / **Thurs – Sat**
– "Wardrobe Doors"
*then alternating weeks – see two plays in one
week!*

Bookable in advance from the box office
50p and 40p
**Special Offer – Monday and Thursday Matinees all seats 45p**

\*\*\*\*\*\*\*\*\*\*\*\*\*\*\*\*\*\*\*\*\*\*\*\*\*\*\*\*\*\*\*\*\*\*\*\*\*\*\*\*\*\*\*\*\*\*\*\*\*\*\*\*\*\*\*\*\*\*

**Nightly at 7.45** (except Sun)
# "Variety at the Clifftop"
Starring
## "LAUREN DU BARRIE"
*The Voice that launched a Thousand Ships*
with

*"Comedian"* **Hughie Dixon**

*"Master of Magic"* **Jonny Adams**

**Miss Penny's Puppets**
The Clifftop Gaiety Girls
Providing the music
**Phil Yovell and Darren Yates**

Bookable in Advance from the Box Office
65p and 55p
**Special offer – Monday evenings only all seats 50p**

The programme

## "WARDROBE DOORS" a farce
in three acts by P.J. Proctor

### *The setting is "Gable's Guest House"*

| | |
|---|---|
| Betty Gable, the landlady | Edith Harris |
| Edward Gable, her husband | Fred Hughes |
| **The guests** | |
| Marcia Duke | Constance Anderson |
| Hilary Peck | William Forbes |
| Doreen Packet | Sue Wilson |
| Malcolm Packet | Edmund Green |
| Lynette Brown | Julia Burton |
| Simon Todd | Patrick Prowse |

## "DEATH NAP" – a thriller in
three acts by Mildred Miles

### *The action takes place in Holkham Hall*

| | |
|---|---|
| Colonel Landau | Fred Hughes |
| Martina Prescott | Sue Wilson |
| Gloria Jarvis | Constance Anderson |
| Linda Jarvis, her daughter | Julia Burton |
| Inspector Cross | William Forbes |
| Sandy Davidson | Edmund Green |
| Samantha Pond | Edith Harris |
| Denis Clark, a solicitor | Patrick Prowse |

The programme

## "VARIETY AT THE CLIFFTOP"

- ❖ **Opus One** – Phil Yovell at the Baby Grand and Darren Yates (percussion)
- ❖ **"Vitality"** The Clifftop Gaiety Girls
- ❖ **"Having a Laugh"** – Hughie Dixon
- ❖ **"By the Light of the Silvery Moon"** – The Clifftop Gaiety Girls
- ❖ **"Strings and Things"** Miss Penny's Puppets
- ❖ **"Magical Moments"** – Jonny Adams assisted by The Clifftop Gaiety Girls

Interval

- ❖ **Opus Two** – Phil Yovell and Darren Yates
- ❖ **"And another thing"** Hughie Dixon
- ❖ **"Give My Regards to Broadway"** – The Clifftop Gaiety Girls
  Introduce
  ***The Star of the Show***
- ❖ **LAUREN DU BARRIE**
- ❖ The Company say "Goodnight"

## *Monday, 26 June*

With Jack in place as the stage doorman, he welcomed back Lauren Du Barrie who arrived swathed in furs despite the warm temperature outside. Jack was pleased to be reacquainted with Milly, Lauren's personal assistant whom he had warmed to the previous year at the Golden Sands. Milly, a quiet mousey little thing, followed behind Lauren who in her usual fashion was throwing her arms about theatrically. "Darling Milly, why do I agree to do these things? Heavens above, I know how the public adore me, but sometimes one wishes for a quieter life. It's the voice, you know; perhaps some hot lemon and honey would soothe it – do you think you could arrange it? There's a dear. I had forgotten we were playing a smaller venue this season, but one must go where one's public needs them."

Jack waved a kettle and smiled at Milly and she smiled back, happy to know that she had Jack there to lend a hand.

Jonny Adams was quietly going through some tricks on the stage and Miss Penny was talking to herself and her puppets about the season ahead. Hughie Dixon crashed through the stage door and startled Jack, who was preparing the honey and lemon.

"Sorry, me old mucker," said Hughie, who appeared to be a little worse for wear. "Just popped into the Fisherman's to check out the local, you know how it is."

Jack raised his eyebrows. "If I were you, Mr Dixon, I would get my act together before Rita Ricer arrives."

"Old Rita, she's a pussycat," said Hughie, steadying himself. "We get on like a house on fire."

"Don't say I haven't warned you," said Jack. "You will find the dressing rooms through there."

Rita came through the door with Jenny. "Hello Jack, was that Hughie Dixon I saw staggering along?" Jack nodded. Handing Jenny her handbag, she walked towards the dressing-room area. "If he thinks I am putting up with drunks on this bill then he has another think coming."

"Oh dear, not off to a good start," said Jenny.

"He may just be in high spirits," said Jack. "First time I've seen him like that and he has been around a bit."

"Well, he won't be in high spirits for long," said Jenny, moving towards the dressing rooms, "not with Rita in charge. Tell me, has young Jonny arrived?"

"You'll find him on the stage with Miss Penny."

Milly appeared and smiled at Jenny. "I take it Miss Du Barrie has arrived?"

Milly smiled again and nodded. "She is in her dressing room."

Jenny thanked her.

"So, how are you, young Milly?" asked Jack, handing her the hot mug. "I had some lemon and honey ready for your arrival, hope it is up to your standard."

Milly took the mug. "I'm sure it will be. I am keeping well, Jack, thank you for asking."

The voice of Lauren Du Barrie could be heard calling, "Milly dear, where are you with the honey and lemon? It's the voice, you know."

"I had better go."

"I see she hasn't changed much since last year," said Jack with a twinkle in his eye.

"She is always the same," said Milly. And then she added, with a wicked laugh and mimicry that amused Jack, "It's the voice, you know."

Alfred was at the box office talking to Maud and Barbara. "How are we looking, booking wise?"

"The variety show is booking quite well but the plays are a bit slow – the opening performance isn't even half full," said Maud. "It might pick up in a day or two."

"Let's hope so," said Alfred, "there's a big ad in the *EDP* tomorrow and in the *Lowestoft Journal* and *Yarmouth Mercury* on Friday."

"I would have thought it was risky to put plays on in the afternoon," said Barbara, adding her fourpenceworth.

"You would be surprised how many older people enjoy an afternoon play," said Alfred, keeping his fingers crossed behind his back. "I have a couple of large parties booked in for next week, so I am hoping I can get them interested."

"How is the hotel doing now you have been fully redone, so to speak?" asked Maud. "Meant to pop over and see you again, but Enid hasn't been too good lately and by the time I arrive here there isn't much time to call my own."

"Things have really started to pick up. I have to say that old Chippy really has done a grand job on the bedrooms and no mistake."

"I had to laugh when I heard that Rita had rumbled that Sandie Cross," said Maud, enjoying the gossip. "Fancy it turning out to be Audrey Audley."

"Well, of course, I had never met Audrey," said Alfred with a grin. "Her face was a picture when Rita challenged her. Fancy trying to pull a stunt like that, she must have known she would get caught out someday."

"Audrey Audley has more front than Blackpool. I always remember her coming along to the Sands, the whole persona was worthy of an award. She went off to Australia on a cruise, you know, with some man she knew. She gave up the agency after the Derinda Daniels affair. You must have read about it in the papers and seen it on the television. Made her look a complete fool really – Audrey, I mean, not Derinda, though she had some bad luck. Audrey Audley coming back to

Norfolk and setting herself up as an interior decorator, it's laughable really. I hope you weren't out of pocket, Alfred?"

Alfred shook his head. "No, all good in that department, settled out of court. I think it will be a long time before you see Audrey back in business."

"I wouldn't bet on it," replied Maud knowingly. "Her sort is always up to something, you mark my words." And with the Maud sigh that followed, the present company concurred.

* * *

Freda opened her front door and let Muriel in.

"What is that you are wearing?" asked Muriel, following Freda through to her living room. "You are supposed to be ready to go to Lowestoft. We mustn't miss the bus."

Freda spun around the floor in a girlish giggle. "I bought it in Norwich, do you like it?"

Muriel looked at the garishly coloured garment in wonder.

"It's a smock-top dress, they are all the rage."

"It's very full," said Muriel, watching as Freda continued to twirl. "There is enough material in that to make several dresses."

"I fancied a change," said Freda, stopping herself before she fell over in the excitement of it all. "I might wear it at the next GAGGA function."

"Not wishing to be unkind," said Muriel, resting her arm on the settee back, "but you'd have been better off buying the fitting room curtains. It's rather full even on your hardly svelte figure."

But Freda wasn't listening as she hastily ran from the room, stomping along like a herd of elephants. "I won't be a minute; I will quickly change for Lowestoft."

She reappeared in her usual attire and picked up her shopping bag.

"Have you noticed there are a lot of people from Scotland in town at the moment?"

"It is that time of the year?" said Muriel, hurrying along, afraid of missing the number one bus to Lowestoft.

"Lots of those Scottish men are wearing kilts," said Freda. "Is it true what they say about them and their kilts, that they don't wear anything under them?"

"I believe so," said Muriel, "but I've never been out with a man in a kilt so I couldn't say definitely."

"Fancy," said Freda.

Muriel put out her hand to stop the approaching bus.

"Well, they do say that people from Scotland are quite mean with their money, so I suppose it saves on the washing powder," Freda added, following Muriel onto the bus.

Muriel found them a seat and, as usual, Freda took up most of it. Muriel paid the conductor and thanked him. "You can pay on the way back. I thought we could have a look round Tuttles and maybe have some lunch in that small café you like near the docks."

"I haven't to rush back," said Freda, fumbling in her bag for a mint imperial. "I'm only doing bed and breakfast this week, thank goodness."

Muriel looked at her watch. "I have to be back by four at the latest. After dishing up I have to go along to Lucinda's for a committee meeting."

"Something must be up."

"It usually is," said Muriel, refusing the offer of a mint. "I think she is keen to go over the accounts again."

Later that evening, Lucinda welcomed Muriel and ushered her into the lounge. "Oh, good, you have brought the account books with you. Please sit down, Muriel. I was just about to have a small port, would you care to join me?"

Unaccustomed to these niceties from Lucinda, Muriel found herself accepting.

"I thought we would be quiet in here," said Lucinda, sitting down. "Most of my guests are out this evening and they don't tend to use this space much, which is a shame after all the expense I went to."

Muriel sipped her port and handed Lucinda the accounts book. "I think you will find everything in order. All the receipts are accounted for and I took the liberty of asking Erica to check things through."

"There is no need to involve Erica," said Lucinda. "You, my dear, are the accountant after all."

Muriel felt herself blush. Fenella had warned her there was jealousy in the camp.

Lucinda looked through some figures and then laid the book to one side. "Well, that all seems to be in order. I would be interested to know your thoughts on holding another day where we invite manufacturers and suppliers to come and demonstrate their wares."

This was something that was normally discussed at committee meetings and Muriel felt she was being put on the spot. She knew that several members thought these events were old hat, a hangover from when Shirley was in charge. Others were of the opinion that they really were a waste of time, as there was little incentive to buy and the only ones who came out on top were the suppliers.

Muriel took a rather large slurp of port and almost choked. "Are you alright, my dear?" said Lucinda, getting up and offering Muriel a tissue.

"Oh, yes thanks," said Muriel gratefully. "I drank a little more than I should have done."

"Let me top you up," said Lucinda, "it isn't often I get the chance for a sit down and a natter."

Muriel smiled. "I think perhaps we should raise the matter of further events with the members. Personally, I find them very interesting, but not everyone holds the same opinion, or so I've been told."

"Really?" said Lucinda, pouring another port for them both. "I wonder that Erica hasn't raised the issue, after all that is what a secretary does, I believe. I am beginning to think that we have the wrong person in the post."

Perhaps it was the port talking, thought Muriel. "Oh no, Lucinda," said Muriel without thinking, "Erica is doing a good job, and after all she is just beginning to find her feet."

Lucinda smiled. "Indeed she is, and are you enjoying your role in GAGGA?"

"Oh yes," said Muriel, "though I have to say I did find it daunting at first, but I think I am doing okay."

Lucinda nodded. "Yes, you are. It is time we threw off the shackles of our old chairman and looked at things from a different point of view. Perhaps as this season progresses we can all come up with some new ideas."

There was a silence between them for a few minutes as each of them enjoyed their drink.

"I was watching a lovely programme on the television the other night," said Muriel, thinking a change of topic might be a good idea as this was, as Lucinda had put it, a natter.

"I don't watch much television," said Lucinda, "but, pray, do continue."

"It was all about India and they mentioned the Taj Mahal which was built as a temple of love from a king to his queen."

Lucinda smiled. "I am sure many a woman would be thrilled to have something built for them in that way."

Muriel nodded. "I think that Dick Boggis did something similar for Freda."

"Really!" exclaimed Lucinda with a quizzical look.

"Oh yes, Dick built a tool shed."

Lucinda laughed. "Muriel Evans, I am surprised at you. I think a sandwich is called for."

\* \* \*

## *Wednesday, 28 June*

Joe Dean had just completed his check of Finnegan's Wake Caravan Park and decided to take a stroll down on to the parade. He had seen the posters advertising the show and the plays that would be on at the Little Playhouse and toyed with the idea of booking some tickets. It might be quite nice to see the matinees. He had heard about the top of the bill for the evening show and thought it might be an idea to give that a try as well. He wandered into Tidy Stores and picked up a packet of biscuits.

"Good morning, Phil," he called, as Phil appeared from her back room.

"Hello Joe, what brings you here on a Wednesday? You picked up your groceries on Monday."

"Fancied a biscuit," he replied, placing the packet of custard creams on the counter. "Besides, it's a lovely morning out there and I fancied a bit of a walk."

Dingle, Phil's dog, who had been asleep in his basket at the back of the shop, woke up and came trotting round the counter and barked at Joe.

"Hello Dingle, me old mate, and how are you today?"

Dingle woofed quietly and sat down and looked up at Joe.

"Come on, Dingle, don't be bothering the customers," said Phil, clicking her tongue, which was Dingle's command to go to his basket.

"Tell you what, Phil, let me take Dingle for a walk along the cliffs, I could do with the exercise. I can pick up the biscuits on the way back."

At the mention of "walk", Dingle returned from his basket with his lead in his mouth and dropped it on the floor.

Phil laughed. "Well, if you're sure Joe."

"It will be my pleasure," said Joe, attaching the lead to Dingle's collar and, with a wave of his hand, Joe and Dingle left the shop.

"And where are you two going?" said the voice of Reverend George.

"Hello," said Joe with a grin. "I thought I would take young Dingle for a walk with it being such a lovely morning, and I admit I am fed up hanging around the park all day."

"Well, it is a beautiful morning," said Reverend George. "Mind if I join you, Joe?"

"Not at all, be glad of the company."

For the first ten minutes the two walked along the clifftop leading towards Hopton-on-Sea in silence, with Dingle trotting alongside enjoying the pleasant sunshine.

"I was thinking of booking to see those plays at the theatre," said Joe, breaking the mood.

"Ah yes, one is a thriller and the other a farce. I read about them in the *Mercury*," said Reverend George. "If what I heard is correct they are going to try out a season of afternoon shows to see if they attract business. I believe Rita Ricer is behind it and of course they are putting on a small variety show in the evenings."

"Sad business about the Golden Sands," said Reverend George, "but there you are, these things cost a lot of money to keep going, as I am sure you know yourself with the park."

Joe nodded. "Oh yes, it is hard graft. Me escaping for a couple of hours this morning is a risk as I could miss a booking, but all work and no play."

They arrived at the pathway leading down beside the Hopton caravan park and into the village. Suggesting they went into the small café for a coffee, Joe ordered a couple of cakes and the two sat down at a window table. The lady behind the counter obliged Dingle with a bowl of water and brought over the cakes and drinks.

"I wonder if you might like to join me one afternoon for one of the plays?" said Joe, stirring his coffee. "Or maybe both, I'm not keen on going to the theatre on my own and I really don't have many friends in the area – those I do have are usually working."

Reverend George smiled. "It sounds a splendid idea, Joe, but I will have to consult my parish diary when I get back to the rectory and see what afternoons I have free. Perhaps we could see them both on different weeks."

Joe nodded. "And if you were of a mind we could see the variety show one evening during the season, break things up a bit."

"Yes, I like the sound of that. I must admit that I do get bogged down with things and when I am supposed to be relaxing, I tend to start something that would be best left until the following day. Yes, Joe, let's do it – can I also suggest that perhaps one evening we go back to the Beach Croft for a meal in their restaurant?"

With Dingle returned safely to Phil, Joe walked along with the Reverend George who said his farewells when they reached the caravan park and carried on back to the rectory. Looking to his left as he was about to cross the road, he saw the local doctor's car parked outside Rose Cottage and made a mental note to call in on Lilly Brockett later that day.

Martha Tidwell was just finishing the dusting in the hallway. "Hello Martha, just seen the doctor's car outside Lilly's cottage – do you know if she is okay?"

Martha put down her duster and put her hand on her hips. "Well, I have heard that she hasn't been seen about much lately, not since she called the wedding off. Not that I am one to gossip, Reverend, as you know, but I don't think that William has been doing her garden like he used to."

"That's strange because he was only here the day before yesterday. I will have to go round and see if everything is alright."

"It may be that she has been writing too much," said Martha. "Seems to spend all her time at that desk in the bay window and rumour has it she has a typewriter now."

"I did know she had been going to classes."

"There were never any classes for cleaning," said Martha. "I had to learn everything for myself and by watching me old mum, of course. Now there are courses for everything. There will be courses for courses before long, you mark my words. Now, I will just go and make you a coffee and then best be off. I am doing old Mr Parkin at twelve."

"Don't worry about coffee, I've not long had one with Joe Dean. I had better see what's in the post tray this morning."

Martha gathered her cleaning materials and returned to the kitchen. *Coffee with Joe Dean, was it?* she thought to herself. *Those two seem to be spending quite a bit of time together lately. I wonder what that is about – and him a Catholic.*

\* \* \*

It was Ida, Lilly's neighbour, who answered the door at Rose Cottage when Reverend George called. Ida stepped aside to let him in. "She has been very poorly, very poorly indeed, your reverence. She is asleep at the moment – the doctor gave her a sedative, and he said he would be coming back this evening."

Ida showed Reverend George into the lounge and asked him to sit down.

"Ida, can you tell me, perhaps you may know, but has William been attending to the garden since they called off their wedding?"

Ida, who was a quiet woman by nature and wasn't one who liked to gossip, nodded her head. "All I know is that they have remained good friends and I think William has been visiting Lilly, though I can't say I know for definite if he has continued to do the gardening. It always looks tidy to me, but then I am not much of a one for things that grow out of the ground, flowers and that. They always look pretty in other people's gardens but I have never been fussed with them myself."

"Perhaps I should call again at another time when Lilly is more up to visitors."

"Wait there a minute," said Ida. "I will just pop upstairs and see if she is awake, she may want a cup of tea. Though she has been having problems keeping things down and no mistake, proper poorly she's been."

Ida returned a few minutes later. "Lilly is awake, your reverence, and would be very pleased to see you – follow me."

Lilly was propped up in her bed by a mountain of pillows, dressed, as far as he could see, in a pink bed jacket. Lilly's face looked drawn and her complexion sallow.

"I will get you both some tea," said Ida, leaving the pair to talk.

Reverend George pulled up a chair from Lilly's dressing table and sat down. "How are you, my dear?"

Lilly spoke softly, the strain of talking made her cough slightly. "I cannot remember being this unwell. I have always been quite strong, but I feel so tired and so weak."

"Ida told me you hadn't been able to keep food down, I expect you have a tummy bug."

"I have never been one to suffer with my tummy," Lilly said, doing her best to smile.

"Perhaps it is all the work you've been doing, writing your books, and then the sorrowful business around the wedding."

Lilly nodded. "Perhaps, but William and I have remained on good terms. He has been here three or four times a week since we called a halt to the nuptials."

"He seems to have taken things very well," said Reverend George.

"He has been making me broths and bringing them over, says they will help build my strength up."

"That is kind of him."

"Brings them over in a flask and I have some when I feel up to it. Quite tasty they are – I am a great lover of mushrooms."

Ida arrived with two cups of tea. "Lilly, I just have to pop back home as I have to put some washing on the line, but I will be back before his reverence leaves."

"Don't worry if you're not. I can see myself out."

They continued to chat about things in general until Lilly's eyes began to close. "I will come and see you again, Lilly," said Reverend George, getting up. He put the chair back where he had found it and took the two teacups down to the kitchen and let himself out by the front door.

Rita and Jenny had called in to the theatre to ensure that everything was in place for the opening on the following Monday. It appeared that some kind of fracas was going on between the actors of the plays, whom Ray was trying to assemble, and the variety acts for the evening shows.

"Darling, this is quite impossible," said Lauren Du Barrie. "My voice will suffer dreadfully if I don't rehearse."

"But, my dear lady," said Ray, trying to be as diplomatic as possible, "we have two plays that need rehearsing on stage and we must be ready for Monday's matinee."

Constance stepped forward. "If I might be permitted to say something, the plans for these rehearsals haven't been properly thought through. There is barely enough space to lay out my make-up backstage with us all sharing facilities."

Alfred appeared behind Jenny and Rita who were standing at the back of the theatre watching the chaos.

"Alfred, I think we need to sort something out here and quick," said Rita. "How would you feel about Lauren using the bar area at the hotel?"

"Sorry, Rita, quite impossible," said Alfred, "we have quite a large party in and the bar area must be available to them at all times."

"Couldn't we ask Lady Samantha if we could use the ballroom in the interim? We open on Monday so it would only be a couple of days," said Jenny adding her own thoughts.

Rita walked about and then turned to the pair. "Look, it is absolutely imperative that those plays are rehearsed on that stage; it's the first time they have done it with the sets properly in place. I am going to suggest that the variety acts rehearse in the evenings, with a full dress rehearsal on Sunday afternoon. They have all been told one costume apiece, but it's different for the actors and actresses who must change their costumes. Besides, all the variety acts know their acts inside out, with the exception of Lauren, of course, who has been changing her mind about her set ever since she was told she had got the contract."

"Shall I sort it, then?" said Alfred.

"Leave it with me, me old lover," said Rita, walking towards the stage. "Could I have your attention, please?"

Constance, who was just about to add something, stopped and looked down at Rita. "Oh hello, I don't think we have been formally introduced, I am Constance Anderson."

Rita smiled. "Hello Constance, I am pleased to meet you."

The other members of the Clifftop Players drifted onto the stage and stood beside Constance while Lauren waved her arms in the air, muttering, "It's the voice you know." Milly appeared at her side with some more hot lemon and honey.

Rita spoke clearly and with some authority. "Apologies, everyone, for this total mix-up of rehearsal space. I am going to suggest this as a solution – the Clifftop Players are to rehearse here for the rest of today and tomorrow; the variety artistes can rehearse in the evenings from eight. All variety artistes have been instructed that one costume per performance is sufficient, with the exception of the dancers."

"But, darling, I have so many gowns to choose from," said Lauren, sipping her drink and feigning a look of worry across her brow.

"Then you must select a frock that you are happy to perform in. Change it every night if you must, but only one frock is allowed backstage. As you are aware, Lauren, these actors have a few costume changes during their roles and it is absolutely paramount that their costumes are kept backstage at all times."

Lauren smiled at Constance. "Well, yes, of course one can understand that actors need their tools."

Constance giggled. "Well, that seems to make a lot of sense," and the company nodded in agreement. "You see, Ray dear, Mrs Ricer here has solved our little problem without the need for amateur dramatics and I am sure we are all most grateful to Lauren and her company for agreeing to the suggestions Rita has made."

Lauren blushed; "her company" – there was something to put on her next entry in a theatre programme.

Ray strutted off to the back of the theatre and through the doors without saying a word.

"Oh dear, I think I may have touched a nerve," said Constance. "Now, fellow actors, shall we get on with *Wardrobe Doors*, without our director, who finds himself somewhat indisposed for the moment."

"Well, that was a storm in a teacup," said Jenny as she walked with Rita out of the theatre.

"These things usually are," said Rita with feeling. "But it is a unique idea, two very different productions running in the same theatre."

Jenny turned and looked at the poster hoardings at the side of the entrance. "But it does look good, doesn't it?"

Rita nodded. "Yes, I agree – let's hope it works. I didn't notice Maud this morning at the box office."

"I think she and Barbara take it in turns," said Jenny, "even with the alterations, two people in that space must be tricky."

They walked along the parade and went to the hotel car park where a designated space had been reserved for Rita to use.

"I am due to see Malcolm this afternoon," said Rita, starting the engine.

"He is a nice man," said Jenny. "We need to do well at the Nest."

"I do hope so," said Rita, "we have a lot riding on these shows. I just hope someone sorts out the Sands."

"So do I," said Jenny. "I miss that theatre. There was something about that place, I always felt a magic when we performed there."

"Ted loved it too," said Rita. "He would be mortified to see what has happened to the old place. Well, it's no good us speculating – we have to deal with the here and now."

* * *

"So, darling Ray – you are expecting me to alight from a wardrobe. Do you really think that the lady I am depicting in this script would be hiding in a wardrobe?"

"Oh, can we please move on from this scene?" said Edith Harris who was beginning to lose patience. "We went through all of this in Earls Court."

"Not wishing to butt in," said Fred Hughes, "but didn't we decide that Marcia, the lovely Constance here, was going to hide at the side of the bed?"

Ray consulted his notes. "Fred, dear boy, you are right – problem averted, Constance."

Constance sighed. "Shall we take it from where I enter?"

Ray waved his hand with a smile. "Play on, dear heart, play on."

"Now I know why they call it farce," said Lauren to Milly; they had been watching from the wings. "The whole thing is a farce. We must get tickets, let's call round to the box office and see if we can get a couple of passes."

# Chapter Eleven *Oh, Sweet Mystery of Life*

*Saturday, 1 July*

"We're nearly there, Mum," said Madge Brinton. "Look, we are just passing Norwich Castle."

Annie Lucas looked out of the car window. "I don't know why we can't go to Blackpool."

"I thought it would make a nice change for you to go somewhere different," said Madge, dropping down into second gear. "Dad has gone on his fishing trip with Uncle Reggie and next door said she would keep an eye on the house."

"She's nosey," said Annie with a sniff. "She likes nothing better than to get a look round my knick-knacks. I told you my china doll with the wonky-looking eyes has gone missing."

"I am sure Poll didn't take it, perhaps you moved it when you were dusting."

Annie sniffed again. "She is always popping in and out to borrow something or other. Your father said we should just knock through and give her the run of the place, it would be easier. As soon as I hear her go "woo hoo" I shudder. I told her she needs to find herself another man – her Charlie has been gone ten years – but Poll likes to play the widow in her black outfits. I am sure that last dress she made was from those black-out curtains she found at the jumble."

"Well, you don't need to go worrying yourself about that now, Mum. I've booked a lovely hotel in Brokencliff-on-Sea.

We can go through to Great Yarmouth, and they have some lovely beaches in Norfolk."

"I hope this hotel doesn't do any fancy food, I don't want anything that's been messed about with. Your father had a Chinese the other night, stunk the place out, him with his sweet-and-sour balls."

Madge smiled to herself; she loved her mother dearly, but she could be a right misery at times. Poppy was meant to be having their parents for a couple of weeks this year, but as usual her sister found some reason why that wasn't possible, and Madge's flat was too small to accommodate since they had sold the house when the children had fled the nest. Basil worked nights and so it wouldn't do to have mum pottering about humming tunes she heard on the wireless.

They arrived at the Beach Croft and Madge checked in at the reception while her mother hovered in the background admiring the paintings on the wall.

"Come on, Mum, we've got adjoining rooms on the first floor and we can take the lift, the nice young man is going to bring our cases up for us."

"Bit posh in here, ain't it?" said Annie, following her daughter. "I could murder a nice cup of tea."

The receptionist pressed the lift button for them. "I will have a complimentary tray sent to your room, madam."

Madge smiled. "That is very kind of you."

"Not at all, madam, it is all part of the service. I'll ask them to send a selection of biscuits."

"Hear that, Mum? The nice lady is going to send us some biscuits and tea."

"Well, I hope they don't send any of those garibaldis – I've never liked them," said Annie, getting into the lift.

Madge smiled an apologetic face at the receptionist and crossed her fingers that this week away was going to run smoothly.

Madge was suitably impressed with their rooms and there was a lovely view from the windows, which she knew would keep her mother happy. Although Madge had only booked bed and breakfast, she decided that a meal in the hotel restaurant would be a good idea. She checked the menu in reception and could find nothing on it that her mother would object to. She intended to take her mother out and about every day in the car and to have most meals out, knowing that this is what her mother would have done in Blackpool. Madge wasn't fond of Blackpool and avoided it at all costs, but her mother and father had been going there for years. But with the promise of a proper fishing trip her father had announced he would be doing his own thing this year, and with Poppy bailing out – the fact was she could cope with her mum and dad together, but not her mum on her own – Madge had stepped in.

## *Monday, 3 July*

Alfred looked in on the auditorium and came back out to the box office. "We are nearly full in there," he beamed happily at Maud and Barbara. "It's better than I expected."

"We're quite busy over the next four weeks," said Barbara, "and the phone hasn't stopped ringing this morning with people enquiring what we have available."

Maud sighed. "You see, Alfred, good box office management is what you have here. Barbara and I have been at this game for years now. We know how to sell a show. When we sell them one play, we offer the other, and if they are less keen on seeing two plays we offer the show in the evening. And on more than one occasion we have managed to book couples and families into all three."

"I knew I could rely on you both," said Alfred gratefully. "We've been advertising the shows and Owlerton Hall in our hotel brochure and bedroom literature, which my friend Maureen thought would be a good idea."

"Well, it's paying off," said Maud. "Let's just hope that what we have got on offer impresses the critics. It wouldn't be good to have a dreadful write-up in the local press."

Rita walked in with Jenny and Elsie in tow. "Good afternoon Alfred, Maud, Barbara. Well, here we are, hoping that *Wardrobe Doors* is going to knock our socks off."

"No, *Death Nap* will do that," said Maud. "I caught the rehearsal the other day and it fair spooked me out. This one should have you rocking in the aisles according to what Barbara said."

"I think it's very funny," said Barbara, "at least what I saw of it the other day, when the wardrobe doors fell off."

"I don't think that was in the script," said Alfred, looking alarmed.

"So, Marcia Duke wasn't supposed to get hit on the head by a flying doorknob then?"

Rita began to laugh. "It had to be Constance Anderson, didn't it? Oh lawks, come on, you two, let's go and take our seats."

"I thought it was quite funny," said Barbara. "Mind you, she did look a bit ruffled. But I thought it was all part of the plot."

"You'd look ruffled if you had been attacked by a flying doorknob," said Maud with a smile to herself. "Oh look, here come the landladies. Good afternoon Muriel and Freda."

The two ladies nodded and showed their complimentary tickets to the usherette.

"What on earth was that Freda wearing?" said Barbara. "Yellow really doesn't suit her, does it?"

"It's best not to ask where that one is concerned," replied Maud, reaching to answer the telephone. "A law unto herself that one when it comes to clothes."

Barbara reached for the can of air freshener. "And what is that dreadful smell, are the drains up?"

Maud covered the mouthpiece. "That will be Freda's perfume, I expect, I heard she gets it off the market."

"What stall, hardware?"

Alfred watched from the back of the auditorium as the lights began to dim and some taped music was played as the curtain rose on *Wardrobe Doors*. Keeping his fingers crossed, he heaved a slight sigh of relief when the first laughs rang out in the theatre after the first five minutes.


"Well, when all is said and done it was very funny," said Elsie. "That Constance Anderson is very good. I can understand why she and her husband, William Forbes, tour so often. I liked that young Julia Burton and Patrick Prowse too."

"Yes, it was very good," agreed Jenny, "though I don't think Constance looked too happy when that doorknob hit her on the head."

"Got a big laugh though," said Elsie, "you see, that shows what a professional she is."

"Come on, you two, let's have some afternoon tea in the Toasted Teacake, I really fancy a scone."

While they were enjoying their tea and chatting in general, Reverend George, who had popped in for a pot of tea and a sandwich to escape his cleaner who was polishing the brasses, spotted Rita and went over and said hello.

"Do join us, Reverend George," said Rita, "we have plenty of room. You've met Elsie and Jenny before."

"Indeed I have," said the Reverend, tipping his hat to acknowledge them. "I won't join you if you don't mind, I have some parish papers to read, but I just thought you would like to know that Lilly Brockett has been very poorly."

"Oh my goodness," said Rita, "thank you for letting us know. Do you know what the cause is?"

"Well, it appears that she has something of a tummy problem, which comes and goes. The doctor has been in to see her and her neighbour, Ida, is keeping an eye on her. I have to say that when I visited her the other day, I was quite concerned."

He excused himself and went to sit at a window table in the corner of the café.

"We ought to pop in and see her," said Jenny, "it isn't like Lilly to be unwell."

"Well, none of us are getting any younger," said Elsie, "and we are more susceptible to things in later life."

"You speak for yourself, me old lover," said Rita. "Maybe we could go round tomorrow. I need to go home and change. We have to be back for the opening performance of the Showtime."

"Oh, I had nearly forgotten about that," said Jenny. "Jill and Doreen won't be best pleased if I don't put in an appearance."

That evening, Lauren Du Barrie was doing some scales as the other acts began to arrive.

"What did you think of *Wardrobe Doors?*" asked Hughie Dixon, who was just pulling on his stage jacket.

"Well, I have to say," said Lauren, enjoying the attention, "that it was very good. Milly couldn't stop laughing – you should see it Hughie, I think you would appreciate the humour."

"I went this afternoon too," said Jonny Adams. "It is very funny, especially when that doorknob flies off and hits that lady on the head."

Lauren was going to say something, but a tap from Milly told her she should leave well alone.

"Well, it will be our turn to impress tonight," said Phil Yovell. "The whole company is booked in to see us tonight and of course we will have the press here too."

Lauren placed her hand on her throat. "Milly, some honey and lemon, dear, please." And the present company turned and smiled at each other knowingly, mouthing, "It's the voice, you know."

\* \* \*

"Mum, I think I will book us in to see these two plays, and one evening we can go to the show, what do you think?"

Annie nodded. "Well, I suppose it will make a change. They have a circus in Great Yarmouth, I like the circus."

"Well, we can go to that, too, one evening," said Madge, trying to get as many things crammed into the week as possible – her mother was a nightmare if she was bored. "We can go over to Great Yarmouth in the car and book the tickets, then have a walk along the promenade."

\* \* \*

## Tuesday, 4 July

As they left the Playhouse, it was apparent that her mother had not really enjoyed Lauren Du Barrie or any of the acts on the bill.

"Not like *The Good Old Days* on the telly," said Annie. "Second-rate, that's what they were, second-rate."

"Well, I enjoyed the show," said Madge. "The next two afternoons we are seeing the thriller and the comedy, so maybe you'll enjoy those better."

Annie sniffed. "Well, I will be the judge of that."

And Madge knew only too well that her mother would find something to moan about. But, as things turned out,

Annie enjoyed both *Death Nap* and *Wardrobe Doors*, though she did comment they weren't a patch on a Brian Rix, who she had seen on the telly.

The circus proved to be a big hit, and Annie even likened it to the one at the Blackpool Tower. Following the visit to the circus, they walked along the promenade and went into the Merrivale Model Village, which Annie also enjoyed.

It was a slightly different scenario when they were walking along Regent Road, checking out the various restaurants for something to eat. The menu boards claimed roast dinners and puddings at very low prices and Annie tutted.

"Their potatoes will be the whitest you have ever seen with no flavour," she said.

"Well, there is a steak house over there – would you like steak and chips?" said Madge, trying to rescue the situation.

"With these teeth," stated Annie, "it would have to be a very tender steak for me to be able to eat one of those."

They walked along in silence and Madge spotted a Wimpy bar. "What about a Wimpy, Mum? You and Dad used to like those."

Annie smiled. "Yes, we used to take you two girls to a Wimpy, as a treat, when you were little. Dad used to enjoy a Knickerbocker Glory afterwards."

With that in mind, the two found a table and ordered a meal, a pot of tea and, for old times' sake, a Knickerbocker Glory to finish off.

They walked back to the seafront and spent an hour in the slot machine arcades, with Annie winning more than she lost. A game of bingo rounded off their outing and Annie came away clutching a teddy bear after winning three games straight off, much to the annoyance of the players around her.

They drove back to Brokencliff and Annie nodded off in the car, leaving Madge to enjoy driving in silence. All in all, it hadn't been a bad week. Looking ahead to their final day in Brokencliff, Madge thought a drive out to Kessingland Wildlife Park would be a good idea and, if time allowed, a visit to Owlerton Hall.

## *Friday, 7 July*

"Miss Anderson," said Jack, as Constance came through the stage door. "I have a letter for you."

Smiling, Constance thanked Jack and took the gilt-edged envelope. She found her husband, William, already applying his five-and-nine in preparation for that afternoon's performance of *Death Nap*.

"Been getting some fan mail?" he said, noticing the envelope Constance laid down on the dressing table. "No doubt from some slip of a lad who finds my darling wife the keeper of his affections."

Constance looked at herself in the mirror. "I am looking more like the Wicked Witch of the West at the moment," she laughed, hanging her jacket up and sitting down. "I didn't sleep at all well and you were snoring heavily – too many sherbets at the bar last night."

William grinned. "A man has to have some pleasures in life. You know, I am not sure if I am playing Inspector Cross all wrong, maybe I should come at him from a different angle."

Constance opened the envelope. "Oh, for goodness sake, darling, don't start changing things, you will give Ray one of his heads, and you know how sensitive he is about his direction."

"All the same, I think my character should be softer, let the audience think he doesn't know what he's doing, gives them something to talk about in the second-act interval – I can hear them now, 'He's a bit of an idiot, that Inspector'."

"Well, run it by Ray first," Constance replied, letting out a whistle. "Well, blow me down. It's a letter from Lady Samantha Hunter at Owlerton Hall."

William raised an eyebrow. "What does she say?"

"She mentions how much she has enjoyed the plays and would like us both to join her and Sir Harold for Sunday lunch."

"Well, I am sure Harold will be delighted to see you after all these years," said William with a wicked grin. "After all, you could have become the first Lady Hunter."

Constance threw her head back and laughed. "Oh my goodness, is that why she has invited us? There was nothing in it, as well you know, husband dear, any more than you and that Felicity person who we worked with on that dreadful tour of South Africa in Coward's *Private Lives*."

"Are we going to accept?"

"Of course we are," said Constance, putting the letter to one side. "I have often wanted to see more of Owlerton Hall. I heard they've had it done up. I wonder how many staff they have."

"No idea," said William, adjusting his wig. "But you can bet none of the female staff will be under fifty, Lady Samantha wouldn't entertain it. You know, I am sure Inspector Cross would have black hair, this ginger wig makes me look like that cartoon character in *The Beezer*."

In the adjacent dressing area, Sue Wilson was having trouble with her zipper.

"Here, let me help you," said Julia Burton. "I seem to have a knack with these malfunctions."

"Thank you, dear," said Sue. "I hope this performance goes to plan. I have to say I am not really getting into characte at all, I find myself confused with the roles I am playing – Martina is very different from Doreen, but whenever I walk out onto that stage I find myself wanting to say the lines of the other character."

"But I heard you were quite an old hand at this," said Julia. "Not that I mean you are old, just that you have done rep before."

"Oh yes, it's true, but these two plays have been written especially for this season, unlike ones I have done before. I enjoy a good Christie or a Francis Durbridge. Coward can be quite fun to play, but not if the great man himself turns up to see a performance."

"Have you met Noël Coward, then?"

"Oh yes, several times. A lovely man, but he can be sharp with his tongue."

Edith Harris popped her head round the partition. "I say, girls, has either of you got a fag? I'm gasping, left mine back at the digs – could have sworn I put them in my bag."

"Have one of my Weights," said Sue, "not my usual, but all I could get at the corner shop."

"Thanks Sue," said Edith, lighting up. "Oh, that feels better. I wonder what the house will be like this afternoon."

"According to that Barbara, it's full this afternoon," said Sue, "so maybe we are in for a good season. Have you anything lined up for after?"

Edith blew a ring of smoke. "Doing Christie's *The Body in the Library* in Liverpool and then touring with it."

"You'll enjoy that," said Sue with a smile. "I was just saying to Julia, I like a good Christie."

"Ten minutes to curtain," said a voice over the tannoy.

"Blast, is it that time already?" said Edith, taking a long draw on her cigarette. "Better pop to the little girls' room or I will be having an accident on the stage."

"Edith seems very nice," said Julia, adjusting her blouse.

"One of the old school," said Sue, "knows this business like the back of her hand. I've worked with her before. Always word-perfect and seems to be able to memorise a part within days of reading it."

Patrick Prowse popped his head round. "If you two ladies are interested, some of us are going for a toasted sandwich and a cake at the Toasted Teacake if you fancy joining us."

"Count me in," said Julia, "my landlady only does bed and breakfast and I forgot to bring a snack with me today."

"Why don't we all meet up later for a proper meal?" suggested Sue. "I think that Fisherman's does food in the evening."

"I have a better idea," said Patrick. "Why don't we all go over to Great Yarmouth and have a bit of fun on the seafront? There are plenty of places to eat over there and Jack mentioned a pub he frequents, Henry's Bar, so we could all end the evening with a few bevvies."

"That sounds spiffing," said Julia. "What about you, Sue?"

"Yes, why jolly not? Patrick, see if you can round up the others at interval. "Be good for us all to go out and have some fun together."

"Great," said Patrick. "Leave it with me. I know Edmund will be tempted."

The voice of Constance called out, "And you can count me and William in, I have been dying to beat him at crazy golf ever since he cheated in Scarborough."

"I say, steady on!" cried William. "You'll give everyone the wrong idea."

"William darling, people have had the wrong idea about you since the day you were born. That wig isn't straight. Try some more spirit gum at the front – we don't want that falling over your eyes during the performance."

## Saturday, 8 July

"Well, Mum," said Madge, "have you enjoyed our stay here?"

Annie looked at her daughter and smiled. "Well, I have to say, Madge, I had my doubts at first, but I have really enjoyed it, thank you very much."

Praise indeed from her mother.

"Perhaps we should book for next year and leave your father at home."

"Dad may want to go to Blackpool."

"Well, he can go with Basil, you and me can come here."

Madge smiled to herself; the thought of her husband, Basil, on holiday with her father didn't bear thinking about.

"I have picked up a little ornament for Poll as a thank you for keeping an eye on the house," said Madge. "It's a seashell lady with 'A Gift from Great Yarmouth' on it."

"Well, I hope it's got wonky eyes," Annie replied. "Poll likes dolls with wonky eyes."

Madge decided it would be best not to answer and turned the car radio on.

As they drove back and were passing the castle in Norwich, Annie piped up, "I would like to go in that castle."

Madge looked at her mother as they drew up at the traffic lights. "Perhaps we can do the castle next year, Mum."

Annie sniffed. "Well, only if you want to, Madge." And with that, Madge had to be satisfied.

## Sunday, 9 July

"Good morning, Penge," said Lady Samantha as he laid the pot of tea and toast on the breakfast table. "Sir Harold should be down in a minute. Tell Mrs Yates he will have poached eggs on toast and I am quite happy with toast and marmalade."

"Very good, your ladyship," said Penge, bowing slightly. "Just by way of information, my lady, the new staff and volunteers are shaping up very nicely. It has been quite handy having extra pairs of hands to call upon."

"I am pleased to hear it, Penge. And have you settled into the cottage?"

Penge nodded with a slight bow. "Oh yes, thank you, I have everything sorted the way I like it and Mr Woods has done a wonderful job on the decoration. It feels just like home."

Lady Samantha smiled and was happy that the cottage was now being put to use instead of standing empty.

"Is everything in order for luncheon?"

"Oh, quite so, my lady. Mrs Yates has prepared a soup course, followed by fish and a roast main. I believe she has made an apple pie for dessert, or there is a fresh fruit salad if the guests prefer."

"That sounds splendid."

"What sounds splendid?" asked Sir Harold as he walked into the room.

"The menu for our guests, Harold dear."

"Oh, I'd forgotten that," said Sir Harold. "I say, Penge, can you ask Mrs Yates for a pair of kippers and some brown bread and butter, just fancy that this morning, what."

Penge coughed and looked at Lady Samantha.

"Harold dear, you are having poached eggs on toast this morning." She smiled. "We are having a fish course at luncheon."

"Gawd damn it, Sammie old thing, can't a man have what he wants for breakfast?"

"Thank you, Penge. That will be all." Penge bowed and left the dining room. "I have told you before about calling me

Sammie in front of the servants; it really is very naughty of you, Harold."

Sir Harold snorted. "I wanted kippers."

"Well, you are having poached eggs. Now, be a dear and pass the marmalade."

* * *

Alfred walked into the dining room of the Beach Croft and was pleased to see that it was busy. The staff were being very attentive and Minnie Cooper's idea of having a waiter greet all the guests as they arrived was in full swing.

Minnie appeared at Alfred's side. "Everything okay, Mr Barton?"

Alfred smiled. "Absolutely, it all seems to be running like clockwork. How are things with you?"

"Very well, thank you for asking. If you have some time this morning I wonder if you might go through a check with me in the linen room?"

"Is there a problem?"

"Not a problem as such, but I think we may need to change the laundry we are using; some of the sheets are not being returned to us properly laundered and pressed."

"Well, perhaps we could do that now," said Alfred, "and then, if you are free, you could join me in the dining room for breakfast."

Minnie Cooper looked at Alfred very seriously. "Mr Barton, I was offered a position here to ensure that your hotel was run efficiently. I do not think that taking breakfast in the dining room with you would give the staff or the guests the right impression. We do not allow staff to partake of meals in the public area or the bar services here, during or indeed after their shifts. I run a tight ship, Mr Barton. Thank you for the kind invitation, which I know you meant well by."

Alfred blushed. "Yes, yes of course, I wasn't thinking."

Minnie turned to leave. "Mr Barton, this way please, the linen room."

* * *

Rita answered the telephone. "Oh, hello Malcolm, this is an unexpected pleasure. What makes you call me on a Sunday morning? Nothing wrong at the Nest, I trust? It all seemed to be going well last night when I popped in."

"Oh no, nothing like that," replied Malcolm. "I was wondering if you might be free for a spot of lunch today? That's if you have nothing else planned."

"Well, Elsie was going to cook a roast and Jenny was joining us."

Elsie rustled her Sunday paper and Rita turned to face her as Elsie mouthed, "Go".

"Malcolm, where had you in mind?"

"I wondered if you might like to join me at home. I do a mean roast dinner and it will be too much for one. I also thought it might give you a chance to have a look round the place, perhaps you can give me some tips on decorating."

Rita laughed. "I rather gather that Inferior Interiors have been given the elbow, then."

"You said Inferior."

"I did," Rita laughed again. "Sounds a better name for them, if you ask me. What time shall I arrive? I'll drive over to you."

"No, you won't. I will arrange a car to pick you up. Be ready for twelve and we can eat about one thirty, if that's okay with you?"

"There is no need to send a car – I am perfectly capable of driving myself."

"No arguments," said Malcolm firmly. "My invitation, my rules."

Rita replaced the receiver and Elsie smiled at her.

"Whatever shall I wear?"

"My dear Rita, I don't think it would matter to Malcolm if you turned up in sack cloth – it's you he wants to see, not your wardrobe."

Rita nodded. "I feel like a schoolgirl on her first date. Whatever would Ted say?"

"He would want to see you happy," said Elsie. "Now, go and get yourself ready. I will call Jenny, and the roast will keep for another day. I fancy a meal out – the Star Hotel will do nicely, and then Jenny and I can have a good old natter and a walk along the seafront afterwards."

Jenny and Elsie enjoyed a leisurely meal at the Star.

"I hope Rita is having a good time," said Jenny, who was feeling slightly worse for wear on the drink front; it was a long time since she had drunk so much, but she did feel relaxed.

"I expect Malcolm is wooing her with the size of his Yorkshire puddings," said Elsie, draining her brandy glass.

Jenny giggled. "That sounded very funny, but wrong."

Elsie grinned and fumbled in her handbag for a tissue. "Sod it, Jenny, we are none of us getting any younger. We have to take happiness where we can find it. I loved old Don a lot, but the months have passed by and, if I am being honest with myself, if the right man presented himself I might just put my toe in the water again, why not, after all we are a long time dead."

This was a complete reversal from a previous conversation the two had had, but Jenny decided not to pursue it any further – it may be the drink talking.

"I say, Elsie, shall we walk down Regent Road? I quite fancy a ride on the snails."

Elsie steadied herself as she stood up. "And after the snails I challenge you to a round of crazy golf, and whoever loses buys the ice-cream."

The two staggered out into the sunshine and walked up Regent Street and made their way towards Regent Road which was heaving with holidaymakers.

A car pulled up in front of the Golden Sands and a lady and gentleman got out and walked towards the pier entrance.

The lady removed her sunglasses and then read the literature she held in her hand for the third time that day.

"It would need a lot doing to it," said the gentleman, as if reading her thoughts. "It has a history. You know only too well the great shows they have had in the theatre, and with some thought and planning the fortunes of the pier as a whole could be turned around."

The lady nodded, her attention caught by the remains of an old poster. "I remember that show," she smiled, "as if it were yesterday."

The gentleman took her arm. "I should think you do, my dear – after all, you were in it."

The lady put her sunglasses back on and the two returned to the car in silence and drove off along the promenade.

\* \* \*

Rita was enjoying the sunshine in Malcolm's garden as he came out of the house with a tray of tea which he placed on the small table that stood between the two deckchairs.

"A nice cup of tea," said Malcolm. "I always like one about this time in the afternoon."

"Ted was the same," replied Rita, admiring the flower beds that had been lovingly tended. "Funny how we all do things in a certain way."

Malcolm sat down. "Would you like to be mother, Rita?"

Rita turned to face Malcolm. "Heavens, no, my mother always told me that if two people touched the same teapot they would have ginger twins."

Malcolm laughed. "Well, I have never heard that one before."

"Oh, she was full them, my old mum. Never trust a man in suede shoes was another one."

Malcolm looked down at his brown suede shoes. "Whoops! I have a feeling your mother wouldn't trust me, then."

"Just old wives' tales, me old lover," said Rita with a grin. "But I am not touching that teapot."

Malcolm poured the tea and handed Rita hers. "It is a nice place you have here Malcolm; admittedly, you do need to redecorate some of the rooms, but it is a lovely house."

"Big enough for two," said Malcolm, sipping his beverage. "I did think of buying a flat, but then I thought a house with a garden that is not overlooked would suit me better."

"You made a wise choice."

"Rita, can I ask you a personal question?"

"You can, me old lover, what is it?"

"Would you ever marry again?"

Rita took a moment to answer. "I suppose that would depend on who was asking."

\* \* \*

Jenny and Elsie walked along the promenade with a cornet each – Jenny had lost at crazy golf and paid up.

"I wonder who those people were, looking at the Sands, as we came along?" said Elsie, enjoying the strawberry soft ice-cream and biting the Flake chocolate.

"Maybe prospective buyers," said Jenny. "I expect they have had one or two of those. It would take a company with a lot of money to take the Sands on. There it stands unused. I do think they could have opened up part of the pier and boarded off the part to the theatre."

"I am sure whoever owns it had their reasons," said Elsie. "I wonder if it will ever be operational again."

Jenny thought for a moment. "It would be nice to have the old place back again, that end of the prom seems a little bit lost without it."

And with that thought in both their heads, they continued on their way to the Pleasure Beach, where Elsie had dared Jenny to go with her on the scenic railway.

\* \* \*

"Well, Harold dear," said Lady Samantha, handing her husband a brandy and soda, "that went off okay. Constance and William were quite charming."

Harold snorted. "He isn't my type. Those theatrical men don't know a day's hard graft. Donning make-up every night and parading round the stage spouting lines."

"Harold, you are being very unkind," said Lady Samantha, sitting down. "You enjoyed the two plays as much as I did. It really is sour grapes on your part."

Harold sipped his brandy and sulked.

"I thought Constance looked delightful in that outfit and she does look much younger in person than one would first expect."

Harold snorted again.

"They both enjoyed the meal which Mrs Yates had beautifully prepared. That joint of beef was melting in the mouth and her apple pie was excellent."

There was a silence only broken by another snort.

"Harold dear, if you continue to snort like that, I shall ask Chippy to build you a sty in the grounds."

And Harold who was about to snort again thought better of it.

\* \* \*

"Well, you certainly charmed Lady Samantha," said William to his wife, who was changing.

"And you didn't do so badly yourself," Constance replied. "I think her ladyship was quite taken with you. She did enjoy your stories about your time in Stratford."

William glowed at the thought. "Yes, she did, didn't she? He was a bit of a stuffed shirt though, no idea what you saw in him."

Constance adjusted her hair and sat down. "Oh, William, you are funny. Can you imagine Sir Harold and me together? Why, it would be like chalk and cheese. Yes, of course he flirted, and maybe I played up to him a little, but after all is said and done I am with the man I love and Lady Samantha has hers, so let's put that baby to bed once and for all, shall we?"

William smiled at his wife and nodded.

## Monday, 10 July

"Have you seen those funny wide trousers the young men are wearing these days?" said Freda, leaning on her garden wall for support, having just returned from shopping.

"They are flares, they're all the rage now," said Muriel, coming out of her front gate.

"I think they look silly," said Freda. "They might as well wear skirts, they are that big. And those boots are so high – I just saw a boy as I came out of Mrs Jary's, he looked like Herman Munster."

"That's fashion for you – stacked boots, flared trousers – we were young once, Freda."

"And his girlfriend was no better – her shoes were so high at the front she could barely walk."

"Platform shoes are all the rage, Freda, just like stilettos once were."

"You wouldn't find me wearing platform shoes," said Freda with feeling.

"I don't think the platforms would support you, Freda, so I shouldn't worry – you would need a couple of platforms from the oil rigs, the weight you have put on recently."

Freda either didn't hear her neighbour or chose not to acknowledge the comment. "What you giving your guests for their meal tonight?"

Muriel looked at her watch. "I've a nice chicken casserole in the oven and I am doing boiled potatoes with some frozen cauliflower and peas."

"Sounds nice," said Freda, retrieving her shopping bag. "Well, I best get in and put the kettle on, my Dick will want his tea. We're having toad-in-the-hole tonight and I've only got four in so it won't be any bother. I wished I'd never started doing evening meals but people nowadays request it."

"See you later, Freda," said Muriel, "just off to pick up the *Evening News*."

Freda opened her front door. "Bye, Muriel."

\* \* \*

"So, I have spoken with Bob," said Rita, "and now he is letting out his house permanently he is more than happy to have Mona go in twice a week to keep an eye on things."

"I hope he has tiles in the kitchen and bathroom," said Jenny with a wry smile. "Mona won't be happy if she can't have her bucket and mop with her."

"Confirmed with Bob, and he also told me there is a lockable cupboard under the stairs where she can keep her things."

"I wonder what his tenants will make of her?" said Elsie. "I mean, 'The Old Rugged Cross' is not everyone's cup of tea."

"Well, I don't suppose they will see much of her," said Rita. "At least it will give her some more hours to make up for the loss of the Sands. I am going to speak to her this afternoon."

"Good luck with that one," said Elsie, "rather you than me."

"Oh, she will probably hum and hah for bit, but when she hears the hourly rate Bob is willing to pay her, it will seal the deal. Besides, he trusts her with keys and that will go a long way with Mona."

"Right, if that's the galvanised bucket sorted," said Jenny, "there are one or two things that need discussing about the shows in Bridlington and Clacton."

Rita opened her desk drawer and took out some papers. "Oh yes, Clacton, this is the one with Mystic Brian on the bill and Bridlington has Roger Davy and the Songbirds – so, Jenny, fire away, I am all ears."

When Rita left the office, Jenny turned to Elsie. "She hasn't mentioned a word about her lunch with Malcolm yesterday."

"Yes, I thought that was strange. She seemed fine when she came in last night. She got in about nine, I think – I had just made myself some Horlicks. That day out had fair taken the wind out of my sails."

"Oh yes, and me too," said Jenny. "I was ready for bed, slept like a top."

"She may mention something later. I don't want to pry, in case things didn't go according to plan."

"But whose plan, hers or his?"

They both nodded at each other and remained silent.

* * *

# *Wednesday, 12 July*

Mona Buckle opened her post and was pleased to find a letter from Bob Scott offering her some extra work.

Monday, 10 July 1972

Dear Mrs Buckle,

I am writing to you in the hope that you will be able to help me out. I have relocated to a London residence and have taken on the responsibility of Rita s Angels agency in Regent Street.

As you may know I have a house in Great Yarmouth and as I shall not be in the area during the foreseeable future I have decided to let the house. This is being managed by a local agent, the tenants that are moving in are known to me. However, as part of the let I have agreed to have the house cleaned at least twice a week, more if requested. The property is three bedroomed with a large lounge, kitchen and facilities on the ground and upstairs floor.

I need a cleaner I can trust with the house keys and I immediately thought of you. I am offering seventy-five pence per hour with extra for travelling expenses. If you are interested I would be grateful if you would speak with Rita Ricer and she will make the necessary arrangements. All cleaning materials are to be paid for from the office in Great Yarmouth and I believe Beverley will oversee this on my behalf.

I appreciate that you are in demand but I hope you will be able to fit my request into your busy schedule. The hours are to be at your discretion but should be somewhere between eight thirty in the morning and five in the

afternoon Monday to Friday and no weekend work will be required.
I very much hope you will be able to help me out and if you have any questions please do not hesitate to ask Beverley who has all the details.

Yours sincerely,
Robert (Bob) Scott

Mona laid the letter down on the table and poured another cup of tea. She smiled happily and decided that a visit to Northgate Street was in order. Mr Scott needed a reliable cleaner and needed an answer. Mona Buckle was going to his rescue, but first she needed to bathe her leg which had been playing up again, apply a new bandage and fetch her best hat and coat out of the wardrobe.

Beverley smiled as Mona presented herself at the reception of Rita's Angels. She was wearing her hat with peacock feathers and a black coat and, to Beverley's mind, looked as if she was about to attend a funeral.

"Good morning, Mrs Buckle," she smiled.

Mona nodded. "I have received a letter from Mr Scott – he needs my help."

"Oh good," said Beverley, "would you like me to take you through what is needed? We can go into Rita's office, she isn't here today."

"I think that would be in order."

Beverley stood up. "Can I offer you a cup of tea?"

Mona looked at the clock on the wall. "It's ten thirty. I never partake of a beverage until the allotted hour of eleven."

Used to Mona's funny ways, Beverley motioned for Mona to join her in the office.

"Mr Scott has been so impressed with your work at the Sands, Mrs Buckle, that when this opportunity presented itself, the first person he thought of was you."

Mona puffed out her chest. "Mr Scott knows who he can trust."

"Let me take you through a list of the duties required," said Beverley, looking at the paper she held. "It would be much the same as you do here, hoovering, dusting, polishing, that kind of thing. You wouldn't be expected to do laundry or ironing, though I believe it was originally requested, but Mr Scott thought that was too much for you to take on."

Mona nodded. "I have never been one to shirk my responsibilities, but washing and ironing has never been part of my daily routine."

"Quite so," said Beverley.

"I have been looking at my busy schedule," said Mona, remembering the words Bob had written in his letter, "and I think I could manage two mornings and an afternoon. I would need to see the property first to be certain what time would be needed."

"I could take you there now if you would like," said Beverley. "I have the keys here."

"That would be most acceptable," said Mona, "and if all is well I could start as early as Friday."

Beverley smiled. "I have the car just across the road, so if you would like to come with me, Mrs Buckle."

Mona heaved herself out of the chair, adjusted her hat and followed Beverley who called out to Julie, "I am just taking Mrs Buckle over to see Bob's house, won't be long."

Beverley arrived back at the office looking shell-shocked.

Julie laughed. "Mona Buckle strikes again," she said. "I think you need a strong coffee."

Beverley flopped into her chair, let out a sigh and called out, "Any brandy on the go?"

Jenny had just reached the top of the stairs, looked at Beverley and laughed. "You've had Mona Buckle here, haven't you?"

Beverley nodded.

"I take it she has taken Bob up on his offer?"

"Oh yes, and the rest," said Beverley, "she wants to have the title of 'house minder' if you please."

"That's our Mona," said Jenny, heading into the office to see Jill and Doreen. "Good luck with that one."

* * *

The season at the Sparrows Nest and the Little Playhouse continued to bring in good houses with "House Full" appearing on many occasions outside both venues. Constance was interviewed live on *Look East* from the Norwich studios and gave away several secrets of what it was like to tour in a company of theatrical players. This in turn boosted ticket sales further and Alfred couldn't have wished for better free advertising.

Christian was interviewed by the local press with a double-page spread appearing in an edition of the *Eastern Daily Press* and the *Great Yarmouth Mercury*. There were a couple of photographs that obviously caught the attention of some of the female fans and single roses and boxes of chocolates arrived at the stage door of the Sparrows Nest, which Christian generously shared with the company. It was a few weeks later when Rita received an unexpected visitor to her Northgate Street offices.

## *Tuesday, 1 August*

"Rita, sorry to interrupt you, but there is a Miss Gaunt to see you."

Rita looked up from her diary. "Miss Gaunt, I wonder what she wants. Best show her in, Beverley, and can you rearrange my eleven o'clock appointment, please? Tell Bernie I will try and see him this afternoon."

Beverley smiled and showed Miss Gaunt into the office.

Rita got up and walked round her desk to greet her unexpected visitor. "Miss Gaunt, I hope there is nothing wrong. Christian is behaving himself, I trust?"

Miss Gaunt tried a smile, but gave up and shook Rita's hand. "Mr Lapelle is a model guest."

"I am relieved to hear it." Rita smiled, motioning for Miss Gaunt to sit down. "Can I offer you some tea? Or a coffee, perhaps?"

Miss Gaunt sat down. "I don't hold with beverages before lunch," she said, resting her black handbag on her lap. "I am meeting an old school friend and I thought that while I was in the area I would take the opportunity to speak with you on a private matter."

Rita sat down feeling slightly puzzled. "I have to say, Miss Gaunt, I am intrigued."

Miss Gaunt took a linen handkerchief from her handbag and dabbed her cheeks. "It's like this, Mrs Ricer, I have a friend who used to be a singer."

Rita nodded. "You say used to be – you mean your friend isn't a singer anymore?"

"Donna and I grew up together, in the orphanage, and she was always singing. The nuns used to encourage her. I was eventually taken in by a kind lady and her husband, but Donna was left with the nuns until she could make her own way in the world."

"And that was through singing."

Miss Gaunt nodded. "Donna Quinn, a stool and a song." Miss Gaunt opened her handbag and took out a leaflet, which was yellowed with age, and handed it to Rita. "I kept this."

Rita looked at the leaflet. "Your friend is a lovely-looking lady."

"Donna was always, what you would say, well in the looks department. I don't hold with the grease women put on their faces, but she did scrub up well and, rumour has it, she had plenty of admirers. Not that I hold with rumours, you understand."

"This leaflet says 'Donna Quinn, a stool and a song. Country and popular music...', and there are some other details I cannot read due to the fading. I have to say that Donna's strapline isn't what one would call catchy – a stool and a song conjures up all kinds of images."

"Donna is short," said Miss Gaunt by way of an explanation. "Always performs sitting on a stool."

"Yes, I see," said Rita, handing the leaflet back to her visitor. "I am not sure how you would like me to help you. Are you asking me to put Donna on my books?"

"It's a bit more complicated than that," said Miss Gaunt, putting the leaflet back in her bag and snapping the clasp shut with a heavy click. "Over the years Donna developed a drink problem. I don't hold with strong liquor. Someone tried to give me a sherry once but I resisted. That said, Donna hasn't touched a drop for a year now and has indicated she would like to go back on the stage. She really has no other form of income."

"And is it Donna you are meeting with today?"

"Oh no," said Miss Gaunt. "Donna lives over in Wangford."

"The other side of Lowestoft, yes, I have passed through it in the car."

"I wondered if you might be able to find Donna some suitable work?" said Miss Gaunt. "I have seen what you have done with the other theatricals you have under your wing."

"Really, I wouldn't have thought that variety theatre would interest you, Miss Gaunt."

Miss Gaunt blushed. "I have seen one of your shows at the Sands and I did go along and see Mr Lapelle a few nights ago at the Nest."

"And did you enjoy the show?"

"Mr Lapelle has a wonderful singing voice, but I didn't care too much for the dancers. I don't hold with men prancing around making fools of themselves."

Rita smiled to herself. "I am sure Christian would be delighted to hear you enjoyed his performance."

Miss Gaunt shook her head. "I wouldn't tell him, I don't hold with getting too close to my guests, it opens the door to liberties being taken."

The thought of anyone taking a liberty with Miss Gaunt tickled Rita and she did her best to control her mirth. "So, I am guessing from all of this that you would like me to audition Donna in the hope I could offer her some work?"

Miss Gaunt nodded. "But Donna mustn't know that I sent you."

"So, how will I introduce myself to her? How will I know anything about her? I can't turn up on her doorstep."

"Donna placed a small advertisement in the local press looking for work. I can give you her telephone number – I am sorry I didn't cut out the advertisement but I think it was in the *Lowestoft Journal*, I'm not sure about the *Mercury*."

"Miss Gaunt, I have to be perfectly honest with you. Only twenty per cent of them might spark an interest in the field I work in. Donna Quinn will have to be someone quite exceptional for me to give her a try. I can make no promises, but I will follow it up."

"That is very kind of you, Mrs Ricer. Now, I mustn't take up any more of your valuable time."

Rita showed Miss Gaunt to the door. "Thank you, Mrs Ricer."

A few days later, Rita sat in the lounge of The Beach Croft Hotel enjoying a cup of tea. She looked at her watch, waved to Alfred as he passed through the area, and looked at some notes she had made.

A small figure came towards her. "Excuse me, are you Mrs Ricer?"

Rita looked up and smiled. "You must be Donna," she said, and stood up to shake hands. "Please make yourself comfortable, can I order you some tea?"

Donna Quinn, who was feeling slightly nervous, shook her head. "No thank you," she said politely, playing with the strap of her small leather handbag. Donna was wearing a black skirt and a white blouse with a bow at the neck. Her legs were tanned with the sun and she wore kitten-heeled black shoes that sported red bows matching the red bow of her blouse. Her make-up was minimal with just a hint of rouge, lipstick and mascara. Her shoulder-length brown hair was neatly arranged with a centre parting and hung in curls that had been blow-dried by an expert hand. Her voice was soft and showed no signs of a life of alcohol abuse.

"I am so pleased you could come along," said Rita, smiling and doing her best to make Donna feel at ease. "As my secretary explained on the telephone, I have a theatrical agency in Great Yarmouth and also one in Regent Street, London. I am always on the lookout for talent and your advertisement caught my eye."

Donna smiled and lowered her eyes and continued to play with her handbag straps.

"I understand that you sing some country music, but also popular songs – I believe you mentioned a couple of Bassey and Cline hits to my secretary."

"I listen to the radio quite a lot," said Donna, looking up. "Music changes so quickly in the pop world, but the great standards live on forever, it seems to me."

"Indeed they do," said Rita. "I wonder if you could tell me a little about the places you have appeared?"

Donna coughed lightly. "Mostly clubs in and around Norfolk and Suffolk. I have also appeared at a few venues in Blackpool, Leeds and Manchester. I did a couple of shows in Dublin a long time ago, but the audience wasn't really interested in my sort of repertoire."

"Have you ever been represented by an agent?"

"I did have one, but he died six years ago."

"And what was his name?"

"Donald Harris, I was on his books for some years."

"I recall the name, I am sure my late husband, Ted, mentioned him to me," said Rita, making some notes. "Donna, when was the last time you sang in public? Your advert seems to imply that—"

"I haven't sung professionally in six years," Donna replied. "I haven't been well."

Rita was beginning to make sense of Beverley's research in addition to what she had been told by Miss Gaunt.

"I wonder if you would care to audition for me this afternoon?"

"You mean today? You mean now?"

Rita nodded. I have use of the theatre along the promenade – the play has just ended and I have arranged for a pianist to come and play for you, if you would be willing."

"But I haven't come with any sheet music," said Donna with a worried frown.

"My friend Phil plays by ear, you can tell him almost any song and he will follow you. I would like to hear your voice and it would be such a shame for you to have driven all the way from Wangford and not sing for me."

"I didn't drive myself," said Donna. "My friend Carl drove me here in his car and will take me back later."

"So, Donna, do we have a deal?"

Donna took a deep breath and managed a smile. "Yes, Mrs Ricer, of course I will sing for you."

"And you must call me Rita," said Rita, getting to her feet. "Let's nip along to the theatre now. I have to say, you have brought some lovely weather with you, Donna."

Donna followed Rita to the theatre stage door and, saying hello to Jack, Rita led Donna onto the stage where Phil was ready at the piano. At the very back of the theatre, and barely visible because of the stage lighting, Jenny, Elsie, Alfred, Maud and Barbara were seated to be judges of the performance that was to follow.

"Take your time, Donna," said Rita. "Please have a chat with Phil and when you are ready sing me a couple of your favourite songs."

"I usually sit on a stool," said Donna, looking around her. Rita walked to the side of the stage and came back with a stool.

Five minutes later, Rita sat in the front row of the theatre as Donna performed 'As I Love You', 'Walking after Midnight' and 'What'll I Do'.

Once her initial nerves had gone, Donna Quinn looked out into the audience and sang with feeling, bringing a tear to Rita's eye. Donna had a wide vocal range which she demonstrated with the songs she had chosen. For someone who hadn't sung for some years, Donna had done herself proud.

Rita applauded and walked back up onto the stage. "That was wonderful, Donna, you have a truly remarkable voice and it is a voice that the public will love to hear again, if not for the first time."

Phil congratulated Donna as she thanked him. "It was really very kind of you to see me."

"Not at all, my dear, now Phil will see you out of the theatre. I need to make some phone calls and I will have Beverley or Julie get back to you in a couple of days' time with your first booking. I think you will do very well and, if you are in agreement, I would be happy for my agency to represent you."

Donna smiled gratefully. "You don't know how much this means to me, thank you so very much."

The ensemble at the back of the theatre were in total agreement with Rita – Donna Quinn had a great voice and they all felt she would be an asset to have on the books.

Rita thanked them and, after they had left the theatre, she walked over to the rear of the auditorium and sat down beside a lone figure dressed in black. "Well, Miss Gaunt, what was your opinion?"

Miss Gaunt looked Rita in the eye. "She did very well, Mrs Ricer, and I really hope that she makes a go of it."

"Tell me, Miss Gaunt, were Donald Harris and Donna romantically connected?"

"I don't hold with gossip, Mrs Ricer," said Miss Gaunt. "The best person to ask would be Donna."

"I am sorry, it was wrong of me to ask the question."

"Least said, soonest mended," said Miss Gaunt, getting up to leave. "Thank you for inviting me along, Mrs Ricer, now I must be getting back to my guest house." And with that, Miss Gaunt walked out of the theatre, leaving Rita with her own thoughts.

"So, where do you think would be a good place to start Donna off in?" asked Jenny.

"I was thinking of the Trawlers Rest as a possibility," said Rita. "It isn't a bad venue. Derinda played it in the past. Providing Donna chooses her material carefully I think she would go down well. I am also considering asking The George Borrow at Oulton Broad – perhaps a Sunday lunchtime spot. I need to make sure that she is okay and it will mean one of us being there to keep an eye on things."

"Well, I am happy to help out," said Jenny.

"And you can count me in," said Elsie. "Who will play for her?"

"The Trawlers has a small band, and for other venues we can always supply a pianist – there are quite a few on our books and they are always on the lookout for extra bookings," said Rita. "I am more concerned about the other problem rearing its head. I don't think Donna has been around drink for a long time."

"I have an idea," said Elsie. "Why don't we appoint someone to be Donna's PA? That way she wouldn't think that management were breathing down her neck and watching her every move. Better still if the PA played the piano as well."

"That's a brilliant idea," said Jenny.

"I agree," said Rita, "and I have someone in mind that would be ideal – Dulcie Gregg, she was a stand in for Maurice Beeney. Dulcie is in her fifties and lives in Lowestoft and I feel sure she would be happy to take on the work. She lost her husband a few years ago and has been taking pupils for piano lessons."

"I know Dulcie well," said Jenny. "I used to get her to play for the girls when our regular accompanist was indisposed. I would be happy to have a chat with her, give her the low-down and, if she is willing, make the necessary introductions to Donna."

"Thanks, Jenny, that would be a great help. I will chat with the venues I mentioned and then run it by Donna. I think we need to approach this sensitively."

"Well, perhaps Alfred would be willing to give her a whirl here in the hotel lounge. I am meeting with him later, so I will mention it," said Elsie. "For some reason he has begun to look on me as something of a mother figure. He likes to run things by me."

"Oh lookout," said Jenny, "he will have you on the payroll before long."

It didn't take long for the wheels to be put in motion. Dulcie agreed to do a trial run with Donna and the two of them met at Dulcie's home where they went through some numbers Donna was keen to include in her act. Rita had arranged a few bookings and the rest would be left to Donna to prove she was ready to return to the world of show business.

# Chapter Twelve    *Murder, She Wrote*

*Monday, 7 August*

"Hello Rita, it's very kind of you to come and visit," said Lilly, smiling as her neighbour Ida adjusted the pillows on the bed so that she could sit upright.

"I will make some tea," said Ida. "I made some gingerbread this morning so I will cut a couple of slices."

Rita sat down beside the bed and took Lilly's frail hand. "This is not like you to be unwell. This has been going on for some weeks and I am sorry I haven't been able to visit sooner. Has the doctor prescribed anything? We are all very concerned about you."

"He wants me to go into hospital for some tests," said Lilly, "but after working in one for so many years I really don't fancy being a patient. Besides, I am best here in my own home. A couple of days ago I was feeling quite a lot better, but when I attempted to get out of bed I fell over – lucky for me that Ida was here. She has been a dear, looking after things."

"I hear that William still pops in and sees you."

"Oh yes, he does, once and sometimes twice a week, if he isn't busy, and he always brings me a lovely flask of soup. He makes it himself, mushroom, it's one of my favourites."

"Wouldn't you be better off trying to eat something a little more substantial?" said Rita, retrieving a couple of magazines from her bag that she thought Lilly would like.

"I don't have much of an appetite if truth be known. Ida does her best to make me eat roast chicken or beef and vegetables, but after a bowl of soup I find it too much and often I get sick, so it all seems a waste of time."

Rita picked up the flask on Lilly's bedside table. "Is this the soup in here?"

"Oh no, that's empty. Ida washed it this morning. When William drops off a flask of soup he then takes the second flask back. This one is blue and the other flask is red."

"So, you ate soup yesterday?"

"Yes, I did, and I believe Ida had some with a roll."

"And have you been sick today?"

"No, thank goodness."

Just then Ida arrived with some tea and a couple of slices of gingerbread.

"Oh, I see you've been reading a Dorothy L Sayers," said Rita, picking up the book from the cabinet.

"Just using it as part of research," said Lilly. "I finished reading it ages ago."

Rita passed a pleasant hour with Lilly and said she would visit again. On her way out she spoke to Ida.

"Ida, can I ask you, please, do you eat William's prepared soup often?"

"Well, I had some yesterday with a roll. But as a rule, Lilly has a bowl at lunchtime and another which I warm up in the evening."

"Have you ever been sick after eating the soup?"

Ida looked quizzically at Rita. "I was quite sick a few weeks ago, but I put that down to being under the weather."

"Can you remember what colour flask you ate the soup from when you were sick?"

"That's a funny question to ask. I can't say as I do remember. You see, William has two flasks which he alternates, yesterday's flask is upstairs washed and waiting for him to collect."

"Ida, I don't wish to alarm you, but can I ask you to keep a note of every time Lilly is sick following soup and what colour the flask is that it came from. I have a theory – I might be wrong."

Ida gulped and put her hand to her mouth.

"Did you know William's first wife?"

"Not really," said Ida, "but William often mentions her. I know he was disappointed when Lilly called off the wedding. But he kept on doing the garden and he likes to visit her. I remember Lilly saying that William's first wife was fond of mushroom soup and when Lilly said it was her favourite too, that's when he started arriving with the flasks."

"Thank you, Ida, you have been most helpful. I must ask you to keep our conversation to yourself."

Ida nodded. "Cross my heart, I am very good at keeping secrets."

Rita squeezed Ida's arm. "Thank you for being such a good neighbour and I will be in touch, I need to do some more digging first."

Ida felt a tingle of excitement as she waved Rita goodbye – why, it was just like being in the pictures.

## Friday, 11 August

Ida put the cup of tea on Lilly's bedside cabinet. Lilly was sitting up in bed flicking through a *Woman's Weekly*. "You know what, Ida, I am feeling better this morning, that egg and soldiers set me up a treat."

Ida smiled. "Well, that's nice to know. Perhaps you could come and sit downstairs today – the sun is fair shining through the lounge window."

"Yes, I think I shall have a warm bath and get out of these bed things."

Ida went to Lilly's wardrobe and took out a dress and a cardigan and laid them on the ottoman at the end of the bed. "I'll go and run the bath for you, put some Radox in the water. I will put out some fresh towels, you finish that tea."

"Thank you, Ida, you really have been a good friend and neighbour to me."

Ida smiled and went to the bathroom.

An hour later, Lilly was sitting in the bay window looking out onto the front garden and waved to Reverend George as he went by. He raised his hand in reply, and was pleased to see that Lilly was up and about and made a mental note to call in later that day.

"Have you got everything you need?" asked Ida. "I must just slip down to the shop and get something in for tea."

"I am fine, thank you, Ida," said Lilly. "I might try and do a little writing; I have been neglecting my readers and I really should put the finishing touches to my latest novel."

Ida put on her hat. "I am sure your readers would forgive you if they knew you had been unwell. I will only be about an hour. Are you sure I can't get you anything?"

Lilly shook her head.

Ida set off down the road to the clifftop and passed by the Toasted Teacake and went into Tidy Stores.

"Hello Ida," said Phil, smiling. "How is Lilly today?"

"Well, I am pleased to say she is much brighter and is sitting in the lounge."

"Oh, that is good news, please give her my best. Now, what can I get you, Ida?"

"That was Ida I just saw going by," said Maud who had been standing near the front entrance to the theatre. "I wonder how our Lilly is getting on. I really should pop in and visit her again."

Barbara looked up from what she was doing. "Perhaps it would be a nice idea to send her some tickets for one of the plays, get her out of the house for an afternoon – it would take her mind off things."

Maud turned around. "What a brilliant idea, Barbara, if we arranged some comps for her and Ida. I will see if I can catch Ida and suggest it to her, I won't be long."

Ida thought the idea was a good one and Maud said that the pair could come along any afternoon. Ida went on her way and called in to see the ladies in the Toasted Teacake and came away with a couple of fresh cream cakes for Lilly. On her way, Ida called in to her own house and picked up the mail from the mat. She put her purchases in the fridge and then, taking the few provisions she had got for Lilly, headed back out to Rose Cottage. Ida went straight through to the kitchen and put away the purchases and then, removing her hat, she hung up her summer jacket in the hallway and went into the lounge. The chair in the bay window was empty.

"Lilly dear, I am back," she called out, thinking Lilly may have gone upstairs, and then on the hall table she spotted a note.

*Ida dear, I have taken the car out for a spin, thought it could do with a little run, especially as William did an oil change for me.*

Ida became concerned. William had been calling a little more than usual and she had seen him working on the car a couple of days before. Remembering her conversation with Rita, Ida reached for the telephone and dialled.

On his way back from his parish rounds, Reverend George headed towards Rose Cottage and was alarmed to see a police car with its light flashing parked outside. He hurried to the front door and a white-faced Ida opened it.

"Oh, Reverend George, the police are here – there has been a terrible accident."

Reverend George listened to the police constable. Lilly had veered off the road in Corton and her car had hit a tree. Lilly was lying unconscious in a hospital bed.

\* \* \*

Rita listened and put the phone down in shock.

"What's the matter?" asked Jenny. "You look as if you have seen a ghost."

Rita grabbed her handbag and car keys from the desk. "It's Lilly – she's been in a car accident."

Jenny and Elsie looked at each other and both got up. "We're coming with you."

Elsie decided to drive so that Rita, who was quite shaken, could sit quietly.

"Oh, I wish I had spoken to the police when I first became suspicious," she suddenly blurted out.

"Suspicious of what?" asked Jenny, taking Rita's arm.

"The soup, the mushroom soup, Lilly was sick when she ate the soup William had prepared. Ida was sick one day when she had some."

"Sorry, I'm not following, what has soup got to do with a car accident?"

"Well, nothing really, but I think it is connected. I believe William was trying to poison Lilly."

"You cannot be serious – why would he do a thing like that? Do you have proof?"

"Ida has kept samples and they are in Lilly's fridge."

They arrived at the hospital and were greeted by Reverend George. "Lilly is still unconscious and a policewoman is sitting with her. She is in a private room on the second floor."

Just then, a police constable came down the corridor. Rita went straight up to him and asked to speak to him in private, and he motioned for her to follow him to the sister's office which the police had permission to use.

Reverend George put his hands together and began to say a silent prayer.

## Saturday, 12 August

"Have you heard about Lilly?" asked Freda, folding her arms, ready for a gossip in the middle of the market place. Muriel had just caught up with her friend who had something of a crowd gathering round her. "Well, they say she might have been poisoned."

Muriel edged her way to get beside Freda. "Freda Boggis, where did you hear that from?"

Freda shrugged. "I heard it from Alice Broom, she is a great friend of Ida's, and I know it's true. They say she could die."

"I heard there had been a car accident," said the voice of Vi Dawson, never one to be left out of a bit of gossip. "They said she was wrapped round a tree."

"You mean someone poisoned her in a car and then wrapped her around a tree? I have never heard the like," chimed in a lady standing next to Vi. "It's happening all over the place, you never know what is going to happen next."

"I think you should come away, Freda," said Muriel, taking her friend's arm. "I am sure we will hear the truth of the matter sooner or later."

Freda huffed. She was none too pleased as she was just getting into her stride. "They say there is no smog without fire."

"Smoke, Freda, it's smoke without fire," said Muriel. "Now, let's get you settled with a bag of chips."

"After the shock I've had, I could do with a brandy."

"Well, you're having chips," said Muriel, gently pushing her way with Freda through the crowd, who had moved on with their take of the events.

"I heard she'd been drinking heavily since that gardener friend of hers called off the wedding."

"I never liked the look of him. His eyes are too close together."

"Wasn't he one of the blokes that got done for illegal fishing at Winterton?"

"I wouldn't put it past him, he seems the sort."

"I am sure it was him that made a pass at our Daisy."

"Who on earth would be daft enough to make a pass at your Daisy? She's no oil painting."

"Well, hark who's talking, you are not exactly the Mona bloody Lisa yourself, Katie Orton. At least our Daisy has kept herself to herself."

"Come over here and say that – I'll have your bleeding eyes out."

"Oh yeah, I'd like to see you try."

Muriel looked back at the scene that was erupting. "You see what you started, Freda Boggis?"

Freda huffed. "I'd only come out for a new mop head."

Muriel sighed. "Two large bags of chips, love, please. Put plenty of vinegar on hers; it might be good for shock."

## Wednesday, 16 August

"The police are holding William Robertson for questioning," said Jenny, coming through the office door. "It's all over the *EDP*."

"Oh, my goodness," said Rita, taking the paper. "It all sounds so awful. I suppose there is no further news on how Lilly is doing?"

Jenny shook her head and sat down. "According to Reverend George, she is still unconscious."

"Poor Lilly," said Rita, "it really doesn't sound good, does it?"

Beverley came through with the post. "Thought you should know that Lilly's neighbour Ida has been arrested on suspicion of poisoning."

"Will someone tell me that I am imagining this?" said Rita. "It is very much like being in some kind of drama that you haven't got the script for."

"I have to say I did wonder about Ida," said Jenny, "especially when I heard that she had been sweet on William herself. Barbara told me."

Rita whistled. "I need some air – coming Jenny? Bev, if anyone calls, please tell them I have been called away on urgent business and that I am unlikely to be back today."

Beverley nodded. "Take your jacket, Rita, there is a bit of a breeze out there today."


Over at Owlerton Hall, Lady Samantha was shocked to hear the news. "Harold dear, it can't be true, can it? That something like this is happening in Brokencliff – it used to be such a quiet area."

"I blame The Beatles and all that rock and roll."

"Harold dear, that was the sixties and The Beatles never did anyone any harm."

Harold snorted. "Bunch of long-haired layabouts."

"Harold, really, there is no need for that. They are quite a nice bunch of young men, I quite like their music and they certainly were not a bunch of layabouts."

"Give me The Seekers any day," said Sir Harold, lighting a cigar.

"Only because you have a thing about Judith Durham."

"Fine-looking filly," said Sir Harold, heading towards the French doors.

The news was being talked about at the Beach Croft. Several of the staff gathered excitedly in the staff room, until Minnie Cooper entered with her clip board. "Now then, we will have none of this idle gossip. I would suggest you all look at your watches – I am sure that at least three of you are not where you are supposed to be. Brian Richards, I would like to see you in my office after the lunch shift, please."

Brian nodded, blushing, knowing he was in trouble for something or other.

"Chop chop, get about your business," said Minnie Cooper with her authoritative tone. "Candy, your apron isn't clean – linen room now, change it at once, please."

Alfred walked into the staff room. "Everything okay, Minnie?"

"Absolutely," said Minnie with a smile. "Everything is running to plan. Now, if you'll excuse me, Mr Barton, I have rooms to check before our coach party of guests arrive. We are fully booked this evening."

Alfred smiled, knowing full well his business was now in the safest of hands.

"I don't think William would have tried to poison Lilly," said Barbara as Maud handed her a mug of coffee. "He just doesn't seem the type."

"They said that about Crippen," said Maud. "They say the quiet ones are the worst. Now Ida is in the mix. No doubt the truth will out."

"I just hope Lilly pulls through," said Barbara.

"So do I," said Maud, remembering Lilly when she worked with her at the Sands. "So do I."

"Of course, darling, one could make a good play out of the material here," said Ray Darnell, tossing the paper to one side.

"To think we could all be murdered in our beds," said Lauren, who had met Ray for a light lunch in the Toasted Teacake. "I shall be locking my door securely from now on."

"Oh, I wouldn't worry too much," said Ray, picking a currant out of his buttered bun. "This kind of thing is usually a one-off. It's hardly *Bluebeard*."

"No, thank goodness!" exclaimed Lauren. "Imagine having that going on under your nose, all those doors for a start."

"My thoughts exactly – the makings of a good farce that *Bluebeard*," said Ray with feeling. "Brian Rix would have a field day with that one."

"Talking of farces, are you planning on touring *Wardrobe Doors?*"

"Oh yes, I'll say, there is certainly a lot of interest in it out there."

"Will you re-cast?"

"Not if the present company are happy to go with it. Some, of course, will already have other commitments. Why, Lauren? Are you thinking of going legit, as they say in the business?"

"I have always fancied doing a play, as it happens. Not such a strain on the vocals, don't you know – with me, it's the voice."

"And we all love it, darling. Several of my 'boyfriends' have been along to see your show and they simply adore you. They say you put them in mind of a Callas, with just the hint of Bassey."

"You are too kind, Ray dear. Of course, I have played around the world to many adoring audiences. I feel their warmth when I walk on stage and they feel my love, my energy – it is quite a burden to carry, you know."

"And you carry it so well, Lauren my dear," said Ray with a big smile. "Allow me to pay for lunch. Perhaps we could take a stroll along the prom and have an ice-cream, or would that be too cold on your larynx?"

"No, darling, that would be divine. I just love holding a cornet."

"Then, dear lady, let me pay the bill so we can have you licking a sumptuous ice while the sun continues to shine."

## Friday, 18 August

Many locals read the news in disbelief. Lilly had not been poisoned, not in so many words. It appeared that Lilly had been trying out a plot for a new book and wondered what effect toadstools would have. She knew they could be the cause of tummy upsets, but could they actually kill anyone? Poor Ida and William had been caught up in one of Lilly's plots – of which neither was aware – and then Lilly having a mishap with her car when she should not have been driving had made matters worse.

Lilly, who was now sitting up in bed in hospital, was facing the consequences of her foolish actions and the local press were having a field day with it. Lilly didn't know where to begin with her apologies; William was magnanimous, but Ida was not so forgiving and vowed never to have anything more to do with Lilly, and was making arrangements to sell up and move nearer to her sister in Cleethorpes. Rita was terribly angry about the whole affair and realised the number of hours she had wasted on nothing more than a run-through of a plotline. Lilly knew she had many bridges to rebuild and decided to cast aside her new story and give her writing a rest, at least until she was thinking straight.

The gossip around Great Yarmouth and Brokencliff was afire, with the goings-on getting more and more exaggerated at every telling.

Freda was full of it. "I have never heard the like, fancy doing something like that. She could have killed herself, which, looking at things now, may not have been a bad thing."

"Freda, don't say things like that," said Muriel, "it is not Christian."

"Well, you can't tell me it was Christian of her to try out something so stupid. That poor neighbour of hers, not to mention William Robertson, they could have been done for murder if Lilly had pegged it in hospital. I shall never be able to look that woman in the eye again."

Muriel nodded. "Well, I agree with you on that score, but then we have always known Lilly was a bit odd in lots of ways."

Freda tutted. "If Lilly's mother were alive she would be turning in her grave."

Muriel looked at her friend in wonder; Freda did come out with them!

From her desk, now back at home, Lilly wrote letters to the many friends she had upset over her own foolishness. In her own mind, Lilly thought that by experiencing what it would be like to be poisoned by fungi, she would write with more in-depth knowledge in her new book. Despite her pleading, she knew she had lost a good friend in Ida, and only hoped that she hadn't turned everyone against her. The flowers from William put aside any ill feeling he should have felt towards her and a visit from Reverend George gave her some hope.

The police, who had been considering a case against her had decided against it after speaking with Lilly's doctor and Reverend George.

Due to adverse publicity, her publisher had decided to cancel her advance on her next book. Putting a stamp on the last letter, Lilly sat back, feeling uncertain where she would go from here.

# Chapter Thirteen *A Time for Every Season*

*Monday, 4 September*

"Thanks Bob, that really is good news. I know Christian has found a summer season in Lowestoft quite a trial. This really will give him a lift," said Rita, smiling down the telephone and motioning for Jenny to sit down.

"I had to pull a few strings," said Bob, "but, thanks to some contacts that I found in Don's old files, I managed to speak to the right people."

"I don't want the boy to spend his career working summer shows," said Rita. "He deserves better, and if the engagement goes well at the Palladium it could open more doors. There is no doubt about it, he has a charm that engages the audiences, especially the ladies, and his voice is pure velvet."

"I will get this off to you in the next couple of days, Rita. Norman has everything in hand here and I plan to go off and see what is happening in Blackpool."

"Thanks Bob," said Rita. "And I am so pleased that you have really settled down well in the job; it must have been a bit of a wrench leaving the Sands, but look at you now, a few weeks down the line and you have nailed it."

"Well, maybe it was time for a change; I had been at the Sands for a very long time. I didn't really know how I would fit in working on the other side of the business, so to speak, but Norman here has been an absolute pal."

Norman beamed a grateful smile at Bob.

"Thank Norman for me," said Rita, "and tell him Jenny may be up there in a few days' time – she is visiting a couple of friends and may pop in to the office."

"If she needs somewhere to stay, I have a spare room," said Bob.

"Oh, I think our Jenny will book in at the Kensington Gardens, she likes to splash out a bit from time to time. Anyway, must press on, nice to talk to you and I will break the news to Christian."

Jenny smiled at Rita. "So, Bob has played a blinder then?"

"Indeed he has," replied Rita. "Two weeks at the Palladium as a special guest star. The Grade Organisation is delighted."

"Christian will be so chuffed when you tell him," said Jenny. "I have watched that boy perform night after night and he really does put everything he has got into his performance. Will you give up representing him, do you think?"

"Not if I can help it, me old lover. Contracting him out is one thing, but we need to retain calibre acts on our books if we are to survive. Now, with Bob getting a real feel for things and Norman flying with it as only Norman can, Rita's Angels will reach heights that even I didn't think possible."

They both paused for thought and Beverley put her head round the door.

"Sorry to interrupt, but I've had Mona on the telephone. Someone has stolen her galvanised bucket."

Jenny and Rita looked at each other and then at Beverley and burst out laughing.

Rita knocked on Christian's dressing-room door that evening.

"Hello Rita," he said, "just doing some warm-up exercises."

"So I heard as I came along the corridor." Rita sat down and took Christian's hand. "Christian, I have some wonderful news for you. We have secured you a two-week booking at the London Palladium. You will be the special guest, and the spot will be twenty minutes."

Christian grabbed hold of Rita and lifted her from the chair and swung her round. "Oh Rita, this is such music to my ears – tonight I will sing like never before. My heart will soar, thank you, thank you, and thank you."

Rita, who was feeling quite dizzy, steadied herself on the dressing table. "You're pleased then," she managed to say when she had got her breath back.

"You have made me the happiest man on earth. If I didn't have a sweetheart, I would go down on one knee and propose to you."

"I say, steady on, me old lover – I am old enough to be your mother, flattered though I am."

Christian kissed her cheek. "But tonight, you are my princess. I shall dedicate all of my songs to you – I want the world to know this great thing you have done for me."

"Perhaps you could dedicate just one song to me."

"Tell me and it is yours."

"My late husband liked 'Hymne à l'amour' – it was a song he used to sing to me when he'd had a few too many sherbets."

"I like sherbets too," cried Christian, unable to contain himself. "I shall buy some from the sweet shop tomorrow and we will share them."

Rita looked at the excited young man before her and smiled; Ted would have loved to have seen this.

* * *

## *Wednesday, 6 September*

"My dear Audrey, what a fool you have been," said Rueben Roberts, making himself at home and taking off his shoes.

Audrey, who was dressed in a flowing kaftan and a long auburn wig with a headband, played with the many strings of coloured beads that hung around her neck. She was overly made-up and smelt of musk oil.

"I didn't think I should try and return to the agency business. Besides, Rita Ricer took most of my remaining acts and is probably raking it in with Derinda Daniels."

"But interior design, dear, you really didn't think that one through. I mean, here in your own home everything looks fine, but taking on projects way beyond even your talents was foolhardy," he said, looking around him at the coloured silks and abstract paintings on the wall.

"But I thought I could do it. I employed some men who assured me they knew what they were doing and could get me some supplies cheap. Reinventing myself as Sandie Cross was invigorating – I felt like a new woman."

"Well yes, dear, I can see that. But employing cheap labour and having a crew around you who barely spoke English wasn't such a good idea. Admittedly, it worked for a while, but then you got careless. You were back to using that old ploy of employing all and sundry at the office. And using the name of Margaret and co again was a stupid idea on your part. Did you really think that no one would rumble you? It took that Rita Ricer all of two minutes to suss you out and you had your back to her at the time."

"But I had some great successes in Ipswich and Felixstowe with those two hotels, they loved my work."

"Yes dear, they did, I read about them in the paper. One was run by a couple of drug addicts who wouldn't have minded what you did to the rooms. The other was a retirement home for very elderly residents and the owner was a friend of yours from way back."

"I thought you had come round to cheer me up," said Audrey, lighting a joint and handing it over to her friend. "When we were on that cruise together, we had so much fun. I forgot that I would have to come back to reality and work again."

"My dear Audrey, we all have to return to reality at some point," Rueben replied.

"Well, I had to tell Mummy the trouble I had got into and she wasn't best pleased, as you can imagine, but she has been a darling and settled all my debts. She even prevented that Barton bloke from taking me to the cleaners. Honestly, the man was out to ruin me."

"But now you are going to have to pay Mummy back and get yourself a job," said Rueben, taking a long drag on the joint.

"But, darling, what on earth am I going to do?" said Audrey.

Rueben Roberts looked at his friend. "There is only one thing you are any good at, and that is being a theatrical agent. You will have to start up the Audrey Audley Agency again and try and get some of your old acts back on the books."

"What, and go into competition with Rita?"

"It's either that, darling, or you could go into business with her."

Audrey looked at Rueben and sighed. "Oh, bloody hell, how can I go cap in hand to her? I'd rather die first."

"What flowers would you like at your funeral, dear, shall I get on to the florist now?"

"You bitch," said Audrey and began to laugh, not sure whether she was really laughing or if it was the effect of the weed.

"There is always one other possibility," said Rueben.

"If you say marry, I shall scream."

"No, dear, let's face it, no man in his right mind would take you on."

"You really do know how to give a girl confidence."

"I am thinking circus!" said Rueben with an edge of excitement. "You could do for animals what you did for humans. You had one or two speciality acts on your books, as I recall."

"Edna and her educated poodles – hardly set the world alight," said Audrey, taking a long drag and inhaling the smoke.

"What about Eric, the bloke who did sword swallowing?"

"He had a dreadful accident during a twice-nightly in Eastbourne," Audrey replied, recalling the day she had received the telephone call. "He hasn't been able to look at a set of cutlery since. His family even upped sticks and moved out of Sheffield."

"Go through some of your old contacts, Audrey, there must be someone you can call upon. Besides, you enjoy travelling and the one thing about circus is, they happen all over the world. Perhaps you should go along and see the show at the Sparrows Nest, there is an act appearing there that may be in need of an agent. Some woman who swings by her hair, it would be worth a go."

"I will look into it," said Audrey, resting her head on the chair back, feeling quite relaxed. "I could murder some toast."

"Let's have another small snifter and then you can call a cab and we will dine out, my treat."

"As long as you don't go on about the circus, I need more time to think that one through."

"Now she wants to think things through already," said Rueben, pouring two generous glasses of vodka. "Ay-Yay-Yay."

The season was drawing to a close and the last of the tickets for the plays at Brokencliff had been snapped up. Lauren Du Barrie had been making herself busy doing personal appearances in the afternoons at hospital garden parties and summer fetes. Barely a week had gone by when Lauren had not been mentioned in the local press. The final week of her show was completely sold out.

The Sparrows Nest had been displaying "house full" and Rita and company sat back knowing they had met their challenge head-on and delivered the goods.

The Beach Croft had seen an upturn in business, and the restaurant, which was popular with the residents, was now becoming a must for locals, so much so that the opening hours had been extended.

Alfred wished now that he had spent less time with the theatre and more time at the hotel, then maybe Jean would have stayed, but what was done was done.

As the closing nights came round, the respective companies had "farewell parties" at Owlerton Hall, which too had seen a turnaround in its fortunes. For the first time in many years, Lady Samantha saw a healthy profit in her books and, with bookings for more parties over the winter months, Penge and his new staff would find they would be very busy indeed.

Although Audrey Audley pleaded with Miss Pauline and Simon, they refused her offers of agency representation. After their summer season on a stage they had both decided that they would never again appear in a theatre venue, much preferring the lure of the sawdust ring.

Christian Lapelle would enjoy many more engagements at the London Palladium and beyond and, reluctantly, Rita's Angels would release their golden boy when offers from others became too much for Christian to resist, but Rita was happy in the knowledge that she and her Angels had helped this promising young artist on his way.

## *Sunday, 10 September*

Deciding to be the first to make a move, Rita visited Lilly and was not choosy with her words. She told Lilly how let down she and many others had felt by her foolish actions.

Lilly nodded in agreement. "No one has replied to my letters of apology and I am now at a loss what to do."

"People will be forgiving in time," said Rita, looking at her old friend, who was not looking her best. "Perhaps you could place an article in the *Mercury*, explain your actions clearly and then let sleeping dogs lie – it's the only suggestion I can make."

Lilly thought for a moment. "Yes, that does sound like a good idea and I am willing to give it a try."

"How is the writing going?" asked Rita, trying to steer the conversation along.

"My mind has been completely blank. I have a story that is nowhere near finished and my publisher has dropped me like a ton of hot bricks."

"I had no idea it had got that bad," said Rita.

"As many will say, 'God doesn't pay his debts in money'. I am finished, Rita."

Rita took Lilly's bony hand. "Something will turn up, you'll see. Another publisher will come along."

"Thank you for your optimism, Rita, but having approached several of the other publishing houses, no one will touch me now. I only have myself to blame."

\* \* \*

"Excuse me, your ladyship, you have a visitor," said Penge.

Lady Samantha looked up from her magazine. "A visitor – I wasn't expecting anyone. Who is it, Penge?"

Before Penge had a chance to answer, a tall lady in a long red velvet coat and hat bounded into the drawing room.

"Samantha darling, I was in the area and thought I really must drop by and say hello."

Lady Samantha got up from her chair. "Cousin Cora, what a surprise. Have you brought Sir Frederick with you?"

"Darling, you know what old Freddie is like, cannot seem to drag him away from the estate. I say, Penge – that is your name, isn't it – do you think you could be a darling and bring in some china tea and a biscuit? I am simply gasping here."

Penge looked at Lady Samantha. "Penge, ask Mrs Yates if she has any cake, and maybe a few sandwiches – it is nearly afternoon tea."

Penge bowed, glanced back at Lady Cora and left the room.

Lady Cora flung her coat down on a nearby chair and sat down opposite Lady Samantha. "Darling, I hardly recognised the place. I hear you have been having some things done to the old place."

"It is amazing how news travels," said Lady Samantha, "even to the far-flung corners of Scotland."

"I think Lady Bagritt visited and did one of those tour thingies. She was full of it when she came back to Stirling. She went on about it for hours – it was a problem to get the old bag to shut up."

"Cora dear, language, please!"

Lady Cora laughed, throwing her head back and breaking into a noise that always reminded Lady Samantha of a donkey braying. "Samantha, you can be so stuffy at times – besides, she is an old bag. I swear it was her that ran off with my silver salvers."

"So, tell me, what brings you to Brokencliff?" asked Lady Samantha, quite used to Lady Cora's ways.

"Darling, I simply had to get away for a few days, we had to have two of the ponies put down and Freddie was quite distraught. I tried to get him to come along, thought the change of air would do him good, but it was the gerbils, he won't leave them on their own and our dear friends the Aleixandres wouldn't look after them – not since that incident with the piano."

"The piano?"

"Yes, darling, you see, Barney and Willow are very musical – they get quite carried away when Freddie plays 'I Love a Lassie'. Well, you see, while they were with the Aleixandres last time, the little darlings got out of their cage one night and were running up and down the grand, if you please, and Sabella was none too pleased, especially as they had guests staying that night."

Lady Samantha sat back in her chair – a conversation with her cousin could be quite exhausting. "So, where are you staying?"

"I've booked into the Beach Croft. I was going to ask you, Samantha, but I know how Sir Harold is about house guests, though I suppose you get quite a lot of those now you have opened up fully to the public."

"But only during the daytime," said Lady Samantha, "though we do have some evening functions on occasions."

"That must be heavenly," said Lady Cora, removing her hat and flinging it across the room to join her coat.

"It pays the bills," said Lady Samantha, "and more besides. It is nice to have the Hall back to its former glory."

Penge entered the room pushing a tea trolley. "Afternoon tea is served, your ladyship."

"Thank you, Penge. Please thank Mrs Yates. That will be all."

Penge bowed and left the room.

"I say, Samantha, he is simply divine, I could do with someone like him at Locke Hill. Instead of that I have two ladies who take it in turns to come in, and my regular gardener, of course, who if he doesn't buck his ideas up will be getting his marching orders. I had to let the Barnabys go, she was getting dreadfully doddery and he was so deaf I spent most of my time shouting."

"Let's have some tea, please help yourself to sandwiches."

"I say, these are scrummy," said Lady Cora, taking a china plate.

"How are you finding the Beach Croft?"

"When I arrived last night, I have to say my breath was quite taken away – what they have done with the old place is amazing. It used to be so old-fashioned and a bit musty."

"Yes, Alfred Barton has done wonders with the place since his wife left him."

"Yes, I heard about that."

Lady Samantha nodded. "Lady Bagritt, no doubt."

"Full of it," replied Lady Cora through a mouthful of egg and cress. "She made it sound like something out of *The Forsyte Saga*."

A cough heralded the arrival of Sir Harold. "Well, upon my soul, it's young Cora."

"Harry Parry darling, how are you?" said Lady Cora, jumping to her feet and flinging her arms around Sir Harold's neck. "Have you been out on one of your shoots, you naughty boy?"

"Oh, do put him down, Cora, you don't know where he's been."

"By the smell of him I could hazard a guess. Let me get you some tea, Harry Parry. Oh good, there is an extra cup and saucer. Darling, do have an egg and cress, I implore you – they really are most delightful."

Enjoying the attention, Sir Harold sat down and beamed a smile.

"Now, darlings, I simply must insist that you both dine with me tomorrow evening at the Beach Croft and we can have a really fun evening together."

"That sounds quite splendid, what say you, Sammie old thing?"

Lady Samantha managed a smile. "Splendid, Harold dear, simply splendid."

The following evening, Stephen Price, the General Manager of The Beach Croft Hotel, greeted Lady Cora Sedgewick as she entered the dining room with Lady Samantha and Sir Harold. "Good evening, Lady Cora."

"Good evening, Stephen, you will know my cousin, of course."

"Lady Samantha, how lovely to see you and Sir Harold again. If you would like to follow me."

Sir Harold snorted. "I hope you have reserved us a decent table."

"Harold dear, don't be an old grump," said Lady Samantha, smiling at Stephen. "I am sure Stephen has everything in hand."

"I hope you are going to behave yourself, Harry Parry," said Lady Cora playfully, taking Sir Harold's arm.

"I thought you would enjoy a window table," said Stephen.

"I am sure that will be splendid," said Lady Cora. "Are you going to sit beside me, Harry Parry?"

"Cora dear, some decorum please. Harold, you can sit beside me and Cora can sit opposite me, we have a lot to catch up on."

Reluctantly, Sir Harold did as he was told and Stephen walked away from the table with a smile on his lips. "Philip, will you make sure that our guests are well looked after, please?"

Philip nodded. "Of course, Mr Price," and he made his way to the table with a wine list and some menus.

The trio enjoyed their meal and, as Sir Harold knocked back the wine, Lady Cora talked nineteen to the dozen. "You see, Freddie does get terribly funny about those sorts of things. I have told him we need to open our doors to the public more often, but he dislikes the idea of strangers trampling through his home and garden."

"But it isn't as dreadful as one might suppose," said Lady Samantha. "I find it quite invigorating to talk to some of the visitors. I do get to speak to some very interesting people."

"And what about you, Harry Parry, do you talk to the visitors?"

Sir Harold, who was now quite flush with drink, waved his hand to speak and immediately had Philip at his side. "Oh, while you are here, young man, a large brandy and soda, please." He turned his attention to Lady Cora. "I try to stay in the background as much as possible — Sammie is much better at all that social chit-chat and she does it very well."

Lady Samantha smiled, praise indeed from her husband. "It is just a case of being able to talk to people at their own level; only the other day I was speaking to a French painter who was so up in the world of the arts it made my head spin, and no sooner had he moved along than I found myself in conversation with a pig farmer who was telling me all about his crops."

"Fascinating," said Lady Cora. "I must come and visit next summer and spend some time with the expert."

"And you should bring Freddie along too," said Lady Samantha. "It has been a long time since we have seen him, and he and Harold get along very well, don't you dear?"

Sir Harold snorted and said nothing.

"How long are you staying, Cora dear?"

"Only a couple more days, I want to go and visit some friends over at Lound."

"Did you drive down?"

"Oh no, darling, I came on the train as far as Norwich and hired a cab from there. I would have driven but the Jag has seen better days and I couldn't get a driver in time."

"I am very lucky with Penge – he drives, he waits at table, and he really is a gem. We had the cottage at the rear of the garden made over for him and he now has a little place to call his own."

"How splendid," said Lady Cora. "Does Mrs Yates live in?"

"Good heavens, no," said Lady Samantha. "We did consider it at one time but she can be a tricky character to deal with and, provided she has clear instructions, is best left to her own devices."

Philip came to the table. "I am sorry to interrupt you, your ladyship, but your man, Penge, has arrived to take you home."

"Oh, darlings, send him away," said Lady Cora, "the night is still young."

"Thank you, Philip, please tell Penge that we will be out shortly."

"I say, Sammie old thing, we could stay a bit longer."

Lady Samantha tapped her husband on the hand. "Now, come along, Harold, you have an early start tomorrow – you are meeting Clive and co for one of your rambles."

"Sorry, Cora old thing, I had quite forgotten about that. It has been a very pleasant evening, thanks for the meal. Will we see you before you go back home?"

"As much as I would like to, my diary is full to bursting."

Kisses and goodbyes were exchanged and Lady Cora made her way to the lift for a much-needed lie down – her cousin could be quite a chatterbox.

* * *

*October 1972*

"Claude Brown, we spoke on the telephone."

Joe Dean shook his hand and invited him in to his office.

"Now, let's get straight down to business, Mr Dean," said Claude, taking some paperwork out of his briefcase and laying it down on the desk. "We have done another survey of the land here and looked at your proposal very carefully. As I think we told you the last time my office was in touch, the application was given the go-ahead by the council and I am here to tie up the loose ends."

Joe heaved a sigh of relief.

"I am sorry it has taken me so long to get back to you, but after your application was passed a number of other factors came into play, as you will be aware of."

"Yes, there was some opposition from certain people in the community."

"You needn't look so worried, Mr Dean, everyone has been contacted and their concerns have been addressed. Having short-let, residential properties in the shape of chalets on this site will not have any effect on property values in the area. The concerns about there not being adequate facilities have been addressed, and I believe the community in general now accept that a professionally run park, as you have proposed, will benefit the area in the long run."

"It has been a very trying few months," said Joe, "and I cannot tell you how relieved I am to be having this conversation."

"You will need to replace the existing perimeter fencing with a brick wall and ensure that there is adequate parking at the side of the properties, thus keeping all vehicles away from the main roads and thoroughfare."

Joe went to his filing cabinet and laid the revised plans before Claude Brown who nodded his approval. "I believe we have received a copy of these at the offices."

Joe nodded.

"You must keep all residents of Brokencliff up to speed on the work that is to take place. Ensure you employ recommended builders and plumbers to carry out the work in a time frame that suits you. Once the work is complete the council will carry out an inspection and give it the go-ahead."

"I am hoping to start work as early as next month if I can get the agreed terms."

"That's good," said Claude, snapping fast his briefcase. "That means you will have things moving before Christmas and, weather permitting, you could see completion by as early as next March?"

"That's the plan," said Joe. "I would like to be ready for the season of seventy-three."

"Strictly off the record, your greatest supporters of this project have been Lady Samantha Hunter, Alfred Barton and the good Reverend George. Not supposed to disclose that, but I thought you would like to know."

Joe nodded his appreciation. "And I can only guess at those that objected."

As Claude Brown stood up to shake his hand, he nodded his head towards the Fisherman's. "I wish you well, Mr Dean, I am sure the improvements here will only bring prosperity to Brokencliff."

"So, you have finally got the all-systems-go-ahead," said Reverend George. "I really am delighted for you, Joe. You deserve to succeed and I am sure the good Lord will show you the way."

Joe smiled. "Yes, I am sure he will. Thank you for all your support, Charles, it really has meant a lot to me."

"Not at all, I feel it is part of my calling to support those in my parish, and not only because I regard you as a friend."

"I know there were some around here that were opposed to my plans," said Joe, "and put it this way, I may be doing my drinking elsewhere from now on."

Reverend George coughed. "Yes, I did hear that a certain lady was against your plans and told everyone on more than a few occasions."

"And we all know why that was," replied Joe. "I wouldn't entertain her advances and it was her way of getting back at me."

"Well, if it makes you feel better I can tell you that the tenancy for the Fisherman's is up for grabs – I understand that Tom is keen to up sticks and go elsewhere. It seems that his lady wife's wandering eye wasn't just centred on you. There have been several others in the area that she has been flirting with."

"I am not surprised," said Joe. "I knew from the off the kind of person she was." There was a pause as he looked straight at the Reverend. "Besides, my interest has always been somewhere else."

Reverend George laid his hand on top of Joe's. "Yes, I know Joe, I know."


Enid sat down with Maud one evening and announced her intention to give up the gift shop. Enid hadn't been feeling in the best of health for some time, though her doctor could find nothing wrong with her, apart from an iron deficiency and the things that came along with age. Maud had been secretly worrying about her sister and knew that, even with her and others' help in the gift shop, it had become a millstone round her sister's neck.

"I don't want to carry on – I haven't ordered any Christmas stock, and the stock that is in there can either be given away or sold for a charitable cause. I should make a good price on the property and with the flat above it someone is bound to snatch it up."

And so, before the final week of October, Enid's gift shop was on the market. She decided to give the remaining stock to The Salvation Army for their Christmas fair in the hope they would make a decent return on it.

It certainly was the season of change, as the *Great Yarmouth Mercury* announced The House of Doris was also closing its door for the final time. Doris had found herself a bungalow with a reasonably sized garden and planned to put her feet up.

Several of Doris's regulars were most upset – where would they go now for their wash and set, perm, or finger wave?

Freda summed it all up in one sentence. "Well, I am not paying those fancy prices at Mr Adrian's. I shall have to do my own from now on, my Dick is quite handy with a pair of scissors when he puts his mind to it."

Muriel took a deep breath and planned to find another hairdresser for Freda, even if she had to take her to Lowestoft to do it. Another fashion malfunction she simply could not entertain.

## Chapter Fourteen    *Blowing in the Wind*

*Wednesday, 1 November*

W ith a furrowed brow, Reverend George read the letter again. He left the coffee that had been made for him and headed for the door.

Martha switched off the hoover and tutted. "Now, where's he off to in such a hurry? No doubt that blessed coffee will be cold by the time he gets back." Martha took a couple of biscuits from the barrel and sat down to enjoy her own cup of coffee and picked up the daily paper to read what her stars had in store for her.

Joe opened the door and was surprised to see Reverend George standing there, a piece of paper in his hand and a worried look on his face.

"Whatever is the matter, Charles? Come on in and I'll put the kettle on."

Charles handed the letter to Joe. "Read this and then you will understand."

Joe switched the kettle on and read the letter letting out a long low whistle.

Charles looked at Joe. "What am I going to do, Joe? My life is here. I don't want to move to another parish."

"Can you refuse?"

"I can appeal, but the Church has the right to move me where they think I am best needed. I want to stay here. All my friends are here, those I regard as friends. I want to stay here. I want to be near you."

Joe took a long look at Charles. "But, Charles, you and I can never be, you said as much yourself."

"But we could be," said Charles, "but it would mean a leap into the unknown. I could give up the Church and then you and I could be together. I know that is what you want and in my heart of hearts I want the same thing."

There was a silence between them and only the meow of a cat outside was heard.

Charles stood up and opened his arms to Joe. "Please can I cuddle you?"

Joe moved forward and held Charles in his arms feeling all the things he had often felt inside. He held Charles tightly and wondered where this would eventually lead them both.

\* \* \*

"So, you can imagine I wasn't that thrilled," said Freda, crossing her arms and refusing the last custard cream that Muriel was offering her. "Bold as brass, there she was on the doorstep, my sister Lena who I haven't clapped eyes on in years and only the odd card at Christmas, if she remembered. Said she has walked out on her husband, Alan, said he was a good-for-nothing lazy lout and she'd had enough of his wandering ways. I never liked him on sight – he had roving eyes and even more roving hands, and if you covered the roundabouts you lost on the swings. So, I said to her, well, you are not stopping here, my girl, so you will just have to find yourself somewhere else to go. I don't think her leaving Alan was pre-medicated and I think she was at a bit of a loss. Can you imagine her and my Dick under the same roof? It would never work and I told her as much."

Freda said all of this without taking a breath. "And another thing I told her, what happened to Mother's pearl necklace and earrings? You are not telling me that her Alan didn't have his eye on them. Not to wear, you understand, but to sell — he's like a mud pie when it comes to taking things. Fingers, that was how he was known, had his fingers in everything."

Muriel put down her cup and saucer. "So, where has your sister gone?"

Freda huffed. "I have no idea. I gave her a few bob and she set off to catch a bus."

"But, Freda, you must be worried about her; I mean, what will happen to her, and what will you do if Alan gets in touch?"

Freda raised her shoulders and let them drop. "I washed my hands of Lena years ago. She ruined my wedding — got herself drunk and made a right spectacle of herself."

"But surely that sort of thing goes on all the time at wedding receptions."

"Receptions, yes, but not in the middle of the ceremony — we were just about to sing a hymn and she strikes up with 'Don't Dilly Dally on the Way'."

"She was probably in high spirits."

"By the smell of her breath, several spirits. No, Muriel, Lena has made her bed and she will just have to buy a new mattress." And with that, Freda chomped down the last custard cream.

\* \* \*

## Saturday, 18 November

"This really is very nice," said Rita. "I had forgotten the Star served such good food."

"A brandy and a coffee, perhaps?" asked Malcolm. "we could move through to the lounge, neither of us is driving."

Rita smiled. "That would be lovely. I'll just go and powder my nose."

Malcolm attracted the attention of their waiter. "Coffees and brandies in the lounge, please, and can you charge this to my room?"

"Very good, sir, room twenty-seven."

Rita found Malcolm in the far corner. "You never did tell me why you are staying overnight?"

Malcolm sipped his brandy and smiled. "I just fancied a night away from home and the theatre only has one-nighters until the panto; we won't be having one of your excellent Christmas shows this year."

"Sometimes it is hard to repeat a success," said Rita, "and besides, I couldn't find the right artists, maybe we will try again next year."

"I wonder if I shall still be at the Nest next year. I think they are happy with my management of the place, but I do feel I could do better."

"Would you like to run a bigger theatre?"

"Oh yes, I would love it. The West End would be my dream."

"And many others, me old lover," said Rita, draining her coffee cup and sitting back to enjoy her brandy. "If only someone would do something with the Sands, I think you'd make a good manager there."

"But surely Bob Scott would want to return."

"I don't think so, he has rather got the hang of the agency and it does give him the freedom to travel around the country."

"I saw some photographs of Ted's bar the other day. That was tragic."

"But magic while it lasted. I don't think I would want it to be replicated. I believe that things happen for a reason."

"Is that what you think about us?"

Rita smiled. "You mean us, like the going-out us?"

Malcolm nodded. "Rita, can I be serious for a moment?"

"Of course you can, me old lover. I know you have been bursting to say something all evening – out with it."

"Rita, will you marry me?"

Rita held eye contact with Malcolm while she finished her brandy and then held out her glass. "Another brandy would be nice."

Malcolm clicked his fingers. "Waiter, two large brandies here, please."

The waiter nodded. "Certainly, sir."

## *Monday, 20 November*

"I've had an offer on the shop," said Enid, looking up from the breakfast table and handing Maud the letter.

"Gosh, that was quick," said Maud, reading the letter, "and they are offering above the asking price. It doesn't say who the offer is from. I hope it's not a chain store, Great Yarmouth doesn't need those, and Norwich is becoming full of them."

"I will accept the offer," said Enid.

"If that's your decision, then you have my backing," said Maud with a sunny smile rarely seen at the breakfast table.

Enid poured another cup of tea for her sister. "Are you sure that you are happy for us both to continue sharing this house?"

Maud looked at Enid. "Well, we haven't made such a bad job of it so far, have we?" She paused; she knew that the prognosis Enid had had from the hospital had not been a good one. "I think we should look upon it as a new start, and I suggest we go away for a week or two and have Selwyn Woods and his men come in and give us a facelift, so to speak. You can choose the colours for your part of the house. I already have some in mind for my own. And while we are about it, I think we could have a new fitted kitchen."

Enid blinked back a tear and smiled. "Thank you, Maud, that sounds like a good plan."

"I shall make a few calls today, how do you fancy Blackpool? We can go and visit Dave and Dan while we are up there. I am sure they will be able to recommend a suitable place to stay."

"Oh Maud, that sounds wonderful," said Enid, feeling a weight being lifted off her mind. "I think I shall treat myself to a couple of new outfits."

"Steady on, Enid," said Maud with a laugh. "You'll be changing your hairstyle next."

And as Enid touched her hair, she looked back at her sister. "Blonde, should I go blonde?"

"Oh dear, what have I started?" replied Maud. "Blackpool, look out."

\* \* \*

In her cottage, speaking on the telephone to Rueben, Audrey could barely contain her excitement. "I put in an offer on that gift shop in Great Yarmouth and, darling, it's been accepted. It has a small flat above and will be ideal for me when I don't want to drive all the way back here."

"You really are going to relaunch the Audrey Audley Agency in direct competition with Rita's Angels?"

"Of course, darling, why not? I was successful once, I can be again."

Rueben smiled to himself; he had to admit his friend had more front than Blackpool. "Aren't you the teeniest bit worried what Rita will do?"

"What can she do, darling? Besides, a bit of healthy competition never did anyone any harm."

"Audrey dear, I do hope you know what you are doing."

Audrey beamed at the end of the receiver. "Rueben dearest, get your arse down here, I feel like partying."

Rueben laughed. "I will be with you in about three hours."

* * *

The Fisherman's Arms had been closed following the departure of landlord, Tom Williams, and his wife, Deanne. The brewery had decided to put the venue up for sale with the hope of attracting a new owner-cum-landlord. Locals were fearful that it may take some time for a suitable buyer to step forward.

Joe Dean had been doing a lot of thinking. Looking through the plans for his newly imagined Finnegan's Wake, something else was playing on his mind – Reverend George's sudden announcement. The two had spoken several times since and it seemed that the Reverend had made up his mind to leave his calling. While this was something Joe felt he should be celebrating– after all, he had carried a torch for Charles for such a long time that this recent turn of events should be one that filled him with new hope for the future –there was Charles's future to think of too. What would he do, how would he make a living? Joe could not visualise Charles living at Finnegan's Wake. Trying to put that thought to the back of his mind, Joe made a list of people to call to get his building works underway and hoped that Charles would come up with his own solution.

Alfred Barton was surprised to see his now ex-wife, Jean, standing before him in the hotel bar.

"Hello Alfred," she said with a smile. "I can see there have been a lot of changes here since I left."

Alfred walked out from behind the bar and took Jean's hand. "Why didn't you let me know you were coming?" He smiled warmly. "It really is lovely to see you. How are the family and Australia?"

"The family are fine. Australia is very different to England, but I like it and I am beginning to make a life for myself."

"You are looking well."

"That must be the sunny weather," said Jean with a happiness in her voice that Alfred hadn't heard for many a year. "I just thought I would pop over and see how you were, to say there are no bad feelings – and I have to say, Alfred, what you have done to this place is simply wonderful."

"I'm only sorry I didn't do it for you," said Alfred with feeling. "Let me show you the rooms. Where are you staying, by the way?"

"I'm at The Claremont in Lowestoft," said Jean, following Alfred's lead. "I am only here for a couple of days and then I am off to London to catch up with a few old friends of mine and take in a couple of shows. I'm going to stop off in Hong Kong on the way home. I thought I might as well do things properly."

Jean was most impressed with the hotel and loved the décor in the bedrooms. Alfred introduced Jean to several of the staff.

"I am pleased to see that you got shot of Janine."

"Oh, I had a little help with that problem," said Alfred. "Janine really would not have fitted in here now."

After the tour, Alfred poured Jean a sweet sherry and showed her the lunchtime menu. "Please stay and have lunch with me, Jean, there is so much I want to hear about."

Jean smiled in reply and nodded. "Thank you, Alfred, I would be very happy to have lunch with you."

Alfred summoned a waiter. They gave their drinks order and Jean looked at the menu with amazement. "You really have turned this place round. This menu is a delight, on a par with leading London hotels."

"I am pleased you approve," said Alfred.

General Manager Stephen Price walked over to the table. "Is everything okay, sir?"

Alfred smiled. "Thank you Stephen, yes it is. Allow me to introduce my ex-wife, Jean."

Stephen bowed. "I am delighted to make your acquaintance."

Jean beamed a smile at Stephen as he turned to leave. "My goodness, I cannot believe I am in the same hotel."

After enjoying a three-course lunch, they retired to the bar for another chat before Jean made her departure.

Over brandy and coffee, Jean mentioned the name of June Ashby and Alfred acknowledged, "She was the star at the Sands in 1969, wasn't she?"

"The very same," replied Jean. "Well, she is a high-flying film and television star in Australia now, and is often in the papers and on the news."

"I remember quite a lot about that season," said Alfred, "caused quite a stir at the time."

"I've heard she is over here at the moment," said Jean, finishing her brandy. "There's a rumour that she is looking for a venture to sink some of her wealth into."

"Well, she won't find much round here," said Alfred. "Unless she fancies taking on the Fisherman's."

Jean nodded. "Or the Golden Sands, perhaps?"

Alfred frowned. "Oh my goodness, now that would be a turn up for the books."

"Indeed it would," said Jean. "I noticed the Fisherman's was up for sale as I passed by."

"Yes, that came as something of a surprise. But the brewery, it seems, wants to let it go and of course it would be an ideal venue for someone starting up in the business."

"So, you have no designs on taking it on yourself, then, Alfred?"

Alfred laughed. "Look, it took me a while to come round to getting this hotel sorted out, and with the theatre as well. Besides, I don't think I would want to have a public house tied round my neck."

"But, surely, with your new-found flair, if anyone could make a go of it, you could. And that is not something I would have said a few years ago."

"I have a lot to thank Maureen Roberts for and, of course, the wonderful Minnie Cooper."

Jean nodded. "Yes, from what I've heard and know about them they are a force to be reckoned with."

As Alfred waved her goodbye, the sense of loss he had originally felt had evaporated. He knew now that Jean's decision to leave him had been for the best, for both of them.

* * *

Lady Samantha smiled at Lucinda. "Well, my dear, that all seems to be in order. I hope your landladies will enjoy their Christmas party here as much as they did last year. Have you laid on any special entertainment?"

Muriel closed her handbag. "Well, we have secured the talents of a local, Donna Quinn – Rita Ricer said we should give her a try – and I have convinced one of the caretakers at the Shrublands to come along as Father Christmas, as this year every landlady will receive a small gift, courtesy of some of the local traders we have been using."

"That sounds most acceptable," said Lady Samantha. "Next year we are having all of the gardens open to the public and, if Selwyn Woods works his magic, there will be a large wooden construction to hold teas and things in any rainy weather. It will also be available for private parties, of course, at a very reasonable rate. Perhaps a summer soirée for those among us who enjoy that kind of thing – your landladies might enjoy a change?"

"That certainly would be worth considering; I shall mention it to the committee," said Lucinda with a gratifying smile. "Now, I have taken up enough of your time."

"I will have Penge show both of you out, Lucinda, a pleasure as always, my dear."

## *Friday, 24 November*

Rita, Jenny and Elsie stood at the front of the Golden Sands pier. The *For Sale* notice was still there and the barricade to keep people from entering the pier still in place.

"It just looks so wrong," said Jenny, shaking her head. "I know it costs a lot of money to keep a pier going, but it has stood idle a whole year and still no progress has been made."

Elsie joined hands with Jenny and Rita. "There are so many memories there. I remember, all those years ago, when Don first became involved with some of the shows in Great Yarmouth, not the big ones, but the one-offs. He loved the Golden Sands and when you, Rita, came on the scene and told him off for being disrespectful to Ted he was well and truly flummoxed. He often mentioned it."

"He was a one-off was Don," said Rita, squeezing Elsie's hand. "A bit like old Ted."

"I remember when my routines were savaged," said Jenny with a laugh. "Looking back now, they were old-fashioned and I didn't have my eye on the ball. One word from Don – and there were many over the years – had me quivering."

"But look at you now," said Rita. "Letting go of the reins was the making of you. Jill and Doreen have regenerated your dancing school and it's now the talk of Norfolk and beyond."

"I wonder if anyone will come forward and buy the pier?" said Elsie.

"Who knows, me old lover," replied Rita, "if I had the money I would buy it myself. I would put in a covered centre walkway so that people didn't get wet when it rained. Put heating in the theatre to keep it open the whole year round. Move the box office to the front of the actual theatre and where the old box office is now, at the front of the pier, I would revamp and put Ted's Variety Bar in its place with stairs to a bar under the pier."

"I knew all along you'd have something in mind," said Jenny, laughing. "If there is a solution to be found, call Rita, she knows just what to do."

"That's why everyone likes working with you," added Elsie, "you are a gem."

"Oh, please stop the sentiment, me old lovers," said Rita, turning her back from the pier, "any more of this and you will have me in tears. Now then, you two, I suggest a spot of lunch in Palmers and then it's back to the office; if I am not mistaken, there is a pantomime for Brokencliff, a cabaret to put together for the Beach Croft and a few more bookings around the country to sort out with Bob and Norman, a few bills that need looking at and then, if there is any time spare, I might just might be able to fit in an appointment with Mr Adrian."

"Well, we best get to it then," said Elsie, adjusting her shoulder bag and taking the lead. The three ladies walked back to the car where Beverley was waiting.

"Palmers, please, Bev," said Rita, "and we would like you to join us for lunch. I have an idea I would like to run by you all."

Beverley started the motor and smiled happily – there was always an idea!

A figure dressed in a black mac had been nearby and had heard most of the conversation. Smiling, she walked back to her car.

"Drive me to the solicitors – the sooner those papers are signed, the sooner I get the men in to do the much-needed work on the pier. The Golden Sands needs a makeover and I intend to see that it gets one."

\* \* \*

"I am sorry to interrupt, ladies," said Reverend George.

"Perhaps you would care to join us?" Rita suggested. "There is plenty here."

Reverend George sat down. "I won't stop too long, but there is something I think you need to know – it's about Lilly Brockett."

Rita put down the teapot and the others sat looking at the Reverend.

"I am sorry to tell you that Lilly was found unconscious in her home yesterday; they believe she may have had a stroke."

Rita looked at Jenny, then at Elsie, and then Beverley. "Please tell me she is okay."

"She is in the General and I am sorry to say that the news isn't sounding good. The doctors feel she may not last more than a couple of days. Lilly had me down as one of her next of kin. I don't know if you are aware, but Lilly did a lot for the church; she was a great believer and, to her credit, had great faith. I will go in later this evening to see if there has been any change."

Tears begin to trickle down Jenny's face as Elsie gripped her hand; Beverley sat in stunned silence and Rita could barely find the words.

"I will go and sit with her; she shouldn't be on her own. Does anyone else know – William, for instance?"

"I have informed William, who I believe is going to contact Ida. They have been speaking with each other on a regular basis and I understand that Ida has forgiven Lilly. She is trying to make arrangements to get down here as quickly as she can."

At that moment, Maud came into the restaurant and spotted the party and waved.

Rita got up from the table. "Excuse me, I think I had better go and have a word with Maud."

Maud listened to Rita and was visibly shaken. "Rita, it can't be happening, everywhere I turn lately I see sickness. I wish I had gone and seen Lilly after receiving that letter from her, but with Enid not being well and the sale of the shop, everything has got a little bit out of hand."

Rita held Maud's hand. "I was thinking I would go and sit with her, would you like to come along?"

Maud nodded. "I will phone Enid from the call box in the corridor and let her know what's happening."

"When you've done that, come back and have some tea with us, we may be at the hospital some time."

A few tables away, Freda was stirring her coffee while Muriel cut a scone to butter.

"I wonder what they are all yakking about," said Freda.

"I expect it's just business, nothing for us to worry about."

"That Reverend fella is just leaving them. Do you think one of them is getting married?"

Muriel passed over a buttered scone. "I would hardly think so, and besides, they wouldn't be discussing it in a department store restaurant."

"People discuss all kinds of things in restaurants," said Freda. "I remember when some woman was in here talking about her wayward husband– mind you, to look at her you could well imagine why. Some couples just aren't suited, unlike present company. Look at me and my Dick."

Muriel nodded. "Yes, you two were certainly made for each other. By the way, is he coming along to our Christmas do? Barry is coming."

"Oh yes, Dick said he wouldn't miss it for the world. Look, I bought him some new aftershave," said Freda, rummaging in her bag and taking out a brightly coloured box.

"What is it called?" said Muriel, wishing she hadn't asked.

"Ramped Up – the aftershave for men with go!" read Freda aloud from the packaging.

"Were they out of Wound Down?" asked Muriel with a mischievous smile.

"I don't think I have heard of that one," said Freda. "I'll ask the man on the market when I next see him. I want to get myself a new perfume."

"Well, just check the contents, Freda Boggis, that last one you purchased nearly had you break out in barnacles, what was it called?"

"Mermaid's Rock," replied Freda. "Dick weren't too fond of that one, but the neighbour's cat the other side of me kept walking round my legs when I was hanging out the washing."

Muriel bowed her head, stifling a laugh.

"I said to her next door, as Tiddles is so fond of my new scent perhaps you would like to have this. She was very grateful."

"I bet she was," said Muriel, "and Tiddles too."

"Poor Tiddles," said Freda. "Got run over a week later, apparently chasing his mistress across the road. She told me she had just left the house to go to bingo and Tiddles chased after her, went under the wheels of a hearse. She said since using Mermaid's Rock the cat barely left her side."

Muriel grabbed a handkerchief from her bag and covered her face. Freda moved round to comfort her friend. She had never known Muriel to get sentimental about an animal before. She had an idea to get her friend some perfume for Christmas. She would keep an eye open for a new one.

"Come on, Muriel love, have some of your tea before it gets cold, and you haven't finished your tuna sandwich."

Rita and Maud turned up at the General Hospital only to be told that Lilly had disappeared from her bed. The police had been informed. It seemed that Lilly's belongings had gone from the bedside cabinet and her hospital gown was folded neatly on the bed. Rita and Maud looked at each other in disbelief, unable to take in what the sister had told them.

\* \* \*

"So, if you would like to sign there, and there," said Mr Wolfe, "that completes all outstanding paperwork and you are now officially the new owner of The Golden Sands Theatre and pier."

"Thank you, Gerald, you have been most helpful."

Mr Wolfe smiled. "A pleasure doing business with you, Miss Ashby, as always."

"Oh please, Gerald, do call me June. I feel you and I will do much more business together in the future."

Gerald Wolfe smiled. "Allow me to show you out, June."

Closing the door, Gerald Wolfe turned to his secretary and, in a less plummy voice than his clients were used to, said, "Well, Deirdre, if she can make a go of that pier, I wish her all the luck in the world. It will take some pot of gold to put that place back in order, it's practically falling down."

Deirdre smiled at her boss, making a mental note to call her friend Beverley at her earliest convenience. This news would certainly put the cat among the pigeons.

# Chapter Fifteen    *Ring out the Old, Ring in the New*

*Friday, 1 December*

Maud Bennett looked at Enid as she lay in bed with flu, the letter laid by her side. "What can I say, Enid love, the sale of the gift shop has fallen through – we will just have to put it back on the market. We may be lucky and get a quick sale."

Enid sniffed. "They wanted to change the usage of the shop, or something like that, and also there were insufficient funds. I had hoped I could have sold it and you and I could go on a nice little holiday somewhere."

Maud sighed. "I'll make you some more hot lemon – you're running a bit of a temperature. I have a good mind to call the doctor."

Enid waved her hand. "No fuss, Maud, please – it is a cold and I will get over it."

\* \* \*

Audrey read the letter and then read it again. "Rueben, are you there? Listen to this, my offer on that bloody gift shop has been rejected. Apparently, I am not allowed to change usage of it from a shop to an office for my agency."

Rueben sighed. "I guessed that would be the case. You were a bit vague with your answers to their questions; I did try to warn you."

"I don't understand why it matters so much. Now I will have to think of something else. I could go back to Norwich; my old offices may still be available."

"Don't make any hasty decisions, my dear. Why don't you come up to London and stay with me for a few weeks? Perhaps we can work out something together."

"We could spend Christmas together. Mummy is going on a cruise so we won't be seeing each other."

Rueben replaced the receiver and began to make a few phone calls. He had some favours to call in.

\* \* \*

Rita stood up to greet her guest. "June, do come in, please, lovely to see you. I heard you were in town."

The two friends hugged and sat down as Beverley brought in some tea.

"Rita, I can't tell you how wonderful it is to see you again. How are things? You must have suffered terribly when fire destroyed the Sands."

"It was a blow, but we soldier on, as they say. Now, what is all this I have heard about you investing in the restructure of the theatre?"

"Well, it is part of the company I set up. My career took off quickly in Oz and I needed to ensure I invested my money wisely. 'Roo Productions' is run by me and three other investors. We viewed the pier on a number of occasions and decided to rescue it. After all, it was the Sands theatre that brought me back to the public eye, and the rest, as we say, is history. We plan to rebuild the theatre and, forgive me, but I overheard a conversation you had with Jenny and Elsie. I intend to use your idea of a fully covered central walkway, have heating installed in the theatre and move the box office to the theatre proper, rather than at the pier entrance. The theatre can then be used as a venue all year round. We can bring in touring productions, mount shows of our own and, of course, have amateur groups stage shows at much reduced costs. I know they struggle with hiring fees. I would also like to reinstate Ted's Variety Bar and place it at the entrance to the pier."

"On the subject of Ted's bar, I would prefer that we let sleeping dogs lie. The original bar was what it was and I wouldn't want to see it replicated. Some things are meant to be." Rita paused before continuing. "Well, it all sounds very exciting. Will you be moving back here to oversee everything?"

"I will fly over from time to time, but what I really need is someone here to keep an eye and to help with the general running of things – someone like you, Rita."

Rita stopped pouring the tea. "I am very flattered, but my time is taken up running the agency."

"But I heard you had Bob Scott on board in London, and you have Jenny alongside, too."

"Bob would be your ideal man – he has his finger on the pulse. What he doesn't know about running a theatre you could write on a postage stamp."

"Would you be willing to release him?"

"June, forgive me, this is a lot to take in. Bob is just getting into his stride with regards to the agency and enjoys travelling around the country. He may not want to be grounded again."

"Well, perhaps you could think it over, unless of course you could suggest someone else."

"There is Malcolm Farrow, currently at the Sparrows Nest in Lowestoft, but I don't know if he would be interested. He has been doing a good job there and his changes have met with approval."

"I would have to know more, but perhaps if an introduction could be made I could get an idea about him."

"As a matter of fact, I am due to have dinner with Malcolm tonight at the Beach Croft over in Brokencliff, perhaps you would like to join us?"

"I wouldn't want to intrude."

"You don't have to worry on that score, me old lover, Malcolm and I have an understanding. Now, let me pour you some more tea and you can tell me about what other plans you envisage."

"Well, if you are certain about Ted's bar, then I have another idea I would like to run by you..."

As Rita and June continued to chat, in an office in the town centre, Dennis O'Connor had gone over the plans with his workforce. The plans had been drawn up by an expert draftsman and each section broken down so that it was clear where the work would begin. It was hoped that by Christmas Eve the pier would be cleared of any debris, the back of the theatre would be cleared and any stalls housed on the pier would be taken away. As June had mentioned to Rita, the idea was to create a centred covered walkway which would have doors at intervals either side in case of evacuation. The walkway would mean that access to the theatre would be more comfortable during inclement weather and, with plans to heat the theatre, would see the theatre open all year round instead of just for the summer season. The box office would move to the theatre foyer.

That evening, Rita met Malcolm in the bar at The Beach Croft Hotel. He handed her a gin and tonic. "So, you have told me a little about June Ashby, but can I be certain that this offer, suggestion – call it what you will – is sound?"

"June is a good person," said Rita, sipping her gin. "If she can sell this to you I think you would be wise to accept it. It could open doors for you. I know for a fact Bob doesn't want to return to the town, I had a conversation with him earlier. He really enjoys being out on the road as much as he is."

"It would mean severing my contract with the Nest."

"I understand that, but what better time to do it? A new manager coming on board would be able to deal with the forthcoming summer season. Besides, we still haven't decided where to live when we get married."

Malcolm pulled Rita close and gave her a kiss just as June entered the bar. "Rita Ricer, I hope you know that man."

Rita laughed. "June, allow me to introduce you to Malcolm Farrow, soon to be my husband."

June looked stunned. "Well, blow me down, you kept that quiet."

"Well, we are going to make an official announcement on New Year's Eve. Alfred is hosting a party here in his newly refurbished basement and all the usual suspects are due to attend," Malcolm replied, "so mum's the word for now. I am very pleased to meet you, June, allow me to get you a drink, what will you have?"

The table in the restaurant was booked for eight, so they sat down in the bar and June began to explain to Malcolm her vision for the Golden Sands and how he might, if he accepted, play a part in it.


Meanwhile, Alfred Barton was looking at the bookings for the hotel and restaurant for the Christmas season and was pleased to see they were going to be very busy. After his wife, Jean, had left him to join family in Australia, Alfred had done what he should have done years ago and had The Beach Croft Hotel revamped. With a new team of managers and staff the hotel had seen a big turnaround in business. Brokencliff-on-Sea was firmly back on the map. The all-important New Year's Party was also on the cards and he hoped, if successful, it would become a regular feature of his much fresher and stylish hotel.

\* \* \*

Other changes were afoot in Brokencliff-on-Sea.

At Owlerton Hall, Lady Samantha was observing the work she had orchestrated to bring the prized building back to its former glory, much to Sir Harold's bewilderment. Visitor numbers had increased and out-of-season business, such as hosting Christmas parties and dinners for local societies, had really taken off. Sir Harold left the running of the Hall to his wife and was more concerned that they didn't run out of his favourite tipple. Penge, their butler and master of the house, had moved out of the main building into a cottage in the grounds that had now been fully restored. Unbeknown to Sir Harold, Lady Samantha had been left a large sum of money by her Uncle Cedric; she had invested the money well and was now able to use some of it to pay for the much-needed work on the Hall and grounds.

Finnegan's Wake Caravan Park, owned by Joe Dean, was also undergoing building works. The purpose was to have holiday chalets to replace the caravans which were now past their best. Each chalet would have proper washing and toilet facilities, with heating installed to allow the chalet to be let during winter months. Joe hoped that, all being well, the work would be completed in time for the following year's summer season. Workmen had begun to make a start and, following a two-week break over the Christmas holidays, it was envisaged that the main body of work would be completed by the end of March.

Opposite Finnegan's, the new owners of the Fisherman's Arms were about to move in, hoping to have the place up and running in time for a New Year's Eve celebration. As yet, no one had actually seen who the new owners were, who seemed to come and go in the darkness of early morning and late night.

"Come on, Roberto Casalino," said his wife, Sadie, "we want to get our accommodation sorted and then start on the pub area. There are a couple more boxes and the furniture van will be here tomorrow morning."

Roberto looked at his wife; there she was, her rotund figure in a dress that hung loose to cover her rolls of fat. Her hair was held by so many grips that she must have kept the metal industry busy, as she was prone to losing them. Finished off with a hairnet, she put Roberto in mind of Ena Sharples in *Coronation Street*, but he kept quiet about that thought. She smoked one cigarette after the other, which only made her skin look older than the fifty years she was. Despite being overweight, Sadie had an energy that meant she liked to be on the go from morning to night. She never slacked in her duties and, as well as managing a business, had always kept a tidy house.

Roberto was tall with a head of curly hair, his body was lean muscle, and his Italian looks made him a favourite with the ladies. Roberto had been born into a circus family, and he and Sadie had met when a travelling circus he was with visited Erith in London where Sadie had been born. Originally part of his family's acrobatic act, with his father and two brothers, he kept himself fit by doing exercises every morning and walking whenever he could, if only to get away from his wife and her constant nagging. The same age as Sadie, he looked at least ten years younger.

Their children – triplets Andrea, Durante and Gerardo – had joined the circus tradition, keen to follow in their father's footsteps. Although loath to admit it, Sadie was secretly proud of her boys but would often be heard to say "they should get themselves a proper job." Roberto would smile to himself, knowing that if ever the boys were anywhere near where they were living at the time, Sadie would be on the front row cheering them on. The boys were always pleased to see their parents and had often spoken of their desire to see Mum and Dad back on the road with them. It was because of his years in a travelling circus that Roberto found it hard to settle, but Sadie was keeping her fingers crossed that this move to Brokencliff would be their last; she was tired of settling into new premises only to move on eighteen months later.

Ahead of their arrival, Sadie had placed an advertisement in the local papers inviting the good people of Brokencliff and beyond to come and join them on New Year's Day lunchtime, from twelve until two thirty. Sadie was providing a free buffet and reduced bar prices. They planned to close the venue for the evening and were hoping to get an invite to the party at the Beach Croft, which Sadie had heard about on the grapevine.

Reverend Charles George was making preparations for what he considered may be his final Christmas services at St Michaels, a thought he had only shared with Joe Dean. He had long been smitten with Joe and the feelings were reciprocated, but the two, other than a warm embrace, had never taken their relationship further. They dined together at the Beach Croft, shared theatre visits and walks. Phil Tidy, who ran the small grocery store, had long suspected that there may be some spark of romance there. She was friendly with both gentleman and one day she would take them both into her confidence and tell them of her own struggles with sexuality.

\* \* \*

## *Sunday, 31 December (New Year's Eve)*

In temporary accommodation in the heart of Kensington, London, Lilly Brockett was reviewing her notes for her latest novel. She had managed to book an appointment with a publishing house who said they might be interested in her work, but certain suggestions before the meeting had Lilly wondering if she was making the right decision. Sadly, her own publishers were not willing to negotiate new terms with her and Lilly felt that she would be somewhat in the hands of those who didn't have her best interests at heart. She had sent word to her solicitor in Great Yarmouth that her cottage in Brokencliff be signed over to Reverend George. Lilly had no intention of returning and she wanted the Reverend to have it, as she had planned to leave it to him in her will. If he should for some reason turn down this offer, the cottage was to be sold.

It was time to make a new life, and whether that should be in London or somewhere else Lilly wasn't sure. She picked up a photograph album and flicked through the pages; there were Rita and Ted, Enid and Maud and a host of other people she had grown to love over the years. There was a lovely snap of Dave and Dan with Stella at the Christmas Day lunch she had shared, but it was the photograph of Jim Donnell that always brought a tear to her eye.

She poured herself a small sherry and raised her glass to absent friends and wondered what the New Year would have in store for her.


Sadie and Roberto opened their doors at lunchtime and welcomed one or two of the locals who were keen on early doors so they didn't miss what free food was on offer. They needn't have worried as Sadie, in her usual way, had catered for the five thousand. A little later, Alfred came in with Rita and Malcolm and introductions were made. Alfred welcomed Roberto and Sadie and said he hoped they would be happy in Brokencliff.

Maud came along accompanied by Barbara; Muriel, Lucinda and Freda decided to pop over to see what all the fuss was about and to have a nose around, and when Reverend George and Joe came through the door it seemed that the party was almost complete.

Sadie was the perfect host and chatted away happily as Roberto made sure everyone was helping themselves at the long trestle table which was groaning with food.

Everyone was in agreement that these new publicans would be an asset to Brokencliff and it was the perfect start to the end of the year, with the party at the Beach Croft to look forward to that evening.

\* \* \*

The Beach Croft Hotel was ready for its biggest night of the year. Alfred, who was understandably nervous, ran over the proceedings several times with General Manager Stephen Price, his assistant Caroline Hutton and Executive Housekeeper Minnie Cooper, who all assured him that everything was in place.

Alfred nervously paced his living room and checked on his appearance several times, making sure his bow tie was tied correctly and that his shoes shone. He looked dapper in his evening suit.

He looked over the invitation list again and again – it was important not to have left anyone out. He had been impressed by the spread and the welcome that newcomers Sadie and Roberto Casalino had put on at lunchtime at the Fisherman's, and he hoped they would prove to be an asset to the fortunes of Brokencliff.

The guest list included Lucinda Haines and her committee from GAGGA, along with one or two of the landladies. Maud and her sister Enid had been invited, and he had even stretched the invite to include Mona Buckle and her husband, Bertie. Lady Samantha and Sir Harold were going to attend, along with Rita Ricer, Jenny Benjamin, Elsie Stevens and Malcolm Farrow.

The basement area was now a splendid dance hall, with a small stage, large enough to hold a five-piece band. There was a bar at one end of the room and the usual facilities leading off from the room. Waiters had been specially employed to carry out the evening's function, along with experienced barmen, and all had undergone a two-hour induction with Minnie Cooper to ensure there were no possible hiccups along the way.

As Alfred entered the basement venue, the band supplied by Vic Allen was playing some seasonal favourites quietly. He made his way to the bar, had a large vodka and tonic and then made his way to the entrance to welcome the first of his guests; it had just chimed nine.

Reverend George, Joe Dean, Maud and Enid were the first to arrive, followed by Lucinda and several of the landladies. Freda had gone all out with a low-cut frock that had a split at the side of it revealing her rather ample legs. Her husband, Dick, was dressed in a blue suit that had seen better days. Muriel was dressed in a rather glamourous red gown and her husband, Barry, in a dinner jacket and bow tie. Muriel was wearing a gold dress with a matching feather in her hair, which had been styled by Mr Adrian earlier that day.

Rita received the most attention from the gathering party when she entered in a cream gown encrusted in diamanté with matching shoes; with Malcolm by her side, the two made a handsome couple and it wasn't long before some of the assembly started to put two and two together.

Roberto and Sadie Casalino arrived an hour later and immediately began working the room, making introductions and being complimented on the reopening of the Fisherman's.

Lady Samantha dazzled the crowd in a shimmering blue gown and a tiara that she hadn't worn for many years completed the look. Sir Harold, who had had a couple of drinks before leaving the Hall, made headway to the bar in order to enjoy another while the going was good.

As the pace of music picked up, couples danced around the floor and Freda proved that she was light of foot as she did an elegant waltz with husband, Dick, who had been under strict instructions not to show her up.

Phil Tidy chatted with Joe and Charles (as she had now been told to address him).

The final guest to arrive was Mona Buckle. It wasn't often that she was seen out with her husband, Bertie, but he had made the effort to escort his wife; their relationship wasn't what one would call a warm one, but on occasions such as these, Bertie knew how to put on a show. Though her leg was visibly bandaged, and her eye watered, Mona looked rather regal in her peacock-blue dress and feather boa. Bertie, who was rather shy at the best of times, did his best to chat to one or two of those he recognised, while never straying too far from Mona – it paid to keep the enemy close.

"Well," said Maureen Roberts as she stood beside Alfred, "it's all going rather well, isn't it?"

Alfred nodded. "Yes, indeed it is, it's so nice to see so many familiar faces here, and even old Chippy seems to be having a good time."

At eleven thirty, Alfred brought the party to order and asked Malcolm to come to the stage. Taking the microphone from Alfred, Malcolm addressed the gathering.

"Ladies and Gentlemen, I have an announcement to make. It gives me the greatest pleasure to tell you that after some months of wooing her, the lovely Rita Ricer has agreed to be my wife."

There were cheers from the crowd and thunderous applause.

"I knew something was going on," said Mona to her Bertie. "I see things, you know, the spirits are never wrong."

Bertie nodded politely and quickly nipped to the bar in order to replenish his glass with a very large spirit indeed.

Lucinda went over to congratulate Rita and wondered what Ted would make of it all if he was looking down on the proceedings. Lady Samantha spoke to Rita and suggested that if she would like to have the wedding reception at Owlerton Hall, she was sure she could offer a competitive price.

The chimes of midnight rang out and everyone made a circle and joined hands to sing 'Auld Lang Syne'. Freda then started a conga and soon all but the faint-hearted had joined the line.

An hour and a half later, the party began to break up and guests began to make their way home, all with the hope in their hearts that the New Year of 1973 would bring them health, wealth and happiness. But that, as they say, would be another story.

Reprint of # - C0 - 197/132/14 - PB - Lamination Gloss - Printed on 26-Apr-17 11:30